FALLING
INTO
FATE

Falling into Fate
Copyright 2014 by Nathanial W. Cook

Published by Piscataqua Press
An imprint of RiverRun Bookstore 142 Fleet St., Portsmouth, NH 03801

www.piscataquapress.com
www.riverrunbookstore.com

Printed in the United States of America

ISBN: 978-1-939739-92-6

FALLING
INTO
FATE

❧ NATHANIAL W. COOK ☙

DEDICATION:

To my father, Dale, who left life too soon,
but who encouraged me from early on to dream and spin my tales;

To my beloved Emily, partner in love, living, and tale-spinning, in
whom I believe, and who believes in me, and who keeps me getting
up, going, and wanting to keep at it;

And to Max and Jack, who dream, make things up, live in made-up
worlds, and bring joy like experts, though they're both only eleven.

Supplementary Documents

Special Agent Maxwell
Federal Bureau of Investigations, Office of

June 3, Max—

Hey buddy! I know how you like the weird stuff, especially XFiles-type things. Well, I got a case here that should be right up your alley.

I received this book and the letter that was with it from a detective working a missing persons up at Boston University. Couple of college kids disappeared. No clues as to where they went, other than the book and letter we found in their dorm room. The book was supposedly written by one of the kids, and the letter is signed by the other, his roommate. I read them, and they both sounded schizo to me!

Well, enjoy the read. We're still sort of working this one, so if you have any insights about it, let me know. And call us one of these years, willya? It's been too long.

Your old pal, 'Billiam'
William F. Marshall
Chief, Boston Metro Police

To whoever reads this...

In case I don't get back, I am writing this so you can tell my parents, and maybe Grant's, too. This is what happened...

My roommate, Grant Donovan, up and disappeared on me a couple days ago. I didn't report it since I didn't want to get him in trouble or anything. I figured another day or two, and I would call his parents. Then, this weird book shows up on Grant's bed. It's in his handwriting, as far as I can tell. It looks like a diary, except he put chapters in it. I read it (he asked me to in the note he wrote in the book), and it was pretty wild!

So I decided to see if what he wrote about is true. I figured, why not? Grant is a little nerdy and quiet, but I never got the feeling he would do something as gay as writing a whole book and leaving it here just to freak me out while he up and disappeared. Yeah, he likes to write anyway, but I don't know. He's not the type to play tricks on people.

Anyways, if you are reading this, I'm probably gone, too. If you want to know the whole story, read the book.

And don't forget to tell my parents!

Sincerely,

Michael W. Alexander

Class of 2017 (rules!)

Chapter One

I'm not the same person I was when you last saw me.

I've seen my first dead body—scads of them, in fact.

You can't gaze at a corpse, or at the faces of the bereaved, without feeling like your own problems don't matter all that much. Dang—I got a bad grade on my paper. How tragic! Oh no! Melissa's eyes glazed over when I started talking to her. It's the end of the world!

I also narrowly escaped getting hacked to death by a large sword. By a large person with a large sword. I even disarmed my opponent and prevailed in the fight. My last scuffle before this one was against Kenny Mahoney on the playground in third grade, and I most certainly did not prevail that time.

Other than that, I grew a beard, shrank several inches, and turned into some sort of elf-like creature, all in one day. Like I said, not the same person...

So how did I end up in another world? Me, of all people! I'm not Mr. Adventure... Mr. Excitement... Mr. Exploration. I'm Mr. Hide-Out-From-Parents-In-My-Room-With-Cookies-And-Soda-In-Front-Of-The-PC Guy. The only times I've ever swung swords were via pointing and clicking a mouse.

And yet, here I am: running with a pack of kickass warriors. They're lunatics, really. Of course I can only write that now, 'cause they're all asleep, but... well, not all of them: The biggest nutjob of the bunch is flashing me a glare at this very moment that, to me, is seeming to say, "Stay cool, little man, for I would like nothing more than to come over there and rip out your throat!"

Eek! Okay... turning away... calming heartbeat... settling stomach... maintaining control over bladder contents...

Ah, where was I? Well I already know that, if any of you back home are getting to read this, you're going to have a hard time accepting any of the stuff I write from here on out. That's all right—sci-fi/computer geek that I am, I'd have trouble believing it myself if it hadn't happened to me. I'll try to make it easier by grounding you in the mundane reality where it all began. And when I say "mundane," I absolutely mean it. My life was anything but exciting, certainly not compared with this. Of course my simple college life seemed like big drama to me then.

I was at my desk, alone in my dorm room, about to start another writing assignment, when something snuck into the fibers of my being, chilled my blood, grasped my insides, and wouldn't let go. It was an awakening of sorts, the opening of a third eye, or the sudden switching on of a formerly unused portion of the brain... a large and scary portion. It was knowledge of conflicts and choices I knew I'd soon have to confront, rising up to tell me it was the second half of sophomore year, it was time. Time to choose a major. Time to think about where I wanted to be tomorrow.

Yeah, there I was, sitting in front of my computer, fingers poised above keyboard, freaking out, realizing my whole life so far had been a path leading to this point. I'd made it through everything, gotten through high school, acing it, now I was doing well in a good college, and...

...? And?

It was like I had been running a race with blinders on. Now, someone had pulled the blinders off, and suddenly I had no idea where I was going. The past was over, the present was just there, and the future was this big, foggy emptiness, with thunder rumbling up ahead. What would I do when I finished school? What was I learning in school (besides how to win good grades)? What would make me happy? Who the hell was I, for that matter? A dizzying uneasiness I'd never really tasted was starting to churn inside me...

When I snapped back out of my "daymare" for a moment, I realized I was holding my breath. I let it out in a big gush. Had to get out. Had to walk, and shock myself out of it with some of that cold city air.

I switched off my computer, grabbed my coat, and headed out.

Down the elevator, out across the street, and toward this nearby strip of overgrown wilderness strode I, the intrepid explorer, on a mission to escape my impending and uncertain future! I had no idea then, none…

The light playing atop the waves of the Charles River caught my eye as usual and drew me to its edge. Thank God for that shimmering ribbon of sanity slicing through this crazy place! The sight of something so constant and timeless grounded me, and pulled me away from my yawning chasm!

And then my gaze settled on a brick utility building by the side of the river. I'd sometimes wondered about these little, blocky structures: Did someone build them and then just forget they existed? I'd never seen anyone enter or leave one of these buildings my entire life. In a split second, my distraction became my cause. I decided to check the place out—after all, it would be as good a diversion as any. It had to be better than standing there, brooding.

When I reached the building, I discovered its door was locked. Not too surprising. And the windows turned out to be too dirty for me to see through. Oh well, mission aborted. I was about to turn and leave when I heard a man's voice coming from inside the building.

"Morrelaine?" the youthful voice was calling. "Morrelaine?" There was a shrill note of fear or concern in the voice.

Extreme curiosity penetrated me, so I wrapped part of my coat around my arm and smashed one of the windows out. Maybe someone was trapped inside? Anyhow, it felt pretty daring: I'd never done anything so "bad" as breaking and entering.

After I'd pulled away a flimsy, rusted grate, I climbed through the window into the building. What I saw (and didn't see) blew me away. There was no electrical equipment of any kind here. Instead, there was a huge hole in the middle of the earthen floor, kind of like a minicrater.

"Morrelaine! What the hell is wrong with you?" came a voice again, this time sounding gruff and impatient. It sounded like a different person. The voice filled the room, and echoed, bouncing off the walls.

I guess I was pretty freaked out by the whole thing, because I lost

3

my balance and toppled over. As I tried to stand, the whole floor seemed to shift, angling toward the pit. I started slipping. I tried to hold on to whatever I could, but the dirt of the floor gave way, and my desperate fingers raked troughs in it as I slid farther and farther. My screams trailed off into the darkness as I plummeted down the hole.

For a little while, I could feel wind rushing by, and I was aware of myself, still falling, drifting in and out of consciousness.

Then, I was aware of nothing.

Chapter Two

I don't know what happened right after that, but when I awoke, the light kept me blind for a few moments. I was lying on my back, and I could sense a group of people standing over me.

"Thank the stars, he's coming out of it!" someone said.

"Morrelaine, what the hell happened?"

I realized as my sight returned that the question was addressed to me. The man asking it was a big, hairy guy dressed in armor of such a dark green hue it almost pulled you in like a black hole. His face was the picture of a Teutonic knight, with a strong brow and forceful, jutting features. He held his helmet at his side and sported a flowing gray cloak. Behind him were three others, also clothed in fighting gear from what I guessed must be medieval times.

"What...?" I moaned, trying to sit up so I could check them all out.

The first of the three was an old guy with a modicum of salt-and-pepper hair left on his head. He wore a purple, velvety robe with gold trim and various symbols adorning it. For some reason—maybe it was the shoulderbag he was clutching anxiously—he looked doctorly to me.

The second of the three was a man who appeared to be about my age. He had long, dirty-blond hair, and wore a swashbuckler's shirt with loose, floppy sleeves and ties crisscrossing up the front, a leather vest, and tight brown pants. A sword was strapped at his side, and a shiny medallion of intricate design hung at his throat. His face looked as if it had become weather-beaten while in the desert or at sea for a long time.

The third person, and the one who most shocked me in appearance, was a nearly seven-foot-tall woman. She was shaped like a body builder, and was big everywhere. She wore a form-fitting, sleeveless leather top, leather gloves, loose black pants with slits up the side to allow for movement, and knee-high boots. Her sword was secured on her back, and she had huge wineskins slung over both shoulders.

"The little mite seems to be quite alright, don't you think, Orlacc?" the woman asked of the knight-type after noticing me staring too long at her bountiful attractions.

The big man gave a slight nod of assent, and then gave me some water from a wineskin he'd been holding. The water tasted really good, and it made me realize my throat had been parched.

"H-How long was I out for? Since I fell through that hole, I mean?" I inquired of my benefactors.

The doctorly dude answered, "Only a moment or so, my little companion. But you had no 'fall' to speak of—you simply slumped to the ground unconscious a few moments ago. Twas most probably an imbalance of your body's humors."

"Perhaps he's confused, Domitrus," the young sailortype suggested. "Give him a moment and he'll be the same old Morrelaine."

"Won't that be lovely?" the woman added. "The same pesky little gnat as always!"

As the others chuckled, I wondered, was I hallucinating? These people knew me? Or they thought I was someone else—someone named "Morrelaine." This all had the ring of some of my more interesting dreams. That, or I'd won grand prize in the hardcore roleplaying gamer's fantasy weekend getaway contest!

"So who are you guys really?" I asked, raising myself up on my elbows. "And where are we? I thought the dorm was right back over... no, it... which way did I come?"

But most of the group had begun to drift down a path that led into the woods. The older man—Domitrus, they'd said—waited for me to get up.

"We've places to go, Morrelaine. You should up with haste, lest you anger Lord Orlacc. You know how he can be after a long day's march."

He offered me his hand and helped me to my feet. I realized

with horror as I stood that, though he hadn't appeared to be more than five feet tall, he was nearly a foot taller than I! Either my sense of proportion was whacked, or I'd somehow gotten shorter! But I couldn't have shrunk, could I?

Panicked, I felt myself, patting down my arms, chest, and stomach to try to figure out if anything else about me had changed. I seemed to be in better shape overall: I was kind of a pale, skinny guy before with hardly a sharp angle on me, but now I seemed sort of wiry—sturdier. I was wearing an outfit of leather too, strung together with leather straps or cords to form a sort of armor. I felt my face and head, but noticed nothing terribly out of the ordinary, except for the fact that I had some hair on my chin. A beard! I'd never been able to grow one before. Oh, how I wished I had a mirror! But that would have to wait, apparently.

"Morrelaine...!" By now Domitrus had noticed that I was again lagging.

"Hey, um, Domitrus... what exactly do I look like?" I asked him. "Am I some kind of hairy dwarf or elf or something? I don't look like some weirdo, do I?"

His brow furrowed as he grimaced and said, "At times I know not whether your words are jests or merely mad mutterings. Well, as you will, Morrelaine. Now let's away!"

What else could I do but march with them? I had no idea where I was or what was around me, so rather than get myself lost in the thick woods, I figured I'd just go along with them for a while. Besides, the forest was pleasant enough. Around us the trees were laden with the sounds of chirping birds and a soft, rustling breeze. The spring smells and the fresh air were amazing. No planes cleaved the sky, no cars, buses, or trains rumbled the earth, and no phones, TVs, or stereos throbbed against my walls. I might get tired of this peacefulness if it kept up, but for now it was oddly calming.

I'll just go along with them, I thought. Eventually I'd find out what was really going on, why I'd been transformed into Dinky the Dwarf, and exactly which medications I needed to be going on. I'd run just as soon as I knew there was a safe place to run to. Things would go back to normal, I resolved, trotting a bit faster. That was just how life worked, right? My life, anyway, which I'd been realizing just that morning, had been startlingly normal… up 'til now, that is.

Well, when we'd caught up to the rest of the group, I decided to do a little questioning.

"So, where're we off to today," I asked the others.

"You know well enough, cretin, that we are bound for West Serra Land," the knight answered without turning his head to look at me as he spoke. I personally had never heard of Serra anything.

"Now press on and be silent," he added in the same snippy tone. "You've cost us time enough already by your weakness and fainting."

Domitrus was more helpful, to say the least. We continued our conversation quietly in the rear.

"I'm afraid my—er—'fainting' spell has left me a little dazed," I muttered. "I'm confused about the details of our travels."

"I'll aid you, my friend, in refreshing your memory," the old man said, bending down to speak more softly to me. "You must forgive our leader for his rough manners. His quest thus far has been largely a failure."

"Why? What's his 'quest?'"

"Since you don't seem to remember, I'll remind you. Lord Orlacc seeks to raise an army to storm and gloriously wrest his kingdom from the grasp of his evil stepfather, Dernalyne."

"And that's why we're going to West…uh, West…"

"West Serra Land. No, we go there to find the Sage, Shan."

"And why are we doing that?" I asked, trying to keep track of the expanding story, which sounded more and more like the plot of some convoluted *Lord of the Rings* mishmash, perhaps penned by one of my D&D-loving classmates.

"To see if he will help us. To see if he can aid us with his fabled magick, enchant our party's spirits, help us to raise an army—anything!"

The knight spun on us, and the party halted abruptly. "I thought I told you to be silent, pilferer!" he screamed at me. "I might slash you in an instant if I weren't so merciful!"

Suddenly, the younger man with blond hair piped up.

"You only attack Morrelaine because you are angry with yourself, Orlacc. Admit it! We are lost! You have led us through endless forests, and we are no closer to finding the Sage then when we began!"

I knew then that I could like this guy!

The woman spoiled the party though by drawing what looked like the biggest damn sword I'd ever seen from the sheath on her back.

"You dare, Parkel, to address Lord Orlacc such? Not while I yet stand. Draw, and face me if you dare!"

The woman's dusky skin was dull with layers of dirt and sweat, but her stance was firm and her jaw was set in an angry challenge. The young man slowly drew his slender blade. The knight's lips betrayed a slight smile of amusement.

"You should listen to me instead of Orlacc anyway, Therra," the boyish man said half-heartedly.

"Ha!" She fell on him, his blade barely parrying hers. He stumbled backwards and nearly flattened me. It was all he could do to avoid her attack, and, within moments, she had disarmed him. His blade lay uselessly at the side of the path, while Therra held the man at sword point.

"Pitiful dog!" she muttered, sheathing her weapon and rejoining Orlacc at the front of the group. They began walking again while I helped poor Parkel to his feet.

"Hey, thanks for taking my side, Parkel," I said after a few minutes had passed. "But you didn't have to fight the woman if you didn't want to. I mean, it really seemed to unnerve you."

It was true: he had looked and still looked so glum that he might burst into tears.

"That woman, as you put it so gently, small one, is no woman, but a queen of hell!" he answered with gritted teeth and a reddening face.

"Yeah, maybe so," I said, "but she sure is a babe, don't you think?"

"Nay, she is perhaps too well-grown, I think," he said, flashing me a quizzical glance. I had been trying to lighten the mood, but he had obviously not gotten my meaning. "I do not understand your prattlings sometimes, Morrelaine."

Then a thought occurred to me. There had been a certain look in his eyes when he was tangling with the woman—a look I was all too familiar with. A look I could read all too well. It was a look of anguish, of frustrated longing for something—or someone—you can't have. To put it simply, he was in love with her!

"Uh, Parkel—what's the story between that woman and Orlacc?" I asked.

"She is his," he grumbled. "He has promised her great power if she will marry him after we retake his kingdom."

"And I take it this doesn't please you?" I prodded, knowing the answer full well already.

"I...I don't know what I think!" he answered with a hissed whisper. "All I do know is that I am driven mad by wanting her to regard me in the way that she regards him! Any man can see how beautiful, how...perfect Therra is! And he is not a good man for her, friend! I just know it!"

I grabbed him by the wrist and tried to calm him. "Don't worry, Parkel," I said. "I'll do whatever I can to help you."

He simply sighed and nodded, and then he returned to walking.

Back home, I had had a knack for getting my friends hooked up with girls. Of course, this was purely by accident—and these were usually girls I was crazy about. It rarely ever failed: if I liked someone, she'd turn out to have the hots for one of my friends. Or, she'd end up hating me and everyone I knew. Still, I had played the reluctant matchmaker successfully before—maybe if I put some effort into this time...and if I got really good at it, I could always take over for Chris Harrison on *The Bachelor* when I got back home.

Suddenly, a shout from up front interrupted my little musings. The others in the group had reached an opening in the trees, and when I'd caught up with them, I saw that it overlooked a valley. Down below were a bunch of huts and other structures made of wood and stone. Smoke rose in gusting clouds over the little village.

"West Serra Land has been attacked!" Therra shouted.

"Shit!" I muttered under my breath. "That doesn't mean we're still going down there, does it?"

But as Orlacc, Therra, Parkel, and Domitrus plunged down the hillside, I realized that we were.

Chapter Three

The town, West Serra Land, had been ravaged by a band of marauders. I'd read in history books about the raping and pillaging that was supposed to have gone on in medieval times, but I'd never imagined I'd end up seeing what the results looked like firsthand. Flames chewed up rickety wooden structures, and bloodied bodies, some with weeping relatives crouched around them, darkened the landscape. Up to this point I can tell you I'd been somewhat nonchalant about my transformation and adventure—I wasn't sure yet whether to believe it was really happening or that it was some sort of psychotic episode, but somehow it hadn't turned me into a quivering jellyfish. Now, as I saw what looked, smelled, and felt like real death for the first time, I began to truly know fear.

The others moved about in the ashes, turning over body after body and swearing. Domitrus was administering some sort of liquid to a wounded man, who convulsed, wracked with pain, and spit it up. Orlacc and Therra began questioning the cowering locals about the identity of the invaders and the whereabouts of the Sage. Parkel, like me, stood and surveyed the carnage with a look of uncertainty wafting with the smoke across his boyish face. His frustration over Therra and Orlacc had been momentarily forgotten. After a while, Orlacc beckoned us together.

"My friends, fear not," he said. "We shall avenge this good village of the deeds perpetrated by those bastards my stepfather sent. But in the meantime, we have been given the location of the Sage's den. I suggest we find him immediately."

We all agreed to that pretty quickly! Anything had to be better than standing around, surrounded by the dead and dying. We followed Orlacc down a few of the village's dirt roads, and soon we arrived at a stone hut. Water dripped from the thatched roof, and tiny trails of smoke from the recently extinguished fires rose into the air. The wooden door had been battered in, and it was half off its hinges. We all looked at each other, and, seeing nothing better to do, we pushed the door open and entered. It was pitch dark inside the hut, and I couldn't make out any people or furniture.

"Maybe he left?" I asked.

"Quiet, Morrela—!"

Suddenly, from out of the darkness, someone leapt on Orlacc's back before he could finish yelling at me. A silver knife blade caught the light. There were sounds of scuffling, and then, apparently, Orlacc pinned his attacker.

"Unhand me! Unhand me!" a shrill voice cried. "Haven't you monsters done enough damage for one day?"

Orlacc's voice growled out of the blackness. "Listen, you little old pip-squeak! We've come for your help—not to harm you!"

All at once, a sizzling ball of luminescence appeared in the middle of the room, flooding it with a watery green light. Orlacc was on the floor on top of a little old Chinese guy in a robe. The skin of the man's face, hands, and feet was spotted with brown and folded into hundreds of intricate wrinkles, and his long ponytail was the color of rock salt, but even with these cues, I was hard-pressed to guess his age—he could have been 65 or 99. His features seemed to shift a bit in the unearthly light.

The rest of us were arrayed about the room. A bloodied dagger lay on the ground.

"Well then," the little old man started, "let me up and tell me who you are."

Orlacc gave him our story and, within a few minutes, the old man had set up some candles and a table for us to sit at. Domitrus applied a bandage to the back wound the old man had given Orlacc. Therra paced the room, and, when she noticed a scraggly-looking snowy-furred cat sleeping in a corner, she went over and shooed it. Parkel watched her anxiously. Just as I was beginning to wonder if we were ever going to get started talking, the little old man spoke up.

"I am the Sage Chueh Shan, formerly of T'ang Di, now of West Serra Land. My friends, you came here knowing of my nature.

Willingly I would aid you, but…" His voice trailed off for a moment, and he seemed sad and far away.

"But…?" Orlacc said in a near whisper, leaning closer to the old man.

"I am tired. Tired and old! My powers are not what they were!" He slapped his hand on the table in anger.

"Can you do nothing?" blurted Therra from the corner.

"Nothing?" echoed Parkel.

"But you are a legend!" exclaimed Domitrus.

"And after what those invaders did to your village!" added Orlacc, with spit escaping his quavering lips.

The old man put up his hand, and then he waited for his gesture to take effect. The room grew quiet as the group bridled its anger. The cat that Therra had scared jumped into the Sage's lap, and he stroked it protectively.

"I did not say that I would not help you," he barked. "It just cannot be by magickal means."

"What, then?" Orlacc groaned impatiently.

"Two things can I do for you, worthy adventurers," the Sage said with his fingers raised. "First, I will offer you the assistance of myself and my aide."

"But you're old and feeble," Therra said. "You said it yourself."

"And where is this aide?" Domitrus added.

The Sage smiled, and he squinted his wrinkle-hooded eyes with the privilege of all-knowing glee.

"Whatever ill effects age may have upon the body do not necessarily affect the mind, my children. Old? Yes. But useless? Never! You must remember that, as a Sage, I am adept at reading ancient languages, finding traps and detecting poisons, and deciphering the hidden intentions of others."

He turned back to petting the cat.

"And this lovely animal upon my lap happens to be my aide," he said. "Her name is Shieda."

Therra huffed and angrily left the hut, but the rest of us decided to give the old man the benefit of the doubt. As far as I was concerned, this was no weirder that anything else that had happened to me since I'd gotten here. I was beginning to think I should be writing some of this stuff down—it would make great source material for one of my writing classes. If I ever got home, that is.

Parkel was gazing after Therra, but I think he was afraid to follow her, so he stayed in the hut. Domitrus didn't seem freaked out at all. Orlacc looked like he was too desperate to give up on the Sage. He merely sighed and said, "How can a cat be your aide?"

"Ah, my friends. Would that we humans could seek an animal's worth beyond mere comfort and servitude. No matter. The cat shall accompany us. You will thank me in time."

Orlacc grimaced, but he didn't give the Sage any argument. Instead, he said, "You said you could do two things to help us. What is the second?"

A pleased expression came over the Sage's face, and he cocked an eyebrow. "I may be able to look around the corner of time. I may be able to peer into the future and perhaps see how best to pursue our quest."

"Astounding!" burst out Domitrus.

"Yes! Yes, by all means do it!" added Parkel.

Yet Orlacc remained grim—his knotted brow casting eerie shadows across his eyes in the weird green light.

"Do what you will, wizard, and we shall see whether the information shall prove useful," he said.

The Sage gestured elegantly again, and the light from the green orb diminished. He then put his left hand across his eyes.

"I suggest one of you retrieve the woman. We shall want to leave as soon as we are done here."

"Parkel!" ordered Orlacc. "Find her and bring her back here!"

The younger man looked dismayed, but he did as he was told. By this time, the old man's lips were working, muttering phrases in some other language. The cat trotted over to me, and it began brushing up against me. I started to pet her, but then I remembered I was allergic to cats.

Aaaaachooooo!!!

Leaping to his feet, the Sage yelled, "No! No! I have gone too far!"

"I'm sorry. I'm allergic," I sniffled.

"Something I saw," he continued, ignoring me. "One of your party...!"

"What is it?" barked Orlacc. "Does one of us perish?"

The Sage looked at each of us in turn.

"One of your party is not who he claims to be," he announced.

Shit! I knew he meant me. The question was what the group would do to me once they'd found out I wasn't really Morrelaine but someone from another world inhabiting Morrelaine's body. Would they help me get back home? Would they still want me with them, or would they leave me to rot in this ruined little village? I held my breath, waiting for the Sage to expose me.

"That's all I know," he said, sighing. "I saw no further. I cannot, I'm afraid, tell you who this person is or what they will do. I'm sorry."

Whew!

Orlacc shook his head and slapped his knee. "Then all we can do is continue our journey and, when the imposter appears, we will fill him full of sword holes!"

Oops. Not "whew!"

Orlacc hopped to his feet and strode out of the hut. Domitrus, the Sage, and I exchanged glances, but none of us spoke. Then, from outside, we heard Therra's booming voice. We rushed out to investigate, and we found our three companions together. Therra had poor Parkel in a headlock.

"Tell him not to give me orders!" she hissed.

"Never mind that," Orlacc said. "The orders were from me. Now let us be on our way!"

Therra hefted Parkel off his feet and then dropped him in the dirt.

"I am ready now," she said.

Parkel rose and dusted himself off, but he said nothing. Orlacc surveyed our group, and then turned and began walking. We fell in behind him, first Therra, then Domitrus, Parkel, and me. The Sage, carrying a walking stick and a pouch, hobbled along beside me.

And then came that damn cat!

Chapter Four

The invading army had left a quite impressive trail of crushed foliage in its wake, so Orlacc decided that the quickest way to get back to his kidnapped kingdom was to follow for a while in their rather pronounced pathway.

By the time we made camp that first night, I realized just how difficult this trip was going to be. Oh, this Morrelaine guy whose body I was inhabiting was in good enough shape all right, but his...er, my legs were so much shorter than everyone else's that I had to work double-time just to keep up. Thank God for the Sage and Domitrus! If they hadn't been there to slow everybody down, I think I would have gotten left behind!

Anyhow, I was damn tired. What I wouldn't have done for a mattress and box springs! Or even a sleeping bag! But, no—like the others, all I could do was find a soft spot and wad up my gloves and outer clothing for a pillow. This world needed to discover Holiday Inn.

The others sat up for a while, sharing stories and passing around a pipe of some sort, but I was too exhausted to try to learn any more about our mission. After a bit, the Sage's cat trotted over and curled up next to me, purring. Wonderful! My sinuses would be a regular Niagara Falls come morning!

"It appears Shieda likes you, small one."

It was the Sage—I hadn't seen him approaching. He gathered his robes up with one hand and sat down near me on a rock. From his lips hung something which looked like a reed, and which smoked a little at the tip.

"I'm sorry to make such a fuss about her, sir. I was just dozing off and, uh, cat hair makes me sneeze."

The old man smiled, his long teeth clenched tightly together, his cheeks round and shiny as apples in the reflected firelight. Laughing to himself, he rocked up and down, and he snorted a bit through his nose. I asked him what he found so funny, but he just sat there, rocking back and forth. Then, after a bit, he drew close to me and let the reed's smoke curl upwards from the corners of his mouth. He put his face right up to mine and said, "You're not from around here, little one, are you?"

Uh-oh. This was it. He did know who I was. But was he going to expose me to the others?

"Well I…I mean…what are you…?" I asked, sitting up hurriedly and fumbling to find words that made me seem confident.

His smile faded abruptly, and he reached for me with his talonlike fingers. His hot breath brought the sweat out on my forehead. He said, "Let us go for a walk in the woods, my well-traveled friend, and I shall tell you exactly what I know."

Moments later, we were hiking through the woods, our boots crunching the rocky pathway beneath us. The Sage's cat followed dutifully behind us as we went. In the moonlight, I could barely make out the Sage's rounded form, but I followed the smoking ember at the end of his reed pipe. When we were away from the camp, he paused and turned to face me.

"Have a bit of this," he said, offering me the pipe. "It will ease your fears." Now that I saw it up close, it seemed to be nothing more that a piece of dried grass, but, when I drew in the smoke, it did indeed relax me. I felt like I was floating.

After a minute, we started walking, and the old man again spoke, this time in more reassuring tones.

"You needn't fear any harm from me. It's true, I know that you are not from this world, but I also know that you are a good man, whomever you are. You are also not the one I spoke of in my earlier prophecy. No, as strange as it may seem, it appears that you are fated to be part of this quest."

"But I…how can that be?" I asked. "This isn't even my own body!"

"I cannot explain everything; magick is not an exact science, my friend. But this I do know: It is not you who bodes evil towards this group of warriors. No. The traitor is another."

By this time, we had reached a small pond, which was fed on one end by a small, bubbling waterfall. I turned, but the Sage was no longer with me. I felt weak in the knees and light-headed, all of a sudden, so I slumped onto a large rock and puffed out the last crumbling embers of the pipe. My head kept drooping, and I finally slid from the rock to the ground.

Later, I awoke to what sounded like splashing coming from out on the pond. I couldn't be sure whether I was dreaming or not, but what I saw at first looked like a young girl and then a young woman, bathing in the silvery waters. Her sinewy, nude body arched out of the lake, jackknifed, and then plunged back in. For a while, she did not reappear, but then, suddenly, she surfaced near where I lay.

Her long, dark hair, dripping against her smooth neck, her eyes, set like green jewels into her angular face, and her high, curved cheekbones rose like an apparition before me. Her skin looked like nothing more than wet marble. Her lips tasted of the night air and cool water as they brushed against my face.

"Don't be afraid. I am your friend," she whispered.

I wanted to say something, to move and to embrace her, but my limbs could not move. Instead, the mists of the waterfall swirled about me as I fell into a heavenly sleep.

I could feel water slowly filling my mouth and nostrils, and it took me a few moments to realize I was drowning. Sputtering, I sat up.

Laughter erupted all around me, and, as the sleep faded from my eyes, I recognized the now familiar group, my fellow adventurers, standing around me in a semicircle. Therra was holding a bowl-shaped rock in her hands, from which, I gathered, came the water she had just finished dumping on my head.

"Do you realize you could have killed me?" I shouted at her. Did I mention I'm not the sweetest person when I first wake up? Also, not the brightest. Well, I'd made the snap decision that I was mad as hell about her bullying, and I wasn't going to take it anymore. In my own sort of tough-guy-wannabe way, I let her have it.

"Y-You don't have to be such a freakin' bitch all the time!"

That definitely struck a chord. The red slowly filtered into her face, and, moments later, the silver emerged from her scabbard.

"Let my actions be my response to your insults," she muttered, and then, down came her steel.

I don't quite know how to explain what happened next. This whole road-trip had been strange to me up to this point, but when Therra attacked me—when I was finally threatened with real physical harm—well, it was like this other sense I never had before took over. Maybe it was the real Morrelaine somehow coming back into his body, re-exerting control? Or maybe, if this was my own hallucinatory, subjective dream world, I wasn't about to let myself die in my dreams?

Well, whatever it was, I jumped deftly out of the way as my gigantic companion's sword hit the rock I had been perched upon in a shower of sparks. The action of battle seemed to slow down. I skittered through Therra's legs and out behind her. In slow motion, she whirled to face me, her sword traveling in a deadly arc towards my skull.

Again, I dove between her knees, only this time, I had a plan. I bounded back up onto the rock, and then I launched myself at her. I landed squarely on her back. She began to writhe and to reach out for me, but she couldn't grab me. To keep from falling off, I gripped her around the neck. A couple of times, her sword-point flashed near my face. Desperately, I started to squeeze her throat with my forearms.

Therra dropped her sword and tried to force me off by exerting her grip against my arms. But my hold had already taken its toll: She was losing oxygen, getting lightheaded. As she grunted with the strain, she began stumbling. Finally, she dropped to her knees and was near collapse when I decided to let go.

My companions, who had whooped and hollered when the fight began, were now utterly silent. Therra's raspy breathing slowly worked its way back to normal. I kept looking at her and then at each of the others in turn. We all seemed to be in shock.

Then, I shrieked at I felt something tickle down between my legs. It was the tail of that damnable cat! I must have looked pretty idiotic—I mean, after felling our group's resident amazon, I go and get skittish over a little ball of fur! Well, I am allergic, after all…

I felt a hand on my shoulder, and I looked up to see Orlacc's battle-hardened face now decorated with a broad, friendly smile.

"Don't worry, little one," he said. "You've proved yourself just now. Perhaps…perhaps we should not place you at the butt of our pranks…so often, at least." He patted me again and then walked away. Therra flashed him a look of astonishment, but she kept her mouth shut.

Orlacc took his place at the front of our party. "Enough!" he said, his voice booming. "We have a long day's journey ahead of us. If we press on well today, we should reach my besieged homeland in three day's time."

And so, we were off once again, back on our trip to wherever it was we were going. As usual, I lagged behind the rest of the group (shorter legs, y'know?). After a while, Parkel dropped back to talk to me. I guessed that his was his aim by the way he hovered around me, staring hopefully, yet unable to speak his mind.

"What is it, Parkel?" I finally asked, tired of him lingering near me with that sad, puppy-eyed face. I guess I had sort of hoped the others would leave me alone for a while and give me time to recover after my fight with Therra.

"I…I wished to speak with you…about…." He motioned with his head in Therra's direction.

"Ah," I answered knowingly, nonchalantly dusting some of the dirt off of my sleeves and vest. "Yeah, she's a toughie all right, but I polished her off pretty good, didn't I?"

Parkel looked confused for a moment—why would anyone want to polish someone else' skin? Though I have to admit, the thought of buffing down Therra's bod did have a certain appeal! Anyhow, Parkel grimaced and went on.

"What I wanted to ask you about was, well, earlier you spoke of…helping me, of turning the woman's affections towards me. How?"

I let out a deep sigh. This wasn't going to be easy. "Hmmm. Okay, well, first you gotta help me out here, Parkel," I said. "It would help if I knew more about Therra. Like, where is she from? What does she like? You know. That kind of stuff."

"She is from Ekhulta, the Barren Land," he began, getting a misty look of reverence in his eyes. "It is in the Western Regions of our great continent. It is a rugged place, and all inhabitants are schooled in the ways of combat."

No kidding, I thought. I'd never have suspected that.

"As for what she likes," he went on, pausing to formulate his thoughts, "I would say only that she cherishes every occasion she has to prove herself in challenging battles."

"Hmmm. Okay, so she likes having a good time. What else?"

Parkel's furrowing brow clued me in to the fact that he was confused yet again.

"What'd I say this time?" I asked.

"I understood you," he answered, "it's just…."

"Wait. Don't tell me: You don't know what else she likes, right?"

He frowned and squirmed uneasily. "We…I've never really spoken at any length with Therra," he muttered.

Ah! Communication between women and men—a mystery for any time or any place! I mused.

I patted Parkel on the arm, and, in my best man-to-man tone, I explained, "Now there's your problem, guy. If you really want the girl, you're going to have to get to know her—you know? Talk to her?"

But his only response was to look dejected, and to shuffle along slightly behind me.

"Don't worry," I said earnestly. "I'll work on it."

He didn't answer, but merely ambled along with a challenged look on his face. I took this to be a good sign at least he seemed to be putting some thought into what I'd said.

Guess things were already a-changin'.

Chapter Five

Okay, the nature scenery was nice at first, but I was starting to get tired of the damned forest after marching through it for a couple of days straight! Trees, trees, and trees and trees! The only sort of civilization I'd seen since I'd arrived here was the burnt-out husk of West Serra Land. Since then, we'd been always on the move, always uphill, always through the endless damned forest.

I kept wondering when we'd finally get to Orlacc's castle. I was dying for a hot bath, a bed, and maybe even a maiden fair or two (hey, a guy can dream—especially in a fantasy world—right?).

Finally, we reached a clearing near an outcropping of rocks at the top of a hill. From here, it was possible to see pretty far, and, you know what? It looked like there was even more forest in every direction around us, stretching as far as the eye could see! Rolling hills, swathed in rustling green, for miles and miles and miles. Awfully pretty, but, um, no castle in sight. SOO-per. Talk about progress.

Orlacc paused at the front, and the rest of us stopped and waited. He seemed confused, like he'd expected to see something else. Were we lost?

"Uh, what's the matter?" I asked.

"Not a thing," Orlacc answered, grumbling. "We shall stop here…rest for a time."

The others in the group looked surprised, but they all lay down their belongings and found stones to sit on. I, for one, was mighty glad for the break.

Wouldn't you know it, though? As soon as I planted myself on a small, flat rock, that damn cat was with me, brushing up against my now-free hands, demanding attention.

"Hey!" I said to her. "Don't you know when you're not wanted?"

But the cat stared up at me, blinking its eyes and purring. I looked over to the Sage for help, but he was already nearly asleep, leaning against his own moss-covered stone.

So, I began stroking the cat's head and neck.

"Oh, all right," I said. "But you'd better bother somebody else next time, Twinklies!"

Twinklies?! I guess the name had just popped into my head. It must've been because of the way the light seemed to dance and glimmer in the animal's eyes, like it enjoyed playing this sly little game with me.

Happy, happy cat.

After more than an hour had passed, we were still there, waiting. Yeah, you guessed it: The cat, in that time, had fallen fast asleep on my lap. Sheesh! My eyes were stinging and gushing a mile a minute!

The Sage was still out like a light. Parkel and Domitrus were discussing something. Therra was tossing her dagger repeatedly into a tree. And Orlacc? Well, he was looking out over the surrounding countryside, apparently trying to get a fix on our location.

Suddenly, he turned, and with a frown said, "You have all had plenty of rest by now, have you not? Well, up! Up! We've a trail to be upon again!"

I had no idea what had prompted his sudden bout of impatience, but no sooner had we all stood up and begun dusting off our backsides than we heard a rustling and the sounds of jangling metal and the clopping of horses hoofs coming from somewhere in the woods. Someone had been spying on us!

No one said anything, but Orlacc, Therra, and Parkel drew their swords. Parkel nodded at me and tossed me a dagger. Guess the "pilferer" was being recruited. Yippeei-o. Domitrus huddled up with the Sage, who, of course, was grasping his cat protectively in his arms. So now the guy finally looks after his own freakin' pet!

After a few more moments of too-eerie silence, we heard a horse snort, and we realized just how near they were—only a few feet behind the tree curtain's edge, barely fifteen or twenty feet from where we now stood. I felt a trickle of sweat drawing a chilly line down the small of my back.

Suddenly, Orlacc screamed, "Show yourselves, cowards!"

Then, through the trees, a torrent of armed knights surged toward us with weapons drawn. They wore the same armor and gray cloak as Orlacc.

"Death to the insurgents!" they shouted, and, "Die in the name of King Dernalyne!" as they swooped down upon us from their horses, hacking with frenzied strokes. I quick-counted ten of them, and reasoned that they were a detachment of Orlacc's stepfather's royal guard, out looking for us.

The wind from a sword buzzing past my skull snapped me out of my daze. I glanced up to see a bearded, sadistically grinning face regarding me.

"You'll eat my steel, little pecker!" he growled, and then he lunged at me, grunting. I bolted to the side, all the while thinking, Wow! They had the word 'pecker' back in medieval times?

As I regained my footing, I turned and found myself again seeing through this Morrelaine's battle-trained eyes. The whole fight became one big panorama to me; some part of my brain was taking it all in and methodically analyzing the scene, which now seemed to me to be happening in slow motion. I saw that the knight who'd attacked me had galloped past me. He had apparently decided not to tackle me again (I was too short to reach from up on a horse, maybe?). Instead, he had joined two of his buddies, who were circling the Sage and Domitrus. They were taunting my unarmed friends, making them run back and forth among their slashing swords.

Meanwhile, Orlacc was parrying blows coming from two swordsmen who had dismounted to face him. Parkel was engaged in a one-on-one sword-fight, while giant, spectacular Therra held four of the warriors at bay—hell, I think she was actually winning!

Assessing the situation, I decided that Domitrus and the Sage most needed my help, so I bounded off in their direction. I let my dagger fly, aiming at the head of the knight who had attacked me before. The puny blade, of course, pinged uselessly off of the man's helmet, but it did serve to attract his attention. All three of the attackers turned towards me.

"You need a lesson, rat!" said my former assailant, and he and the others rode at me.

I was just thinking about which way to run when a voice cried out. "Stop! All of you, stop!"

Immediately, all of the action of battle died. Everyone looked in the direction of the voice and saw Orlacc on top of one of the knights. It had been this knight who had shouted, and it wasn't hard to see why: Orlacc had him pinned, with his sword across the man's throat. A quick shifting of Orlacc's body weight was all it would take to decapitate the downed fighter.

"Now tell your men this, Kryfalikk," Orlacc said to his captive, practically spitting the words into his frightened face. "They shall drop their weapons and back away from my party. Do it!"

Clearly unnerved by his predicament, the man called Kryfalikk complied in a somewhat timid and hoarse tone.

"Y-You heard what he said."

Stumbling, the other nine men tossed their weapons to the ground. There was quite a clatter as swords, daggers, and one metal-tipped club-thingie hit the rocky dirt.

"Collect them," Orlacc said to our group. Domitrus, Parkel, and I shuffled around, picking up the discarded steel. I decided to procure myself a decent sword, and I snagged a fine little number—sturdy-looking as all get out. For some reason, Therra didn't seem interested in acquiring any of the stuff. Parkel took the rest of the swords and held them bundled like firewood in his arms.

When we'd finished, Orlacc hissed to his captive, "Don't ever forget that I could have slaughtered you this day." With that, he rose to his feet and let Kryfalikk up.

Orlacc motioned to Parkel to give him one of the swords. He then handed the weapon to Kryfalikk, saying, "I give you this, for one day soon, you will use it to serve me."

"Not likely," said Kryfalikk, brushing himself off and straightening his cloak. But he accepted the weapon anyway.

"You and your men leave us be," said Orlacc, and with action-hero flourish, he added, "And don't forget to tell that false king, Dernalyne, that I am coming for him."

As his men preceded him into the forest, Kryfalikk sneered and said, "Don't worry: I won't." He climbed onto his horse and left, and, with some more jangling and clopping, they were gone.

We all stood silently for a little while, and, as my heartbeat gradually returned to normal, all I could think was *whew!*

Chapter Six

"Therra and Morrelaine shall have the first watch," said Orlacc that night as we made camp.

Great. That was all I needed. We had decided to put two people on watch shifts each night, just in case Kryfalikk and his men decided to attack us again. As the fire crackled low and the others prepared for sleep, I looked over at Therra and found her regarding me with a look of disdain. Oh, how we so loved each other!

I spent the first part of my shift scribbling notes about my adventures thus far in a little book I had gotten from the Sage (which you are now reading, smarty-pants). I was beginning to think all this would make for a good novel or movie. Maybe Spielberg could produce and direct it (title it "Crouching Dwarf-Boy, Hidden Courage")—if I ever made it back home to show it to him, that is. Which was looking less and less likely—nothing I'd seen in the past few days led me to believe my original theory: that this was some sort of elaborate joke. The evidence said this world went on forever, that these people were real and genuine, that this was all really happening. Either that, or I'd gone psychotic, and this adventure was taking place inside my head! It was probably some cosmic accident, but it was the truth—that much seemed apparent.

I wasn't sure what to put down about how I'd gotten here in the first place. I mean, was it one of those things where I had hit my head, and this was all one long, vivid dream? Was I going to wake up at some point and say, "Gosh Auntie Em—there's no place like home?" Or had I really crossed over into some other time or dimension or something? I wanted to talk some more with the Sage about it, but of course he was asleep.

While I was writing, Therra was making some annoying noises by digging in the dirt with her swordpoint and flicking pebbles off into the woods. A couple of the mini-rocks bounced towards me, and one finally hit me in the forehead.

"Must you?" I asked, throwing her an irritated glare. As soon as I'd said it, I wondered if I might've just picked another fight with her. But she just kept flicking the gravel with the blade.

"Leave me be, Grimnell," she said.

"Excuse me? Grim...Grim...what?"

"Grimnell. It's what you are, is it not?"

Now I was intrigued. I was what? I had figured maybe I was an elf or something. I just had to know.

I closed my book and hopped off of my rocky perch. As I sat down next to her, she stopped toying with her weapon and glanced apprehensively over at me.

"I know this might seem strange, Therra, but...well, can you explain to me what a Grimnell is? I can't seem to remember."

She scrutinized me for a few seconds. I could only guess what she might have been thinking. I mean, I would've thought it was mighty strange if she'd asked me what a big, seven-foot-tall woman was—although I would have enjoyed explaining it to her.

Finally, she spoke to me in cautious tones.

"A Grimnell is what you are—a wood people...the small folk of the forests. In fact, Grimnells come from the Allarraban Forest, to the south and east, though you are said to have left there and struck out on your own some time ago." She looked me over, and I nodded, as if recalling my life in the forest.

"You're a fat and feeble race, full of sloth—this I do know also," she added, and she went back to digging in the dirt.

"Oh, well, I see you know everything then!" I snapped, pissed that she'd managed to insult me yet again. "What makes your people so wonderful?"

I expected her to launch into some tirade about how strong and perfect her people were, and how they never lost a fair fight, and blah blah blah, but Therra was strangely quiet. She stopped digging and remained still. Then, to my surprise, she shifted a little, and I noticed by the firelight a lone tear falling from her eye.

"Therra, I'm…." I stopped. How do you apologize to a seven-foot Amazon? But it was she who spoke.

"My people are not, as you say, 'wonderful.' They are hard and cold. And I have exiled myself from them."

For several minutes we said nothing, and the only sounds were the snaps and pops of the logs on the fire.

"What made you leave?" I asked, when I thought she might be ready to continue.

"I-I was to be executed," she began, and her voice was softer and warmer than I'd heard it before. "In Ekhulta, I was considered the property of my father, Mik'Kun. Though the women of our race are trained to be competent fighters alongside our men, we are subject to the whims of our 'owners,' be they our fathers or husbands.

"You might think it strange, seeing me now, but I tried quite hard to be a good and dutiful daughter when I was growing up with my father. I served him food and wine, watched his back in battle, and even wrapped myself from head to toe in the black Ateh robes that the women of our clan are required to wear."

I pictured her then, living in a village that sounded somewhat like a strict Islamic society on our world. What a drag!

"When it came time for me to be married off, only one man showed up to claim me. He was Uran." She swallowed, then continued. "I did not want to marry him. It was rumored that he had deflowered my best friend, Chellah. I knew this to be true. In our society, when a woman is deflowered before marriage, she is done away with. It matters not whether she was willing or not, she is considered 'spoiled,' and is put to death. Though I wanted with all my being to please my father, I could not bring myself to marry Uran.

"But, because he was my only suitor, I had no choice; an unmarried woman means no heirs, which is unacceptable. Still, I went to my father and pleaded with him to help me avoid such a fate. My father…"

I noticed that she was having difficulty talking about this subject. Now, the tears were running freely down her cheeks, softening her once impenetrable mask.

"He…did what a father must do when his daughter refuses to give herself to a man, to obey the Law," she continued. "He turned me over to the Deathmen. They decided I was to be beheaded."

"Yeesh! How did you get away?" I asked. "Did Orlacc save you?"

"In one sense, he did, I suppose. I escaped on my own by night, and I made it to a town several days' walk away from the borders of Ekhulta. There, I pondered my next move. I had heard of the troubles occurring within Terasskos, Orlacc's kingdom, and had even considered selling my services to his army. Then, to my surprise, I discovered that the usurped King Orlacc was passing through the very town to which I had fled! His warriors sought me out and informed me that Orlacc had heard tell of my prowess in battle. He was there to recruit me into his army of liberators!"

Wow. This place was full of weird coincidences. She meets up with Orlacc while running for her life, and he just happened to be in town looking for her? Well, at least I could finally see what she saw in him—a way out.

Almost as if she had heard my thoughts, she added: "Orlacc has promised to put me in charge of his armies once we retake his kingdom. Then…hah! Then, I shall lead a charge westward, and I shall personally subjugate Ekhulta! Aye! Then you shall see the rules of our society turned on their ears!"

"But, that seems like a lot of stuff to have to do before you can bring change to your people, doesn't it? I mean, don't you also have to marry Orlacc?"

Therra grimaced bitterly. "'Tis true. And though I see fit to marry no man, 'tis a small price to pay to bring about my desires. Orlacc is a good man."

She began to examine the blade of her sword more closely again—a sure sign, to me at least, that she was uncomfortable and did not want to talk about this anymore. And that was fine with me. Not that I didn't enjoy talking to her, especially if it meant I was going to start really learning more about her and the others. No, I liked talking to her, or, rather, listening to her, but right then, I really needed to take a pee. I got up, but saw no need to excuse myself since she wasn't paying attention to me anymore anyway.

As I trotted off into the woods, I remembered my relief a few days ago when I had first had to go to the bathroom in this new world. When I'd looked down then, and I discovered that Morrelaine's anatomy was at least biologically the same as my own had been, I'd felt a huge weight lift off of my shoulders. Now, it had reverted back to being just second nature to me. My biggest concern now was keeping enough of the firelight in view that I could find my way back without tripping over anything. When I'd gotten about thirty feet away from the camp, I found my spot and started tinkling away. Ahhhhh!

In the dim light, I could just make out the shape of the tree I was facing. And then, slowly, I noticed something weird—a white oval shape started appearing from out of the side of the tree trunk. Or was it behind the tree? It was at about my height, and had two dark patches in it, like...

Eyes!

There were three things I did then: Number One, I screamed—a full-throated gargle of fear. Number Two, I ran, arms flailing, face smacked by twig, leaf, and branch alike. And Number Three, I tripped and fell on my face. The next thing I knew, I was being yanked up off the ground by my arm. I looked up and saw Therra, towering over me with her blade at the ready. I could hear panicked voices coming from behind her near the campfire.

Great, I'd awoken everyone.

"What is it Morrelaine?" she asked. "You shouted...?"

She let go of my arm, and I scrambled to regain my footing. Was whatever it was still out there in the woods?

"I saw someone, Therra! Behind a tree, looking right at me!"

A skeptical expression crossed her face, but she peered into the forest just the same. A moment later, and Orlacc, Parkel, and the rest had joined us.

"If it had been Kryfalikk, we'd all be dead now. Right, Orlacc?"

"Aye, Domitrus. Kryfalikk's men would not be so foolish to

waste their time frightening lowly guards like Morrelaine."

I let out a deep breath to try to relax myself, and I dusted myself off. I was still a little shaken, so I wasn't about to argue back to Orlacc, even though it was clear he didn't believe I'd seen anyone.

"Which tree was it, Morrelaine?" Parkel asked.

"Well, it was right over…"

I stopped. As I was pointing, we all noticed the same thing: there was something white sitting at the foot of the tree. We all stared, and then nearly jumped when the thing started moving towards us. It floated, or crept over the dark earth, slowly, silently. And as it approached, I saw that it looked like…like…

My heart sank, as we all saw what my "ghost" truly was: The Sage's cat!

As I glanced around, I noticed that the others were all glaring at me. Uh-oh.

"Your ineptitude has cost us again, weasel!" Orlacc said. "I don't know why I shouldn't slaughter you here and now, and leave you for the forest worms to eat."

"Leave him be."

It was Therra. I had been about to say something to defend myself, but she'd cut me off.

"We're all tired of marching through these endless woods," she continued. "The animal could have taken any of us unawares."

Well! It looked like I'd found myself a new champion!

Clearly biting back his anger, Orlacc could only manage a weak, "Perhaps." Then, he turned and headed back towards the campsite. Over his shoulder he said, "Parkel. Domitrus. You take the next watch."

Later, as I struggled to get comfortable on the rugged ground, I overheard Orlacc and Therra talking to each other.

"Need you address me in that way in front of the others?" he asked.

"I said nothing wrong," Therra responded.

"Yet you rebuffed your Lord and Leader before his underlings! How am I to enforce my authority if you act to undermine it?"

"I leave that to you to decide."

There was an uneasy pause, and then I heard Therra unsheathe her sword. The thought crossed my mind that they might fight, but then she took a stone and began sharpening her blade.

"I care not whether you truly love me," Orlacc hissed, "but if you wish to share with me my kingdom, you'd best learn to respect me. In public, at least, I expect compliance."

There was no reply. Therra continued sharpening her sword, and, after several minutes, Orlacc left her alone.

From where I lay, I could see Parkel by the firelight, sitting on a rock, keeping watch. I guess he must have heard the conversation too. How did I know? Well, you should have seen him smiling!

Chapter Seven

The first half of the next day's march passed without incident. No one said much of anything to each other, and nobody bugged me about my hapless encounter with the Sage's (damned) cat the night before. I think we were all too tired from the monotony of the daily march to harp at each other.

Parkel did ask me if I'd learned anything about Therra on our watch together. I didn't have good news for the boy.

"She's tough, but she's had it tough, too. And she thinks she's got good reasons for throwing in with Orlacc," I said to him, quietly enough so the others wouldn't hear. "You might be able to relate to her by talking about battle strategies and stuff, but I wouldn't ask her about her family life."

"Battle strategies, eh?" he said. He seemed to take this notion under advisement, and, soon, he was off in his own little world of thought again, as was I.

And so it went. We all just trudged along, marching uphill mostly, and then, when we'd reached another crest, we at last saw what we had all been looking for! In the distance stood a nice, solid, big gray castle! It looked a lot different than I'd expected—in the movies, castles always seem to be perched atop craggy mountain peaks, or are at least situated in very difficult-to-reach places. This castle was just nestled in the heart of the forest, surrounded by redwood-sized trees, and it would probably be pretty hard to spot from too far away.

I peeked at my companions, and, sure enough, we were all doing pretty much the same thing—staring, dumbfounded, with our mouths hanging open. Even Orlacc, which surprised me, since you'd figure he wouldn't be so bowled over just from seeing his own home again (I mean, what had he expected to find here? A McDonald's?).

Finally, Domitrus said, "Castle Orlacc, I presume?"

And I noted keenly, "It seems so small, and so… peaceful."

"Be still!" hissed Orlacc. "I am certain that even now we are being observed!"

It seemed a little too tranquil to be believed, like it was a movie backdrop, not the real thing. There was absolutely no noise coming from the direction of the castle or from the surrounding woods. Even the birds were silent. From the stillness, it wouldn't have surprised me if we'd entered the gates and found the place deserted. Parkel looked at me quizzically, and I shrugged, unsure. Nobody else looked to me, quizzically or otherwise, so I shrugged a second time to myself. I didn't have a clue what was up!

Orlacc mustered his nerve and took a cautious step forward. Nothing happened. Therra, with more determination, followed suit. Nothing happened again. The rest of us—Parkel, Domitrus, the Sage, and I (and maybe the cat—I wasn't looking)—each lifted a foot and took a single step. The forest was bone quiet. And then …

… a man in armor stepped out from behind a tree trunk. It was Kryfalikk!

Orlacc's muscles stiffened. "You!" he spat.

"Undeniably," Kryfalikk answered with a sly smirk.

Drawing his sword, he added, "And I am here to carry out your execution, traitor."

"You must be joking," Therra said, relaxing her guard. "Even if you alone could best our leader, you surely know that the five of us would not stand aside and let you slay him."

But Kryfalikk kept grinning, and he lowered his weapon. Then, he made a noise that sounded like, "Eeeeeyyyaaauppp!" And then, from behind seemingly every nearby tree trunk, armored men emerged. The woods came alive with the echoing sounds of whooping and of steel blades being drawn from scabbards. My friends and I tensed, and we all readied our own weapons.

"I would ask you if you'd prefer surrender over death, Orlacc," Kryfalikk said once the din had subsided, "but I know you better than that."

"This is how I am to die then?" Orlacc asked. "At the hands of my own rogue soldiers?"

Kryfalikk frowned bitterly. "You gave up the right to lead these men when you turned against your own father."

Then, Orlacc began to tremble with rage. His jaw clenched, and his face grew all purple-y. "He. . . is. . . NOT...my...father!!!"

Seeing that Orlacc was about to come unhinged, Kryfalikk's soldiers started closing in around our group. It was becoming apparent that we were about to get "sliced and diced."

I heard myself mutter, "Pardon me, but SHIT!"

Suddenly, Orlacc let out a roar and threw himself at Kryfalikk. Swords clanging, the two tried to hack each other apart. The rest of us didn't have a chance to say or do anything, because as soon as our leaders crossed swords, the gathered army of soldiers poured onto us like tackling football players, 'cept these guys had swords and spikes and clubs (oh my!).

I didn't even get an opportunity to look back and see how my friends were faring—I was too busy fighting and being shoved around! It was all I could do to dodge every sword, mace, dagger, or fist that was tossed my way. Every once in a while, I was able to get in a good parry, and even a thrust or two. But I definitely wasn't making any headway.

I could hear the anguished grunting of Therra and Parkel, who were fighting behind me. I could only hope that Domitrus was somehow able to protect himself and the Sage ("Meow!" Oh, and the cat).

Finally, I couldn't take any more. My arms were getting tired, and I knew that, before long, some of the enemy soldiers' weapons were going to start making it through my defenses. And then, before I knew what I was doing, I found myself running. I put my arms up, waved my sword in front of me, and just charged through the enemy lines. Some of the men swung at me, while others just jumped out of my way. I guess they were surprised. I felt a few blows whiz through the air over my head, but none of them connected.

When I'd reached the edge of the battle, I turned around,

afraid that some of the men might have come after me. But it seemed that they were more interested in finishing my larger companions now. I gazed at the scene: All I could see were hordes of gray-cloaked men, all converging on one central point. And there was Therra, in the middle, her dark hair swinging as she spun to face fighter after fighter, her sword arm rising and falling with seemingly inexhaustible strength. What a warrior! But she was the only one of my friends that I could make out through the fray. Had the others already fallen?

I felt that I should get back in there to try to help out, but I just sat there, paralyzed and out of breath. I collapsed on a rock, promising myself that I'd only sit there a moment. That was when I caught sight of the figure.

About twenty feet from where I was resting was a person, dressed in a black robe and mask, kneeling, watching the fight. The person's robe was adorned with shiny objects, and they were what caught my attention, gleaming in the sunlight. Almost as soon as I'd spotted the figure, it noticed me too. Our gazes were locked on each other for a moment, and then it turned and scurried off into the forest.

What the hell? I thought to myself, and then I got up and raced through the woods after the interloper. I was tired of all these people—or creatures—hiding out behind trees, watching what was going on in mine and my friends' lives. I decided it was time for answers.

But this character was fast, and he or she seemed to know where he or she was going. The figure led me deeper and deeper into the forest and into thicker and nastier brush. It was jumping over fallen tree trunks and ducking under branches, while I was running full into everything. But I was determined, so I kept charging through.

Finally, the person stopped and stood stock-still. I couldn't halt my forward motion in time, so I slammed right into him or her. The figure grabbed me and held me close. And then the ground seemed to fall away beneath our feet. We started dropping.

"Careful," the figure said. "Don't move, or you may fall."

But all I could see around me was blackness. We seemed to be on a little platform of earth, descending like an elevator into the very heart of the planet. Above me, the tiny circle of sky was fast disappearing. I glanced down, but there was nothing to see. It was all black.

And I thought once again, *What the hell?*

Chapter Eight

I'm not quite sure what happened right after that. The circle of light above us gradually disappeared, and we were engulfed in utter darkness. The figure still held me, but I realized that it was not in a menacing way—it was more like the way a mother grips her child after it has nearly fallen from the sidewalk into a street full of traffic. We said nothing to each other on the way down.

Then, something seemed to change about the air—it was like the whole atmosphere got thicker and heavier. I coughed a few times, trying to deal with it, and then I passed out.

When I came to, I was lying at one end of a long bridge that spanned a huge, subterranean cavern. The whole place was lit by flickering wall-torches, and by an eerie blue light that came from somewhere below. I looked around for my guardian figure, and I found it standing in the shadows behind me with its back towards me. It was taking its mask off, and I could see a long mane of brown hair cascading down its back to between its shoulder blades.

"H-Hey?" I ventured in a croaking voice.

It turned and faced me, and I saw, at long last, that it was not human. It had an impossibly thin face, a tall head, and high, arched eyebrows. I couldn't tell for sure whether it was male or female—it looked sort of like a large, effeminate teen-aged boy, so I guessed it was a he. His eyes were long and slanted upwards towards the outside of his face. There were hardly any whites to his eyeballs—instead, his sockets seemed filled with dark, brown, swirling liquid. And, his mouth appeared to have been carved into a permanent grin.

"You are awake," he said. "Cool."

Cool? "You speak English?" I asked, "I mean my, er, like Twenty-first Century-type of English!?"

"Like, yeah, I do," he answered beneficently. "I can speak pretty much every language that's ever existed. Butt-wipe."

"Butt-wipe?" I moaned. "Wh-Why'd you call me that?"

"Sorry," he explained. "Just wanted to prove I knew some of your insults too."

He moved towards me, and I sat up cautiously. The last thing I wanted was for him to grab me again. He noticed my fear and stopped, still smiling at me.

"It-It must have taken you a long time to learn all those languages," I said.

He cocked his head to one side, and said, "Time? I suppose you could say that, yes."

He started towards me again, and when I began to freak out, he said, "Don't worry. I just want to make sure I haven't damaged you in some way."

"I'm fine," I said, scrambling to my feet. I felt a little dizzy and hot, but I was still in one piece. I patted myself down to make sure I didn't have any gaping cuts. Then, I asked him, "By the way, what are you?"

"Well, if you must call me something, I'm an Ilf. My name is Argothrex."

He put out his hand, and I shook it. "I'm Gra...er, Morrelaine. I'm a, um, Grimnell."

"I know what you are, Grant. Only you don't," he said, pointing at me. Then he put his arm around my shoulders and guided me along with him. "Come with me. Let's cross that bridge, now that we've come to it."

And we started to traverse the giant cavern. The bridge seemed sturdy enough, but when I looked over the edge, there seemed to be no bottom to the pit we were crossing. There was only that strange blue glow.

I glanced over at my guide again, and, noticing his pointed ears, I asked, "Argothrex? You said you're an Ilf, but don't you mean elf?"

He shrugged, and answered, "No, that's something completely different—a made-up character. I'm an Ilf, and all those of my kind are Ilves."

We were nearly halfway across the bridge when strange rumbling noises started coming from all around us. The whole place was shaking! Below us, the blue light was making hissing and popping sounds.

Argothrex calmly put out a hand and stopped me in my tracks. "You'd better hang on to something," he said, "you won't want to fall."

"Fall!?" I shouted, but I did as he said, gripping the bridge's railing tightly with both my hands. Meanwhile, the whole cavern grew brighter, and it seemed as if the blue light, whatever it was, was rising up around us. The place started to shake violently, and I was sure we were about to experience an underground earthquake.

And then it happened. Like a gunburst, the blue energy shot up through the room, engulfing us in its fury.

For just a moment, I could make out Argothrex's form, but then he was swallowed by the light. I looked down at myself, but I could no longer see my arms, hands, feet, or the rest of my body. I wondered if I was disintegrating, and, then, the next thing I knew, I could feel myself screaming.

Then, I forgot who I was and where I was. I wasn't anyone anywhere. The only thing I could distinguish was a feeling of enormous pleasure, washing over me, and lifting me up. I seemed to be high for a while, even laughing so hard I was crying, spilling myself all over myself. And then images started to congeal in the space around me like huge, suspended water droplets. I began to realize while looking at them that some of these images were of my life, of things I had done or felt. I reached out and took one of these droplets, and I bathed my head and body with it. I don't know what prompted me to do it, but it gave me a rush of orgasmic happiness. I felt knowledge and endless possibilities radiating through me, answers to everything—I could have cured cancer and AIDS in a second. That's right, I thought to myself, everything's so wonderful!

And suddenly, I was back in the dream I'd had by the pond a few nights before. I heard the water splashing all around me, and I felt the cool night wafting over me, tasting me. And then she was there, my green-eyed, darkhaired night angel, bent over me, kissing me. "Don't be afraid," I heard her say again, "I am your friend."

And then she vanished, and the blue light faded.

I was back in the cavern, lying on my back on the bridge with my hands still clamped on the railing. Good old Argothrex was standing near me with his eyes closed.

When he opened them, I asked, "What the hell was that?"

"That, Grant, was the Thrum. Beautiful, wasn't it?"

"Y-Yeah, but what was it?"

"That may take some heavy explaining, but, I promise you, we'll get to it when the time is right," he answered. He put out a hand, helped me to my feet, and then we proceeded to finish crossing the bridge.

When we had reached the other side, another of Argothrex's kind (an Ilf, I suppose) was approaching us from the opening of a dark passageway. When he saw us, this other Ilf threw us a sour look. Argothrex stopped me and then introduced us.

"Grant, this is Boolean. Boolean, this is Grant."

"What'd you bring him here for?" Boolean growled at Argothrex, while completely ignoring my outstretched hand. "We never bring Outkind to our domain. It could ruin the Chaos Bounce!"

"Ah, but it could strengthen the Bounce as well, my friend," Argothrex countered. "Remember, as Sol Siggund once said, 'Embrace the Chaos—Jostle the Jewel Quite Often!'"

"True enough, but I might refer you to the words of the great Sol Dileggi," said Boolean with narrowed eyes and a waving finger, "'Beloved Chaos is as fragile as Despised Order—Guard its Mysteries!'"

"Yes, but Sol Biggerus succinctly stated..."

"Guys! Guys!" I wailed when it looked like they might go on with their philosophical debate forever. "I know you guys are, like, Ilves and stuff, and I can guess that you're pretty much all-powerful in this place, and I know I'm only a puny human, or whatever I am right now, but..."

They both stared at me, looking perturbed.

"...Well, I really have to go to the bathroom. And then I have to get back to Earth, or wherever I've been for that last couple of days, to help my friends. Is that too much to ask?"

"No, not at all," Argothrex answered sheepishly. "We can certainly accommodate your needs."

"He has made a point, Argothrex," Boolean said, again accenting each of his words with a finger wave. "Show him the Jewel and its workings, if you must. But tarry him not too long here—he must still play out his role."

Argothrex nodded his compliance. With that, Boolean tottered off across the bridge, and we entered the darkened corridor.

After letting me stop off in a room to one side of the passageway where I could, uh, "take care of business," Argothrex guided me to another larger room.

There were four metallic braziers, placed haphazardly about the room, each spitting a smoldering, crimson light. Near the center, there was a raised area of rock, like a giant table, and, in the middle of that, there was a deep, dark pool of water. Argothrex motioned with his hand for me to gaze into the pool.

"I don't get it," I said. "What's this supposed to be?"

"Watch," my guide answered.

And as I did so, a blue glowing sphere appeared in the water, and it slowly seemed to grow larger as it moved towards the surface. I wondered if I should be scared or awed or something, but I peeked over at Argothrex, and he still looked pretty mellow, so I just watched and waited as the ball of light rose up out of the water and hovered in the air. Once it had cleared the surface, I saw that it was, in fact, some kind of jewel or gemstone. I noticed that there were shimmering green highlights within the depths of the crystal. The colors made me think that the rounded gem looked a lot like the Earth, and for some reason that worried me.

"S-So? So, you've got a floating diamond in your bathtub. What's the big deal about that?" I asked.

Gazing worshipfully at the jewel, Argothrex answered, "That 'diamond,' as you call it, is no simple precious stone– It is a refracted representation of The Entirety."

"The entirety of what? The world?"

"Yes, but not just your world. The Entirety is all worlds, all possibilities. As the Old Ones phrase it: 'Every Time, every Place, every Drama, every Dream!'"

I looked back at the jewel, and then slowly back at him. His smile seemed to have grown even larger than it had been. He was entranced.

"All righty then—so you have a representation of everything—The Entirety or whatever. Why?"

"Well, that's simple, really," he said, approaching the pool so that he was now standing next to me. "It's our job to turn the jewel."

"Uh, well...pardon me for asking a lot of questions, but why?"

"Because Order must encounter Chaos, that's why." He must have noticed me gazing dumbly at him, because he went on to elaborate. He extended his hand towards the jewel, but stopped with his fingers about a foot away from it. He held his hand there, as if he were feeling the heat from a campfire.

"Here's how it is, Grant: Each facet of the jewel represents a new possibility, a twist, if you will, on the way reality is right now. Whenever we turn the jewel, a new possibility slides into place. Something Chaotic happens. The twist becomes the new reality. Everyone gets thrown for a loop."

"Waitaminute! Is that how I got to where I am? I mean, to where I was—with Therra and Orlacc and everyone else?"

"Exactly—well, pretty much," he said, nodding. "Let's face it, Grant—you needed a little Chaos in your life." He withdrew his hand, and stood looking at me with his arms crossed.

"Now hold on," I said. "What gives you the right to...?"

"It's not my right—it's my task, my job. Order needs to be met with Chaos. And we Ilves are the chosen Agents of Chaos. Have been forever."

"So what am I supposed to...? What's going to happen?" I wanted to ask him a million questions all at once, and I started to babble. But just then the whole room started shaking. Even Argothrex seemed startled by it.

"Crap! I'd better get you back," he said, steadying himself. The jewel began to sink back into the pool. "Are you ready?"

The jarring of the earth had knocked me on my ass, and I was struggling to regain my footing. "No, wait! There's so much more I want to know!"

"Believe me," he interrupted, reaching his hand out to help me up, "there's a lot more I'd like to tell you—and I will, I promise, when I can. But right now there are other things that need doing. Are you all right?"

I was back on my feet, thanks to him, but the whole place was still rumbling and quaking like a scene on the *Star Trek* bridge. Cracks were beginning to form in the walls, and steam started billowing through the fissures.

"I'm okay," I answered, "but I don't want to go back 'til I find out some more stuff."

"No time," he said more forcefully this time. He gestured, and a piece of the ground broke off and rose up beneath me, lifting me. "We'll talk again. I promise. But I've got one last word of caution before you go: Now that you've seen all this, you may find that you will perceive some things in your new reality a bit differently—with greater acuity. You may notice some things that you weren't able to before. Try not to let them worry you."

"I-I don't understand," I said.

"Don't be afraid. Trust me."

And with that, he waved his hand, and the chunk of earth I was on shot up towards the ceiling. I thought I was going to be plastered against the roof-rock, but I merely passed through it into a dark emptiness.

I was moving faster and faster, and I could no longer sit up. I fell to my back, lying flat on the stone platform as it raced through the black nothingness. The motion pulled tears from my eyes and sucked the air out of my lungs, until finally I passed out.

Chapter Nine

The first thing I noticed when I opened my eyes was that it was still pitch black all around me. The second thing I noticed was that I had stopped moving. I sat up and tried to see what was around me, but I couldn't make out anything in the darkness.

"A-Argothrex? Where am I?" I called out. My throat was raw, my voice hoarse, and I immediately started getting the bed-spins. My words echoed around, and from the reverb I could tell that I was in some sort of large chamber, maybe even a small cave. I started to smell the mustiness and taste the gritty damp in the air. I began, finally, to be able to make out a faint bit of light, apparently coming from a window placed high up on one of the walls.

"M-Muh-Muh-Morrelaine? Is that y-you?" It was Parkel's voice, but he didn't sound too good. I went towards the source of the voice, feeling my way along one of the walls.

"Parkel! It's me! Where are you?"

He coughed, choking on some phlegm. I could tell, though, that I was getting closer to him. I felt my way along, but when I got to where I thought he was, there was still only bare wall. I called to him again, and then I heard his choking sound above me.

"I am suh-sorry, my f-f-friend," Parkel said. "It's duhd-difficult f-for m-me to t-ta-talk."

I straightened to my full height, such as it was, and I felt something tickle my face. I reached up to touch it, and then I realized what was going on: It was Parkel's hair that had tickled me. Which meant he was hanging upside-down!

"Oh shit, Parkel! We've got to get you down! You're gonna die like that!"

"W-We will all puh-probably d-die soon a-anyway."

"No! No way, man," I said, jumping up to see if I could reach whatever bonds were holding him to the wall. But I couldn't seem to get any higher than his face. "Damn! There's no way to get you down, and if the blood rushes to your brain..."

"It may not be as hopeless as that, small one." Another voice! It seemed to have come from the other side of the room.

"Sage? Is that you?" I peered through the dark, and I thought I could see a rounded shape huddled in the corner.

"Indeed, Morrelaine—I am here with you and Parkel."

I started moving towards his voice. "You're not hanging upside-down too, are you?"

"Fortunately, no—I am merely bound with some rope, over here in the corner. I suppose the soldiers deemed it unnecessary to tie such an aged prisoner to the wall."

I finally reached him in the dark. I patted him down, and, sure enough, there were ropes wound tightly around him.

"Don't worry, my friend. I'm not hurt," he said.

"I can get these off you pretty easily, I think," I offered, and, as I worked, we talked some more.

"So why didn't they tie me up?" I wondered aloud.

"Perhaps they did not perceive you as much of a threat," the Sage answered. "You were unconscious for quite some time, after all."

I have to admit it irked me a little to be seen as less of a threat than Parkel and even the Sage. I was getting tired of being thought of as inconsequential, and, sometimes, as a burden. On the other hand, I did feel a little guilty about having run out on the others during the fight with Kryfalikk's army.

The Sage seemed to have read my mind, because he said, "Don't trouble yourself, Morrelaine: the soldiers' oversight may lead to our escape."

I shrugged and continued to work on his bonds. I'll admit, I was grateful that it was too dark for him to see me blush.

"So, I can assume, then, that we're inside Orlacc's castle?" I asked.

"Yes. We were brutally outnumbered, of course," the Sage answered. "The soldiers brought us here, and I suppose that Orlacc,

Therra, and Domitrus are in another dungeon."

"So everyone's alive, then? That's wonderful, but I figured they were going to just kill us."

The Sage's shoulders moved in a shrug. I almost had him freed. "Perhaps Orlacc's stepfather prefers to mete out his 'justice' against us personally."

I had finally gotten the ropes off of him. He stretched out his arms and legs, and I could hear his joints cracking.

"Can you get up?" I asked. "We need to try to get Parkel down from the wall over there."

"In a moment, small one," he said. I could see the gleam of one of his rings as he moved his hand to wave me off. "I need time for the blood to revive my legs and arms."

Then an idea hit me: "Hey, Sage! Couldn't you, like, work some magic to get us out of here? You know! Blow a hole in the door, or teleport us away or something?"

He clapped his hands together, as I had seen him do back in his village, and a little flare of green light started to form between his palms. But then he said, "I am afraid, now, that you have overestimated me, my friend. I'm too old and tired for any of those tricks. But perhaps I can do something..."

A sphere of green energy rose from between his fingers. It was like the one he had made before, except that it kept zapping in and out of existence, sort of like a TV set does in an electrical storm. Still, I was at last able to see him and the place we were all in. As I looked around the room in the flickering light, I could see piles of old bones, probably left there to scare us. I saw pieces of metal from, I guessed, manacles that had rusted and fallen off of the prisoners' emaciated limbs. And there was poor Parkel, inverted on the wall, and, in the opposite corner from where the Sage and I were sitting, another person, a woman, I thought, and nearly naked, I guessed, from the sight of her white form. I was just about to point her out to the others when the glowing orb zapped out again.

"Hey! Light it up again!" I shouted. "There was a woman, there, in the corner!"

Grumbling, and shifting on the floor, the Sage clapped his hands again and reproduced the light. I strained to see the opposite corner, but there was no one there this time. She'd either disappeared, or I was going nuts—though, to be fair, I had been through a lot in the past few days.

"Wh-What happened to her?" I said, jumping to my feet. I paced over to the corner, but found only a pair of old skeletons, chained to the wall. In between them, I saw something moving. Was it a small white rat, or...? Then I realized I'd been fooled again by that damn cat! The Sage's damn cat—Shieda, he'd called her. I picked up the little beast, and walked over to where her master sat, chuckling.

"A present for you," I said as I handed her to him. "I guess they didn't see fit to tie her up either," I groaned as I sat down again.

"And that could be their fatal mistake, my friend," said the Sage. He seemed suddenly animated—excited about something. "I'm still too tired to use my magic, but you—you can pick the lock! Then, you can send Shieda out to prowl! She can explore the castle without being detected, and she can find the safest route for our escape! And when she reports back.... "

"Waitaminute!" I said, as I reached over and petted the cat's head. "She's only a cat. And what makes you think she'll do all this stuff when we let her out? And even if you've got her trained really well, how can she 'report' anything? Cats don't talk! Or do they here?"

The Sage had a strange expression crossing his face, sort of a deflated look at first, changing to an uncomfortable grimace.

"There's something weird about that cat, though," I noted. "She's come out of nowhere to surprise me several times, and I've mistaken her for a person twice now. And I was so sure I'd seen a woman over on that side of the room the first time I looked."

The Sage 'ha-rumphed,' and, when I looked at him again, he appeared somewhat angry, or stern.

"Nonsense," he said. "She's a resourceful and welltrained animal—that's all. There's no magic in her."

I began to think I had somehow upset or offended him, and it worried me. He'd been pretty darn helpful and friendly to me so far—plus he was the only one of the group who knew I wasn't really Morrelaine. I tried to think of some way I could get back in his good graces, and I said, "You know, I bet I could pick that lock. Then maybe I could sneak around and..."

"You won't be sneaking anywhere, runt!"

That nasty voice had been accompanied by the sounds of a heavy door being unbolted. A moment later, a cadre of seven soldiers entered the room. One of them strutted over towards me. When he'd noticed that the Sage was untied, he stopped and motioned for two of his men to come over.

"This little rat's gotten the old man free," the lead soldier said. "Be careful of him—he could work a spell."

"You oughtta be worried I might do something!" I blurted before I'd thought about what I was saying. "I'm the one who freed him, you know!"

Slowly, the soldier turned to face me, drawing his sword as he did so. I, of course, had no weapon, so I just sat there. Smiling, he placed the tip of his blade at my throat, and said, "Perhaps you are right, Grimnell. Perhaps I should kill you right now for having threatened a knight of the royal court."

Then, he put his foot against my chest, and he kicked me to the floor. I landed hard on my back, but I bounced quickly to my feet and stood there just glaring at him. He twisted his blade in the air while he mocked me, saying, "And perhaps we would have bound you, dog, had we not found you, fainted away like a woman in the woods, a good distance from the battlefield."

At this, all of the knights broke into laughter, but their leader raised a hand to silence them.

"We have no time for jokes!" he said. "Bring them, and get that other one down from the wall."

As three of the knights moved to undo Parkel's bonds, the leader smirked at the Sage and I, and muttered, "Quickly, now—the master has waited a long time for this!"

Chapter Ten

Our captors tied our arms tightly behind our backs, and they chained our feet. Then, they proceeded to drag us through the passageways in such a manner—with a knight on either side of each of us, each with an arm thrust through one of ours, lugging us along by our armpits—that I was afraid one of my shoulders might get dislocated. After we had gone a few hundred feet, the procession stopped. Orlacc, Therra, and Domitrus were being rousted out of another cell by a separate group of knights, and they soon were carried along ahead of us in a similar fashion as we continued on.

In a short while, we passed through an arch and entered into an immense hall with a ceiling that must have been at least a hundred-or-so feet high. Colorful banners with battle scenes depicted on them hung along the walls at regular intervals, and a purple-and-gold-trimmed carpet covered most of the room's floor. I noticed that the weird designs on the carpet were actually the letters of a huge text, so that a person standing on the ceiling would see the floor as a giant document. I resolved that, if we ever got out of this, I'd ask Orlacc what it said.

The room was filled with people—not just with the twenty or thirty soldiers guarding us, but also with noblemen and their wives, and, of course, a few dozen servants. We had been led in through a side entrance, and now, as the soldiers turned us towards one end of the hall, we finally found ourselves face to face with Orlacc's stepfather, King Dernalyne.

Well, not quite fact to face: he was still about fifty feet ahead of us. He sat on an elevated throne at one end of the room. From where I was, I could tell only that he was a very ornately dressed old man with a crown on his head. And, also, that there were eight royal guards standing behind him with twelve-foot pikes in their hands.

The guard at the king's immediate right shouted, "Prisoners!

You are now in the presence of His Highest Majesty, King Dernalyne the First!"

With that, our captors threw us to the floor, from which I, at least, struggled to get up and back on my feet. But then the king in a booming voice said, "Guards, I want these ants on their knees! Make them kneel!"

His men did as they were told; we were all yanked by our elbows and hair into a kneeling position.

"You know why you are here," the king began, "and you know what will become of you when we are finished here. But, on behalf of the good citizens of this kingdom, we shall undertake the task of formally sentencing you for your crimes, so that all may know what a great folly it, indeed, is to plot against the rightful ruler of this most honorable and holy kingdom."

"Liar!" Orlacc screamed, and he managed to get out "Beast!" "Fiend!" and "Infernal traitor!" before his captors kicked him in the stomach, pitched him to the ground, lifted him up, and stood him back on his kneecaps again. Afterwards, I could tell he was still reeling from the blows by the way he was rocking back and forth unsteadily.

"And now that that insignificant outburst has been quelled, we shall continue!" the king went on, and I noticed, now, that there was something a little weird about him. I couldn't quite put my finger on what it was, though. While I was searching my mind for the answer, two more men entered the room through a little door to one side of the throne. Both wore long robes, but they looked quite distinct from each other. The man who stood to the king's left was tall and well built—he looked like he could be just another one of the king's guards, only dressed differently and perhaps slightly older than most of the other men. His robe was of a deep red velvety material, and it was decorated with designs stitched in gold and silver thread. Also, he was carrying a large scroll.

The other man was a good bit shorter and older than the first, and he had a salt-and-peppery beard on his puffy, pockmarked face. His robe was plain black, but he wore a black beret-type hat on his head. Both men stood in front of the king, facing us, and crossed their arms sternly.

"For those of you who are not of this kingdom, I shall introduce my royal enforcers. To my left is Tholem, who shall read the charges against you."

At the king's introduction, Tholem bowed low.

"To my right is Frouder, my loyal court wizard. He is here to insure that those of you who practice the Art do not attempt to move against me."

Frouder, who seemed rather nervous, bowed his head only slightly and then stood there glaring at us with shifty eyes.

Tholem stepped forward, unfurled his scroll, and began reading the charges: "The six of you present stand charged of the following crimes against the Kingdom of Terasskos: Treason, Conspiracy to Depose the Rightful Monarch, Conspiracy to..."

As he was reading, my thoughts drifted back to the king, and the strangeness I had sensed about him. What was it, exactly? Was it something in the way he spoke, or in the way he looked...? And then I realized that it had to do with the way he moved, or rather, the way he hadn't moved—not one bit. He hadn't stood, raised his arms or hands, or even turned his head. In fact, I couldn't even see his lips or mouth move when he spoke (though I was pretty far away from him, I should have at least been able to detect that he was talking by some facial movements). Why, for the life of me, the king seemed almost like, well, almost like...

... a wax statue!

Just as this thought leaped into my head, something weird happened. No one but me noticed at first—after all, Tholem was still reading the charges—but the king's head began tipping ever so slightly to one side. I watched, then, with my mouth hanging open, as his head slowly lolled backwards and to the left and his crown spilled off onto the floor with a clatter.

The whole room fell silent. For a moment, everything seemed frozen. And then, from behind the throne, a voice was heard: "Shit! Curses and damnation!"

Out stepped Kryfalikk. He reached down, picked up the crown, and addressed Orlacc. "I-I'm sorry, Your Highness. We thought we had prepared him adequately."

"Never mind that now!" Orlacc said with disgust. "The game is up. Now get me out of these chains!"

All our eyes were on Orlacc, as his captors unlocked his manacles. He rubbed his arms and legs as he stood.

Finally, Therra asked, "'Your Highness?' But what is this about?"

"What became of King Dernalyne?" said Domitrus. Parkel began to struggle against his bonds, and shouted, "I demand you release us! Answer why you contracted us to serve you, and why we are chained now if you are indeed in command in this place! I demand it!"

Orlacc, massaging his wrists, turned to face Parkel. He had a mischievous grin on his face, and, as the seconds passed, his grin grew into a wide smile, and the smile, finally, into a laugh. And then he stopped and looked each one of us in the face, as though waiting for some expected response.

"Alas, have none of you guessed it as yet?" he said, as he slowly began making his way towards the throne. "I slew old Dernalyne some time ago—had him poisoned as a matter of fact. And then, cleverly, I had my stepfather's body preserved—well preserved—as you can see."

By this time, he was standing beside Dernalyne's body. He grasped the head and twisted it so that he was looking into the corpse's eyes. "Truly, Terasskos has been a land ruled over by a dead king for quite some time now."

The crowd began murmuring. Clearly, they were as surprised as we were. Only Kryfalikk and a few of Orlacc's top aides did not appear shocked.

"But why?" I asked Orlacc, as if on cue.

"And why did you deceive us?" Domitrus asked. "And recruit us to a false cause?" grumbled Therra.

Orlacc let his stepfather's head droop. He took the fallen crown from Kryfalikk and placed it on his own brow before turning to face us again. "As to Morrelaine's question about why I would govern in secrecy for all this time, well, I shall answer that anon. But for the reason I selected you for my noble cause? Well, that is simple enough to explain."

He came down from the dais and began striding among our shackled forms. "Come, surely you must be guessing at the reason! No? Very well, then. The five of you are perhaps the greatest fighters from your own nations. Sitting here in my castle for so many months, I had heard of all of you and of your exploits. I reasoned that, were I to decide to launch a Grand Campaign to take over the five other nations of this continent, I would do well to have subjugated each nation's greatest champion. What better way to strike terror? And here you all are."

"But…that makes no sense," I said, partly to him, and partly to myself, after considering his words. "'Greatest fighters?' You kept telling me yourself how weak I was, and that I'm just a 'pilferer.' And Therra—she's not even welcome in her homeland. She's under a death sentence! And Parkel…you kept having him beaten up. Now you say we're 'champions?'"

"Fool!" he sneered. "Do you not remember the talks we had about Destiny and Fate when first I wooed you to join my quest?"

(Er, no, I didn't, but I guessed it was probably because it happened well before I'd fallen into the driver's seat of Morrelaine's body.).

"My words then carried dual meanings," he continued. "It is not the fighters you have been, but the champions you are becoming I need defeat. My wizard has assured me of this. His scrying revealed that it is not your prowess in battle, but your unconventional ways of thinking I must guard against. And so I have. But Frouder is not the only wizard—there are others, and their mutterings have reached your own countrymen. Despite what you believe, you are becoming known, which is why my victory today shall be total. By dispatching all of you, I will assure my future as ruler of all Aeron! As they once did for my father and his father, your peoples will kneel before a Lion Liege of Terasskos!"

He looked down at Therra then, and said, "Take her, for example: the warrior men and women of Ekhulta are sure to doubt their chances against me—at least a little– when they learn that mighty Therra has fallen by my sword."

"Never!" Therra hissed. "The warriors of my nation will no more than glance at your puny armies before rushing over your arrayed forces like an unconquerable river. My people know not the meaning of fear!"

"Silence, bitch!" Orlacc said, and he backhanded Therra across the cheek. Then, regaining his composure, he smiled at her. "Do you think you hold some sway over me because I claimed to love you? Is that it? Well then, think again! I used you even more easily than I used these others. I can have any of the women of Terasskos. Why, then, would I choose such a manly, overgrown giraffe as yourself as my consort?"

At that, Parkel went crazy, straining so hard against his bonds that he nearly fell over. "You!" he screamed. "You set me free, you tainted snake, and then deign to mistreat her again! Let's see what will happen then! Set me free and you'll see!"

Orlacc angrily lunged and gripped Parkel by the hair, yanking his head back with a snap. "Cur!" he spat into Parkel's face. "How many times I wanted to run you through and be done with you when we were on the trail together! How many times! I think there were so many, I cannot count them! But now, what's to stop me? Why should I wait any longer?"

He turned to one of his knights, and said, "Guard, give me your sword!"

I thought I was about to see Parkel's blood spattered all over the floor, and I tried to think of something I could say or do to halt Orlacc's fiery rage. But before I could come up with anything, the Sage spoke up:

"Lord Orlacc! Or perhaps I should say 'King Orlacc.' You have spoken many truths here today. You have revealed much of your true self. But, in at least one respect, you have lied to this court."

Orlacc's arm, which had been outstretched to receive his guard's weapon, fell to his side, and his bloodlust seemed suddenly muted. He ignored Parkel—and the rest of us—and strode over to where the Sage was bound. "Well, well, old man. As dried up and used up as you are, you've succeeded in gaining my attention. Now kindly tell this court what, exactly, you meant by that last remark."

"A moment ago, you said you could have any woman you wanted," the Sage answered. "But I know that there was one woman you wanted—one whom your own father, whose power and influence far exceeded yours, could not win for you. And though you vowed to find and conquer this woman, you could not."

Orlacc shrugged and began to walk away, but then the Sage added, "And something more: I know what became of that woman."

At that, the angry king halted, and he turned around again to face the old man.

"You mean she did not die?" Orlacc asked.

The Sage laughed. It seemed he almost could not contain his glee at having turned the tables on Orlacc. "You were meant to think so, indeed," he said, "but no. No, the woman called Kayleah is very much alive."

Again Orlacc descended upon him. He put his face right up to the Sage's, and he lifted him up by the front of his robes and shook him. "Very well then, wise one. Tell me what you know of her, and perhaps you might stave off the execution of your friends a while longer! Perhaps I shall not execute you at all but allow you to live out your days as my captive! But you must tell me! You must tell me now what you know!"

The Sage coughed a little, and some spittle ran down his chin. Then, in a rattled voice, he said, "Please, my lord—as you've said, I am old and weak, and my bonds are restraining my blood flow so that I can barely remain conscious. Unchain me, and I'll tell you all that I know of her."

Orlacc hesitated a moment, considering, and then the Sage added, "What can this 'dried up, used up' wizard possibly do to move against you, after all?"

After a few moments more of deliberation, Orlacc made his decision. He dropped the Sage to the floor and motioned for one of his knights to approach. "Release the old man. But watch him closely."

While his guard took out some keys and unshackled the Sage, Orlacc, who now seemed quite disturbed, strode back up to his throne, thrust his dead stepfather's body aside, and seated himself. After the Sage was freed and was able to stand under his own power again, he looked up at Orlacc.

"With your permission...?" the Sage asked.

Orlacc leaned back in the throne and said, "You've gained my attention, old man. In fact, you've intrigued my entire court, it would seem, judging by their silence. You've won a momentary reprieve. Now tell your story."

Chapter Eleven

The Sage dusted himself off, faced the crowd, cleared his throat noisily, and began his tale:

"First of all, for those of you who do not know me, I am the Sage Chueh Shan, shaman, formerly of T'ang Di, lately of West Serra Land, a town recently trampled by your king's rather enthusiastic troopers, I might add.

"Nearly twelve years ago, I think it was, a young woman stole into our little village. When I say 'stole,' it is because she was very secretive, and was, in fact, traveling incognito. She wore a long purple cloak with a hood, which she kept raised at all times. She had with her a small entourage: four well-trained eunuchs, armed with sabres, and an elderly handmaiden.

"Though she was young—barely a woman, in fact—she had journeyed far and wide, had experienced much, and was very learned. In hushed whispers, it was rumored she had a natural talent for the Mystic Arts, and she was called a White Witch by some. Whatever the case, she came to our village, West Serra Land, to 'hide out for a while' (as she put it), and she must have heard talk of me, for she soon sought me out.

"When she first came to see me, I immediately sensed her potential. I was struck by her youth, and I asked her her age.

"'Thirteen,' she said—she was even younger than I had suspected. I marveled. I asked her why it was she had wished to see me.

'I am training to become a White Witch,' she said. 'I have been pursued by demons, and also by many human foes. I want to attain mastery of the Arts so that I can defend myself when necessary, and so I might bring a measure of peace to my homeland.'

"And, realizing that she had the capacity to become a great and noble Practitioner, and, in all likelihood, a doer of good deeds, I consented to complete her training. So that the villagers—who had been kind enough to take me in when I had fled my own homeland so many years earlier—would not be uneasy, I adopted the young woman as my daughter, and she dismissed her servants. She told me her name was Katherine Leah Krabbe, but that she usually went by 'Kay' or 'Kay Leah.' The villagers tended to run the two names together, hence 'Kayleah.'

"I continued my new daughter's training for five more years, and she excelled. Still, her youth made it difficult for her to focus her own great powers, and I realized that it would be a few years more before she could truly defend herself from most forms of attack, magickal or otherwise. Nevertheless, we continued her practices.

"That same year, Orlacc's true father, King Ottallo, journeyed with his armies throughout his kingdom to demand that his villages increase their tributes to him. When he arrived in West Serra Land, which was then a province of Terasskos, he had the members of our ruling council stripped, whipped, and beaten, and then put in stocks on a stage for public display. Kayleah and I were in town that day at the markets, and, when the king caught sight of my blossoming daughter, he took a keen interest in her.

"The king removed his glove and touched Kayleah's hair and smooth skin. Then, with a lustful grin, he said, 'I have a son, Prince Orlacc, who is about the same age as this precious jewel of yours, old man; this son of mine soon shall require a wife. This woman might prove adequate. Give her over to me, and I shall look favorably on your village.'

"I must admit, I trembled at his proposition, for though I was mighty in the ways of magick, I had always been lacking in the skills needed to manage verbal confrontations. Yet, while I stood there stammering, Kayleah spoke up for herself, saying, 'I am neither his to give nor yours to take. Furthermore, I have no desire to be made a prince's plaything.'

"I was shocked by her forceful response, and, while I stood trembling, the king's face went from white to red to purple, and he screamed, 'I want the leader of this town and all members of its council beheaded! Their families shall be tortured, and their houses burnt to the ground with all their possessions inside! And the tribute owed to me by this pitiful village shall be increased a hundredfold!'

"Before he could continue his rant, I begged him for forgiveness. 'She is young and impetuous,' I pleaded. 'She often does not think before she speaks!'

"The monarch paused for a moment, though his wrathfulness had not entirely abated. 'How, then, do you answer my offer now? What do you propose to do to save your town? Speak! Speak, old man!'

"Before I knew what was happening, I was mouthing words that were not my own. The words that escaped my own throat were: 'Why not take the woman to a private dwelling, my lord, and, there, examine her for yourself? If she still pleases you, you may claim her for the prince.'

"As soon as I had pronounced these sentences, I knew what had happened: My own daughter had forced me through magickal means to speak them. I wanted to deny what she had made me say, but no such denial would have turned aside the king's reawakened passion for Kayleah. I could see that fantasies of enjoying her flesh were dancing across his face and throughout his very being.

"'Your plan has merit, old man. I shall give your daughter a second chance to please me. Guards! Bring her!'

"They disappeared into our public hall, which was, at that time of day, deserted. His men stood guard while I waited, and trembled, and worried until I was nearly sick. And then, less than twenty minutes later, the two of them emerged from the building.

"King Ottallo looked ill—his face was a pasty green hue, and his lips were quavering. Kayleah bore a self-satisfied smile on her face as she stood in the doorway of the hall.

"The king merely climbed upon his steed and said to his men, 'We go back to the castle. No more shall we ride through the land.'

"'But what of this woman? The council? This village?

"'What of the tributes?' his soldiers asked.

"'Forget them all. Leave everything. To the castle!' And with that, he spurred his horse, and they rode off.

"Later, I asked Kayleah what had happened, what she had done that day. 'I put a sickness into him, Father; or rather I loosed the sickness of his spirit upon his physical body. He did deserve it, you know.' I agreed with her, though I was firm with her. I told her I was worried what might become of her should the king recover his senses. And I told her I was not pleased that she had used my voice to initiate her plan.

"Well, as most of you know, the king never did regain his senses—or his health. A short time later, we received word in our village that the king was dead.

"I took my daughter aside and told her that I feared the king's knights might return to punish her. I was nearly certain that they would connect his death to her.

"'What shall I do, Father?' she asked. 'I've nowhere else to go, and I do not wish to leave your side!' I pleaded with her to escape, but she insisted that her foes would find her no matter where she hid, especially if she had not yet finished her training with me.

"Finally, after examining all the alternatives, I decided upon the only one I felt was a safe option.

"'I can hide you through magickal means, Daughter. I can conceal you in a fashion that none would think possible. But there is a price: You shall lose much of your powers for a time, and even, perhaps, you shall lose your humanity. Such a charm of concealment has not been attempted for many years, but I feel it is our only hope.'

"After we both had shed many tears, she consented.

"And then, I worked the charm.

"Several months later, a small army of Terasskossian soldiers entered our village. These knights were led by their new monarch, eighteen-year-old King Orlacc. He soon came to me, and, with vengeance in his squinted eyes, he demanded I turn over my daughter to him.

"'Would that it were possible, Liege, I would do so,' I answered, 'but I'm afraid my daughter has died.'

"'Oh? Is that so? When did it happen, and how?' he asked, doubtfully.

"'This past winter, my lord. She fell through the ice on Lake Etab'hi and was drowned.'

"As I had expected, young Orlacc did not believe me. He had his men tear apart our town to search for Kayleah, and, when he did not find her in the village, he made his knights examine the woods surrounding the lake. Finally, empty-handed, he abandoned the search, but, before he left our village, he hissed a curse at me, saying, 'One day I will discover your secret, old man. I shall find out what magicks you have wrought, and I shall have my revenge.'

"Yet I have carried my secret with me 'til this very day, and your king, it would seem, has forgotten his vengeance and turned his mind towards other matters."

After he had finished his tale, the Sage bowed at the waist, and the people of the court seemed almost ready to applaud him for spinning such an entertaining yarn. But then Orlacc jumped up from his throne.

"You would dare to mock me in my own palace!? Are you mad, old man?" He then took a sword from one of his men and approached the Sage, who now seemed to cower. "You forget, magician, that I have you and your friends at my mercy!"

He grabbed the Sage and held the sword to his throat.

"True, I had forgotten our unfortunate earlier encounter. 'Twas many years ago, and you were just another fleaeaten old crow to me, even then! Why would I even care to remember you? But now...now that you have reminded me of your offense—and worse, that of your daughter's, there shall be a reckoning! My kingdom's misfortunes began the day my father died! His chief vizier, Dernalyne, soon married my mother and usurped power, telling this court I was not yet 'mature' enough to rule. When Mother died soon after, he must have thought his hold on the crown secure, but he was no conqueror and no king, and I showed him otherwise. Still, in his time on the throne, Terasskos declined, and it is now but a shadow of its former self. And to think...it all began that day in your village!"

He gripped the Sage even tighter and glared, saying, "So reveal to me now where your bitch daughter is hidden, or I shall spill your blood upon this court! I swear it in the name of my beloved father, Ottallo!!!"

"Very well," said the Sage, struggling to get his words out (for Orlacc held him tightly). "You scream 'bitch,' but I'll tell you you've got the wrong animal. Shieda! To me!"

At his command, the cat strode out from behind me, walked over to where her master stood, and stopped a few paces in front of him.

Before Orlacc could grasp what was going on, the Sage thrust out his open palm and shouted: "Shieda—become! Let the spell we cast now be undone!"

A charge of energy seemed to ripple through the room. I felt the hair on the back of my neck jump to attention, and everyone else appeared to sway uneasily. The atmosphere of the hall swam, and a burning smell permeated the air. And then, as if I had blinked and missed something, a beautiful naked woman stood where the cat had been. I recognized her at once! It was the woman I had seen swimming in the lake several nights back—the woman who'd kissed me—my night angel!

She seemed dazed by her transformation, but then, so did everyone else.

Except the Sage.

With Orlacc still stunned, the Sage yelled, "All secrets burn, now let the tables turn!" And then to us: "Run, friends, run!"

He raised his hands and chanted staccato words in some unknown tongue. Blue energy radiated from his fingers, and bolts of electricity or some other force snapped through the air. Orlacc's sword leapt from his hand. Then, his soldiers' weapons seemed to magnetize their swords and pikes flew about the room, crashed together, and fell to the floor in piles. Their armor, too, became charged, and their arms and legs attached themselves to those of their companions.

The Sage gestured again, and our party was affected; our manacles fell to the floor, and our armor and weapons materialized on our bodies. Another gesture, and a leather-skirted armor appeared from thin air and covered his daughter's body.

Finally, he said to her, "Shieda... Daughter. Go. Lead them out of here."

"F-Father?"

"I have only so much power, Kayleah! Go! You must!"

"Will you be... ?"

"Just go!" he screamed, and then he brought his hands together above his head, sending a fireball racing wildly around the chamber. Orlacc's guards and his gathered court, already staggering, dizzy, and off-balance, dove to the deck; but Shieda, er, Kayleah...well, the darkhaired, once-a-cat, formerly-nude-but-now-clothed-in-leather, adopted-daughter-of-the-Sage person waved us on, and we followed her out of the room.

And we knew we were running for our lives.

Chapter Twelve

It was difficult for me, with my shorter legs, to catch up to the Sage's daughter, but I somehow managed. She turned her head slightly as she ran, and she flashed me an awkward smile, as if to say, "I know, I know—I've got a lot of explaining to do, but not right now." But I, of course, being me, couldn't wait for a better time.

"I wanna ask you something!" I screeched over the sounds of our footfalls.

"Not a very good time for it now, is it?" she huffed. I noticed for the first time that she had an English accent.

"I need to know ..." I stumbled and nearly fell as we turned a sharp corner, but I regained my footing and caught up with her again.

"I need to know, first of all, what I should call you?"

"For now, Shieda. It's been my name for... well, a long time. It means 'Shadow Walker,' my father said."

We turned another corner, and I realized we were reentering the prison area.

"Where are we headed?" I asked.

"These dungeons should all be connected to a central trough that leads to a waterway. They use the trough to wash all the waste from the cells."

"You mean, like...a sewer?"

"A sewer...yes, that's right."

"But why?"

She glared at me again, nearly melting me with her green eyes.

"Do you know of another way we can get out of here with all those guards roaming around?"

True, I thought, and I shrugged. There were a plethora of doors and windows throughout the castle, to be sure, but Orlacc's men would be looking for us to escape that way.

We stopped in front of a door, and Shieda peered into the cell through the bars on the window. Then, she said, "This will do. Can one of you break open the door?"

"Stand aside," Therra answered, and she lunged forward and grappled the door. As she pulled, her arm, leg, and back muscles shook and swelled from the effort. The wood of the door creaked and shuddered, the metal lock and hinges groaned and stretched, but nothing else happened. The door would not be budged.

"Move away," she said at last. "I shall batter it down."

Parkel put his hand up to stop her, and he stepped forward. "Wait. I believe I can force the lock."

Therra's eyes looked like they were about to bulge out of her head when he said this, and I thought she might just charge the door anyway, even with Parkel standing in the way. He ignored her anger, instead removing a small, sharp-looking object from his shirt and kneeling in front of the door. I guess he figured he could pick the lock.

"Hurry!" I exhorted him. Just then we heard footsteps—many of them. The soldiers had nearly caught up to us!

Therra and Shieda assumed fighting stances and waited for our pursuers to round the corner. I shouted (bravely), "Hurry! They're almost here!"

"Fight or run, weakling," Therra yelled, "but do not whine!"

Domitrus, who had finally caught his breath from our first flight, muttered, "Would that I could cast some spell, as the Sage might, but my powers work only through charmed objects and carefully mixed potions. I fear we are lost!"

Just then, I heard a loud clunk. It was the lock falling to the floor. Parkel had done it! Now, he pushed open the door and rushed into the cell. I dove in after Shieda and Therra, pulling Domitrus along with me, and, as I slipped through the doorway, I saw the soldiers entering the hallway where we'd just been standing. One of them saw me and shouted, "They're here! Get them!"

"Hold that door shut—now!" Shieda said when we were all inside. "Parkel, come help me get the grate open. The rest of you make sure those guards don't get in."

While Domitrus (barely), Therra (just about singlehandedly), and I (okay, at least I'm willing to admit I'm a stubby-limbed wuss with little strength) kept the door closed by leaning against it, Shieda and Parkel worked at prying a metal grate up from a hole in the floor in one corner of the cell. I must admit, I was a little jealous that she had picked Parkel to help her instead of me. I thought that she had, maybe, you know, kind of preferred me in a special way, but...oh well.

So far, just seven guards had reached the hallway outside the door, and Therra was doing okay at holding the door shut on them. But we all knew there would be more of them arriving soon, and, with greater numbers, they'd be able to storm through the door. Parkel and

Shieda seemed to be getting nowhere with the grate.

I looked around the room. Something caught my eye. On the floor was a wooden pole, five feet long and sturdy looking, with metal hooks fastened at each end. After a moment's consideration, I reasoned it was used to carry the buckets of water used to wash out the cells (certainly not to bathe the prisoners). More than that, though, it'd make a great lever.

I rushed over and grabbed it, and then I joined Shieda and Parkel at the grate. "Watch this," I said, and I slipped the pole through a couple of holes in the grate. Together, the three of us pulled on the bar and were able to yank up the grate. Success!

Shieda glanced at me and smiled briefly. I nearly forgot where I was! Then she said, "Right. Now, all of you—into the hole. Quickly!" She waved at Domitrus to come over, and he ran away from the door and plunged down the opening. Parkel followed, and then Shieda indicated that I was to go next. When I hesitated, she said, "Don't worry. We'll all make it." I jumped down.

It was about a fifteen-foot drop to the bottom. When I'd landed, I looked up and could barely see Shieda near the opening. I thought I had heard her shout to Therra, but now she was just sitting there, stock-still. Suddenly, Therra came leaping through the hole, bellowing, and I had to jump to avoid her. After she'd landed, I looked up again, but Shieda was still crouched near the edge of the precipice. I was sure the soldiers would get her before she could jump! Then, I heard a crackle, and I thought I smelled something burning. At last, Shieda turned and leaped after the rest of us.

Once she regained her footing, I asked, "Wh-what happened to the guards?"

"Fire," she answered matter-of-factly, and then, realizing that I still didn't get it, she added, "Tell you later. Let's away before more come."

We took off sprinting down the course of the sewer. Of course, it smelled simply joyous, but at least there weren't any rats or other creatures around and there wasn't much standing water in the place to slog through. After we'd gone a few hundred feet, we came to a place where a part of the floor opened below us. It was kind of a big chute, and, when we looked down, we could see a river flowing by.

"This is it," Shieda said. "Whenever you're ready, take the plunge."

And then she did. One by one, the others followed. Then, I took one last look at the water rushing by below me, closed my eyes, held my nose, and plunged.

Chapter Thirteen

I could kid you by claiming I swam down that mighty river, but in all honesty its current was so strong that it was all I could do to just stay afloat.

I was washed along, rolled over and over into submerged rocks for, I'd estimate, a good half-a-mile. I tried to locate the others, but the commotion of the rapids made it impossible to see if any of them were nearby. I began to think about making a last-ditch push to swim to shore, when something subtly changed about the sound and pull of the river. I spun around in the water, and was horrified by what I saw.

Not far ahead, the river disappeared, or fell away—I was coming to a waterfall!

I had no way of knowing how bad the drop-off was, but the fact that I couldn't see the river beyond the edge of the falls made me realize I didn't want to find out. I started paddling like a panicking animal, but, though I was in better shape as Morrelaine than I had been as Grant Donovan, my arms and legs were so short that I couldn't seem to make any progress. The sinking stone of death chilled my insides as it tumbled through my desperate soul.

But then I heard a shout above the roar of the waters, and something splashed near my head. I bobbed my head up, and saw Parkel leaning towards me. He had his shirt off, and was tossing it out like a fishing line. Instantly, I realized this was my only chance. With all my strength, I leaped and grabbed the sleeve of Parkel's shirt.

As he reeled me in as best he could with one arm, I saw that he was being held by Therra, who was hanging on to a tree, using a hastily-fashioned harness made of her own and Parkel's sword belts. I thanked whatever gods there might be here that I had such ingenious and quick-thinking companions! This thought led to another: If I died here, would I return to Earth, or would I go wherever people go when they die?

When they'd hauled me out and laid me on my back, I stayed there for a while, just gasping for precious air. Once I could speak again, I asked Parkel if everyone else had made it okay.

"Aye, Morrelaine—you were the last out," he said, smiling. "And a lucky Grimnell you are indeed."

"Lucky?! But I could have died! It was horrible!"

"It could have been more 'horrible,'" he replied, and he held up his shirt to show me that the sleeve was half torn off from my pulling on it. I swallowed my outburst. Time to shut up, Grant.

"We cannot afford to tarry here, listening to his moaning," Therra said, reattaching her sword.

"No, you're right," said Shieda. "Orlacc's men will be combing the countryside, trying to find us. We've got to get as far from here as possible by nightfall. Get up, everyone. We can dry off as we go."

"Aren't you worried about your father?" I asked, climbing to my feet.

She thought for a moment, then answered, "No. If he's alive, I'm sure he'll be able to find us. If not..."

"But what if they've imprisoned him again? Shouldn't we try to rescue him?"

"He...won't let himself be captured again," she said. Then, she took a deep breath, put a brave smile on her face, and added, "I know him well enough to be certain of that."

Without any further discussion, we began jogging through the forest, trying to keep a pace we could all maintain. I found myself wondering what Shieda's deal was. She was a sensuous dream that night I encountered her by the lake in the woods. Naked, wet, and playful, she'd seemed like a child of nature, a wood nymph, or a spirit of the water, longings answered in the blue shadows. That night, I'd felt a strange, overwhelming sense of love emanating from her, and it was a feeling I'd found mirrored in my own heart, a feeling I'd carried with me ever since. I'd imagined that, if we ever met again in the daylight world, we'd fall instantly in love.

And now, here she was in front of me, flesh and blood, a seemingly natural leader, practical and pragmatic, confident and businesslike. I admired those traits too, and my attraction to her was still there, but the connection between us seemed to have disappeared. She'd barely acknowledged me, let alone showed she cared anything at all for me. I wondered if that night I'd first encountered her, when she'd seemed like a sensuous dream come to life, when we'd seemed like two halves of the same dream, come together at last...maybe it had been only a reverie after all.

These melancholy thoughts raced around in my head, while my feet pounded the forest floor. We jogged, stopped, and jogged and so on for several hours, until, finally, the sun began to sink. Shieda announced that we should look for a spot to set up camp for the night. Parkel scouted around for a bit, and he soon found us a small clearing below a cliff near the river where it would be difficult for anyone to spot us coming from most directions. While Parkel and Domitrus worked at catching us some fish for dinner, Therra, Shieda, and I gathered wood for a fire. By the time the sun had disappeared completely, we were nursing our sore feet and dining on some fresh, flame-broiled riverfish.

Later, when we were sitting around digesting, I took Shieda aside and said, "I have to talk to you."

"I know," she whispered back, "but wait until the others are asleep."

She volunteered us to take the first watch, and, after the rest of the group had settled in for the night, we strode off into the woods. We stopped when we were still near enough to be able to keep an eye on the camp but far enough away that we could talk. I leaned up against a tree, while she paced back and forth a bit, scuffing at the tree's roots with her feet.

When we were pretty sure the others were asleep, she said, "We have to figure out our next move. We need a plan. I assume that's what you wanted to discuss with me, right?"

Man! And I thought us guys were supposed to be the clueless ones when it comes to relationships! Not in this world, apparently. I calmly uncrossed my arms, looked into her eyes, smirked, turned red, and blew up.

"Excuse me? It'd be nice if we could 'discuss' what's going on between us! Or what's not going on, now, at least! You remember, don't you? Me on my back, you, naked, leaning over me, a little kiss by the pond, oh, say, about a week ago? It all really meant something to me! I thought it might to you too, but I guess not!"

For a few seconds, she just stood and stared at me. I wasn't sure whether she was going to laugh in my face, walk away in disgust, or what. Then, catlike, she stretched her arm out to my shoulder and slowly drew me towards her. We kissed, and she eased her body up against mine. I was in ecstasy again—though I was confused, too. But I didn't care at that moment—she was loving me again, and, this time, it wasn't a dream. Somehow, I knew in my heart that we'd work this whole thing out.

Finally, she drew back a little, and said, "Now you have to stop worrying about this. We don't have the time right now."

"I know," I admitted. "I was being stupid. We do have to think about getting away from Orlacc's forces—they are trying to kill us, after all! It's just...if you had any idea how unsure of everything I've been..."

"Well, what do you expect? You haven't been in this world very long now, have you?"

"Y-You know about that? But... ? God! It seems like everybody knows!"

"If you're referring to my father, well, he knows about you and your strange origins because he's old, wise, and magickal, and he's able to divine such secrets. But if you're wondering how I know? Well, I could sense it, I believe, because I come from the same place as you— Earth."

What? Was that really possible? I puzzled over this one for a minute, but, actually, in a weird way, it seemed plausible. I mean, if I'd managed to fall through that hole in the utility building that led to this world, someone else could have done the same thing. Whew! Well, if things keep up at this pace, the whole of the student body at my college could end up here by the end of the semester! Anyhow, it had seemed a little strange to me that Shieda didn't converse in the same "medieval speak" that the others had. And now, I knew why.

"So, um, what were you doing out there, poking around that utility building?" I asked, trying to be a little cute. But she just looked at me quizzically and shook her head. I tried again, asking, "Oh, you weren't a freshman or something, were you?"

"I-I'm not sure what you mean... are you asking about university or something like that?"

"Well, yeah. I just assumed, 'cause that building is right behind my dorm and all."

"What building?"

"The building I broke into that led me here. To this world." When I saw she still wasn't getting me, I got impatient. "C'mon...it's on the Charles, in Boston, near the college. Don't you remember how you got here?"

Finally, she seemed to make some connection in her mind. She smiled and put her arm around me, leaning up against the tree trunk alongside me. It was a little unsettling, with her being about a head taller than I was, but I wasn't about to worry myself over that right now. At last, she said, "Do I! How I got here? Hmmm. Well, I was in San Francisco, California, visiting relatives, when the ground starting shaking as if someone were jerking the earth back and forth. It was a terrible, horrible earthquake, which caught everyone off guard. I lost my footing, and then I was falling into the pitch darkness, falling and falling, and then I lost consciousness. When I next opened my eyes, I was here, in this strange world."

I wasn't sure why, but a shudder ran through me just then. It was as if an echo of the quake she'd just described had reached me after having traveled some nearly unimaginable distance. I'd never been in an earthquake, but I remembered watching the coverage of the San Fran quake in '89, when that bridge ...

"Hey, wait a minute!" I said suddenly, realizing there was something weird about her story. "What year was that—when you left Earth? Do you remember?"

"Of course. It was nineteen hundred and six. Why?"

Now, I let out a whoosh of air. 1906?! I faced her, took hold of her shoulders, and looked her in the eye. "Shieda...Kayleah...do you want to know what year it was when I fell through the hole that brought me here? You might find it hard to believe."

She thought it over for a moment, and answered, "Well, I can guess it was after I came here. I've been here perhaps twelve years, so, if you departed terra firma a little over a week ago, it must have been 1918 back home. What was happening then?"

I gulped. "More than you can imagine. But that's not... Well, the thing is, when I came here, when I left Earth, it was 2014."

After I'd named the year, her arms dropped and went slack for a moment, and then she tensed up again. At first I thought she was going to push me away, but then I saw she wasn't angry, but she was grappling with her emotions. I felt my own worries, swirling at the back of my mind: What might this all mean for me? If I ever do get back to Earth, will something like 110 years have gone by? But I tried to suppress these fears.

"Are you okay?" I asked her. It almost seemed like we'd both been away for a while, and that we'd just snapped back to the present. She looked up at me and caught my gaze. Her eyes looked tired.

"Well... it... it takes a moment... to sort of come to terms. Everyone I knew is probably dead or extremely old by now. It's so... "

"Did you ever try to make it back home? Is that why you tracked down the Sage—to ask him for help?"

"No, I... I had other reasons. I... " Her voiced trailed off, and I suddenly realized that I might have been pushing her a little too hard too soon. She had just found out, after all, that her whole sense of time had been screwed up by almost a century. That had to be a tad difficult for a person to take!

Apologetically, I pulled her close to me and held her tight, rocking gently from side to side. "It's okay," I said softly. "Don't worry about it now. Everything's fine the way it is. We can figure this out another time."

In a little while, I felt her put her arms around me. Thoughts and questions were racing through my mind, but I forced myself to ignore them—to just not hear them anymore.

We stood there together like that, saying nothing, until Parkel and Therra came to take the next watch.

Chapter Fourteen

We had run for two hours without stopping the next morning, following a straight-line course away from Orlacc's castle, when we came to what was apparently the forest's edge. Beyond us, rolling plains, covered with knee-high grass and scattered scrub bushes, stretched out for as far as any of us could see.

While we were catching our breath, Shieda spoke to us.

"Now is the time for us to make our plans. Once we leave the cover of this forest, we'll be easy to spot from far away on the plains out there. We'd better figure out where we're going, and then we have to get there as quickly as we can."

Parkel was the first to break the resultant silence: "We should raise an army to attack Orlacc's domain. We five are the only ones not of Terasskos who know of his plans to wage a 'Grand Campaign.' All our peoples will be taken unawares if we do nothing!"

"I'll go back there and cut out his heart myself!" Therra hissed. "I need no army to support me."

"That would be certain death! You couldn't... " Parkel stifled his critique once he spied the expression it had brought to Therra's face. Shieda came to his rescue.

"There's no question that we'll need an army if we're going to strike back at him. Can we count on your people to help us, Therra?"

Now Therra's angry expression soured into bitterness. "We...cannot. I am an outlaw amongst my own folk, and I fear they would be more likely to carry out my death sentence than listen to me, though my words might very well save them. Oh, my people love their retribution, their vengeance against rule-breakers! Orlacc knew this when he selected me for his quest, and now he shall play it to his advantage. I fear he has insured himself too well against us."

"Aye, 'tis the same for me," said Parkel. When the rest of us looked quizzically at him, he elaborated: "As a boy, I joined a pirate crew, and, with them, ransacked the boats of the people of my nation, Ruzal. I was later captured and expelled from my country."

"Well... the people of West Serra Land would be unlikely to feel any strong allegiance towards me, I'm fairly certain," Shieda said.

"Most of the families there have roots to the town stretching back a century or more. I was an outsider living there, as was my 'father.' On top of that, I know some of them blamed us for risking a Terasskossian reprisal when King Ottallo died after visiting our town. And common folk like the West Serrans tend to want to keep magick practitioners like us at arm's length anyway."

"Might they join us still? If only to fight against Orlacc?" Parkel asked.

"Yeah!" I shouted, enthused. "They've gotta be pretty pissed, er, angry with him."

But she shook her head. "Perhaps, but the confusing political situation might play havoc with our attempts to explain things to them: First we'd have to convince them that it was, in fact, Orlacc who ordered the raid against them. We have no proof beyond our words that Orlacc's the real king. My people still think that Dernalyne is in charge. And don't forget that the last time Orlacc strode into West Serra Land, he was with you people, and he was posing as the heroic liberator, 'outraged' at the wrongs done to my village. We'd have to work hard to overcome that perception. On top of that, the previous kings of Terasskos conquered West Serra Land time and again in the past. Compared with his predecessors, Orlacc's exhibited a lot of restraint towards my people: they'd likely be afraid to invite his wrath."

"That leaves only Morrelaine's people," Therra said in a flat, dismal tone.

"W-Wait! Wh-What about Domitrus?" I stammered. I suddenly sensed that everyone's eyes were trained on little old me! But I couldn't let on that I didn't even know any of my own people!

"Morrelaine, you know that Domitrus's folk are not made for warring! They are a peaceful, learned order," Parkel scolded (and, damn it, if he hadn't become a lot more assertive since Orlacc had "left" our party!). "Still," he added with a note of reconsideration, "they could, perhaps, assist us with their wisdom."

"My friends," Domitrus said, coming forward at last. "Your conversation forces me to speak of a matter I was loath to bring up earlier. I am afraid I must speak of it now." He paused, and, crossing his arms nervously, he began kicking the dirt. "Perhaps...perhaps there are some of us who do not wish to engage Orlacc again."

Therra's face came to life again. "Surely...you can't allow him to get away with all that he has done to us? To you?!"

He glanced up at her, but turned away quickly, casting his gaze towards the ground. "It is only that...I fear I have been little more than an impediment to our endeavors thusfar. I must admit also that I have learned to fear combat, especially against well-trained warrior knights. I no longer wish to seek it out."

"Well... why did you seek it out in the first place?" I asked.

"I suppose... well, I had hoped I could be a force for good," he answered. "Perhaps I felt that I could accomplish more by joining you and fighting the oppressor powers than I could through the continuation of my priestly studies at Auriggido Mountain. There I was removed from all the affairs of the world. But I felt that our order was founded to foster good amongst the peoples of this world, and that perhaps we needed to do our service amongst these selfsame peoples. I was looking for a new way. But now I see that I was wrong."

"No! You were not wrong!" Therra spat.

"I say that I was!" Domitrus yelled back, staring Therra square in the face. His eyes glowed with a mournful pink light. Then he added, less forcefully, "I meant what I said, and nothing that you might say will make me change my mind."

We all stood in silence for several minutes. I could certainly understand Domitrus's feelings, but I definitely didn't want him to leave us. For one thing, he was the most calm and approachable person in our party, and, what the hey—cooler heads do sometimes prevail in certain situations, after all. Not only that, he was the first member of our group to cut me some slack back when I first fell into this world. Yeah, I had to admit I'd kinda miss the guy, with his shiny bald head and creased brow!

After a while, Shieda looked up at the sky and seemed to notice that the sun was getting near its zenith. She turned back to us and said, "Well, Domitrus—what is it you want to do?"

"I must return to my mountain home, to my studies."

"Well then," Shieda said, addressing the rest of us, "I think we should escort Domitrus back to his homeland. We owe him that much."

"What?! We should do what?!" Therra came totally unhinged now. She speedily drew her sword and waved it in the air, violently punctuating her pronouncements with stabs into the air.

"If this simpering old fool wishes to abandon our war against Orlacc, let him! But do not say that we should join him in his folly! We haven't the time! It takes time to raise an army! To devise a battle plan! To train many warriors to fight as one! And yet you say we should fritter away what time we have 'escorting' this...this failed wizard back to his precious sanctuary? Fah! I'll have no part of it!!!"

As Therra ranted on, Shieda closed her eyes and massaged her temples. When Therra had finished and was standing still with her sword aimed outward, seemingly awaiting a response, Shieda opened her eyes and calmly replied, "By doing this, we should be able to outwit Orlacc. Remember, he'll be expecting us to try to raise an army to oppose him, but he won't be expecting us to head for Domitrus's homeland, a place full of peaceloving cenobites. By going to Auriggido, we'll stand a better chance of eluding his knights. Once Domitrus is safe, we can go about rounding up an army. This is the best way, and it's fair to Domitrus as well. Don't you see? If you or Parkel or any of us wanted to quit now and go home, I'd do everything I could to help. And I still will, if any of you decide you've had enough. But this is what I've decided to do now, and I hope you stand ready to do the same."

For a while, we stood there. None of us appeared very sure of what we should do. But each side had made its case. Now, it was time for our decisions.

"Come, Domitrus," Shieda said finally. "Now we are wasting time. Let's go."

"You... you needn't accompany me, Shieda," Domitrus stammered. "I warn you, the journey is three days from this place, or perhaps more, by foot."

"That's not far," Shieda replied, stepping out of the forest and onto the sunlit pampas. Domitrus followed her. Then, to me, she said, "Morrelaine? Are you coming with us?"

Of course I would have followed her anywhere! But I answered, "For now," and I climbed out of the shady woods and stood with them.

"Parkel?"

"I...I'm afraid I do agree with Therra in principle," he said. "Still, perhaps you are correct. Perhaps we will throw Orlacc off our trail by doing this. I...I'll go with you, unless Therra intends to stay and fight. I do not wish to leave her...without assistance."

At this, Therra dropped her sword arm to her side, and she relaxed her taut fighting stance for the first time since our argument began. She seemed genuinely surprised, maybe even touched, that anyone would take her side against the majority of the group. After reflecting for several moments, she, too, stepped out into the daylight.

"Very well. You... you are my friends, and your judgment has brought us safely this far. I shall trust that judgment a while longer," she said, but then added, "However, if I see that any of you are lingering too long in any one place, and if I deem that you are foolishly delaying our true mission, I will raise an army myself and crush Orlacc's kingdom. And then, if you should come to me seeking the benefits of my friendship, your pleas will fall on deaf ears. Mark my words!"

She gazed sternly at each of us in turn, but her glare lingered longest upon Shieda. Finally, Shieda said, "Understood," and we all nodded our approval.

Parkel leaped out of the forest's fringes, and we took off running across the open plains.

Chapter Fifteen

As we went along for most of the day across the seemingly endless ocean of windswept green, we held to a particular formation: Domitrus, out in front, led the way; Shieda and I followed; and Therra and Parkel guarded the rear. I had been noticing with some regret that our party was becoming polarized into these three factions of a fairly regular basis. I was starting to worry that, if we had any more situations in which we had to take a vote to decide our course of action, we would end up with a 2-2 split vote every time once Domitrus had left. I mentioned this to Shieda.

"You don't think we can count on Parkel?" she asked, wiping the sweat from her forehead.

I stole a quick glance backwards to make sure Therra and Parkel were not within earshot.

"I don't know. It's kinda strange: he told me before how he's been in love with her for so long, but how she never paid any attention to him when Orlacc was around. But ever since Orlacc turned on us and humiliated her, she's been sorta warming up to him. I guess I'm a little nervous he might vote with her just to, you know, win her over or something."

"I see your point," Shieda answered, "but I'm afraid we'll have to wait and cross that bridge if we come to it. Let's hope we don't."

"Well, I've got another dilemma for you to ponder, too," I said, moving even closer to her to avoid being overheard. "And I know I seem to be full of worries, but that's just the kinda guy I am. Anyhow, here's the problem: You said our plan is to eventually go back to my village to recruit an army after we've dropped off Domitrus. But how am I supposed to appeal to my people when I don't even know my people? I mean, you and I both know I only dropped into this world about a week ago!"

"You may not know your people, but they do know you. You'll pull through."

"You mean they know Morrelaine! But I'm not Morrelaine!"

She flashed me a grin, and said, "Are you so sure?"

I wasn't quite sure what she meant by her question, so I went on.

"What I'm saying it that I have no idea what this Morrelaine was like before I got zapped into his body. I mean, was he married? Does he have any kids? Do people like and respect him? All that stuff is important for me to know if we're gonna pull this off! On top of all that, I know nothing about Grimnell customs and practices. How am I supposed to convince them to join up with us?"

Shieda put her arm around my shoulders to calm me, and we walked on like that for a while together.

"As far as their customs, I can fill you in a bit about those," she said. "I've traveled among the Grimnells before, though it was a long time ago, I'll admit. As for your other concerns, well... haven't your instincts served you well up 'til now? Why not trust in yourself? You might be surprised to find in yourself a leader after all."

I realized that, of course, there was a lot of truth in what she'd said. Morrelaine's battle-trained instincts had kicked in a couple of times before, so maybe his other faculties would take over when they were needed too. Still, I couldn't help being a little apprehensive. Well, actually, I was more that a little apprehensive—I was petrified!

"I guess I wish your father was still here with us," I said, and, as soon as I'd gotten the words out, I realized I'd hurt her feelings. As she pulled away, I tried to put my arm around her, but she shrugged it off. I suppose it had sounded like I was saying that I didn't have much faith in her leadership abilities, and that the Sage would have come up with a better plan. That wasn't what I'd meant, but I knew that any explanation I offered her would sound half-assed. I managed to mutter, "I'm... sorry, Shieda," but even that went unnoticed in the commotion that followed.

Domitrus, who had been traveling about 100 feet ahead of us, had stopped, and he was shouting for our attention. I peered through the rippling heat of the late afternoon and saw what it was he was hollering about. Up ahead in the distance was a village—or a small outpost—of about four buildings. There were shapes moving about near these structures. People? Or... they looked more like horses!

Parkel, Therra, Shieda, and I had all caught up to Domitrus. We were sweating and out of breath. Now, all our eyes were locked on the distant settlement.

"What are we waiting for?" Therra asked, her voice croaking from thirst. "They must have food and drink, and perhaps we can acquire horses." And, as we started towards the apparent oasis, she turned to Parkel and said, "Mayhap our destinies are blessed, as you said."

The largest of the four buildings was an inn and tavern with a sign out front that read: "Ye Olde Inne and Taverne at the Woodesyde." Wow, I thought, bad and trendy misspellings as a form of advertising has even reached this mysterious corner of the universe!

There were twelve horses tied up outside, and a few meek-looking villagers were mulling about the place. We decided (due to our intense hunger and thirst) not to bother with them and to go directly into the tavern.

The place was gloomy and smelly—with beer and smoke—just like any bar back home. I counted sixteen men and five women in the room. The men were loud, boorish, and covered with dust, sweat, and spit. A few were leaning up against the bar, but most were sprawled out in chairs around the five tables in the place, laughing, lying, drinking, farting, burping, and feverishly groping at the few women around the room, who seemed to be serving wenches from what I could tell. They—these loose-garmented waitresses—were busy navigating from the tables to the bar and back again, taking the men's orders, allowing a small amount of their patter and pawing, and fighting off their more zealous assaults. Like I said, it was just like any bar back home in the city.

The exception to the rule with the men was, of course, the bartender/owner of the establishment. He had to be about the hairiest man I'd ever seen, here or on Earth. He was short and stocky and seemed to be hunched over, but he looked compact and muscular, not fat. Glaring out from beneath his frizzy heavy metal hair and from behind his spittle-crusted ZZ Top beard was the most severe, cruel, dour, un-jolly, unfriendly, and un-funny pair of yellow Charles Manson-y eyes imaginable. I guessed that "The Customer is Always Right" was probably not his motto. Yuck!

Of course, just like in any good (or bad) Western film, all eyes bored into us as soon as we entered, and the room fell silent.

Being perhaps the most courageous (and thirsty) of our bunch, Therra headed towards the bar and said, in a parched and pleading voice, "Good sir, my friends and I are hungry, thirsty, and tired. We would ask that you attend to our needs, but we, alas, have no means with which to pay you. Could we beg... ?"

At her utterance of the word "beg," several of the tavern's patrons burst out laughing. One of the men standing at the bar slapped another on the back, and they both nearly spilled their drinks. One drunken voice shouted, "You women can always find a way to pay... on your backs!" More uproarious laughter.

The bartender's expression did not change, and his probably-frowning mouth remained hidden behind his mass of facial fuzz.

Therra, her face set in a vengeful mask, was drawing her sword, when we all heard a thud near the door. When we all turned to look, we saw Shieda sprawled on the floor. She was covered in a sheen of sweat, and was turning her face from side to side, groaning softly.

I rushed to her side, shouting, "Shieda! Shieda!" I started to yell for someone to get her some help, but my cries were drowned out by the sounds of men's boots stomping as they leaped out of their chairs and flew to Shieda's aid. Before I could collect my thoughts, several pairs of hands were lifting her limp body and carrying her towards a stairway. A voice screeched, "Get her to a room! She needs rest!" Another shouted, "Bring some water—cool, but not too cold!"

Our party followed as the tavern crowd bore Shieda upstairs and into one of the inn's four bedrooms. They lay her on the bed and threw open the room's windows. The strange bartender stood at the foot of the bed and barked orders to his serving women: "More water! Bring some cloths! And get a plate of our best dried fruits! Quickly! Go!"

The rest of us were dumbfounded, and I, of course, was extremely worried about Shieda. But, within a few minutes, she was sitting up a little, sipping water and sampling from a dish of sweet fruits. Not only that, but two of the women were toweling the sweat from her body.

After a short while, the patrons cleared out of the room, and only the bartender, his workers, and our party remained. He turned to us and said, "You may stay here 'til the lady recovers, but no longer. When she is well, you must begone—we need the room available for our paying customers." Then, he spoke to Shieda, saying, "My women shall attend to your needs. Call when you require aid. I'll...I'll take care of your...friends." He motioned for us to follow him, and said, "Come. I have food and drink for you too."

The rest of the group went with him downstairs, but I waited. When they were gone, I shut the door and crouched at Shieda's bedside. She looked up at me with tired eyes.

"Are you okay?" I asked. "That really surprised me back there."

Her eyelids fluttered, and she moaned, "Kiss me." I did, and from the way she reciprocated, you would have thought she wanted something else besides water. Not that I was complaining! Whenever we kissed, I forgot everything that had been troubling me—my body-switch, our mission, the dangers, all of it. When I finally pulled away, I saw through the window that the sun was finally setting outside, and it was getting cooler. I started to ask if she wanted to be left alone to sleep, but then I noticed she was smiling coyly at me.

"Wh-What's so funny?" I asked. "Did I kiss you weird or something?"

She rolled her eyes, and giggled, "No, silly! It's just that I'm surprised you fell for that bit of acting back there!"

I thought about it for a moment. Then, a realization crept over me, and I said, "You mean you weren't really sick at all?"

"Of course not! I don't wear out that easily! What do you think I am? A 'mere woman'?"

I huffed, and answered, "Well, I know for a fact that there's no such thing as a 'mere woman,' but you were right to judge that others here don't think that way. It was a nice trick you pulled, and now we get free room and board out of the deal."

"Thanks. The 'damsel-in-distress' routine never fails. And, actually, it's a trick I learned from a friend back on Earth. It seems to work everywhere, though. 'Big, strong' men never fail to jump when a 'frail lass' needs help."

"It's lucky for you we didn't end up in a bar full of Amazons," I joked.

"Then you or Parkel would have had to 'faint,'" she quipped. Then, she popped a grape into my mouth. "Here you go, sweetie. You need food and water too. In fact, if you wish to join the others downstairs for their meal, you shouldn't let me stop you."

I took a slice of peach from her next. "Nah. I think I'd rather stay here with you... you know, to make sure you're really okay and all. I mean, I really should watch over you, like any good strong male ought to."

The sun had completely disappeared below the horizon outside, but I could still just make out her form in the blue evening half-light. I saw her hands reaching up to unfasten her leather armor. And then she spoke, sending shivers up and down my back:

"Hadn't you better come here and protect me, then, you sturdy Grimnell warrior, you."

I gulped, but obeyed. I was in another dream, but better, it was real. Zowie!

Chapter Sixteen

In the morning, I awoke with the sun in my eyes. I was buck-nekkid in bed, and Therra, Parkel, and Domitrus were asleep, propped up against the walls in various spots around the room. Seeing them made me feel sort of guilty about snagging the only bed in the room, but then again, it had been for a good purpose! I don't know if other people's 'first times' were as good as mine; it had been a dream come true for me—literally!

Shieda was standing in a corner, pulling on her boots. She had already put on the rest of her armor.

"You're not going somewhere, are you?" I asked her, shielding my eyes from the morning light. "They won't let us stay here if they know you're up and about."

She turned to me and put a gloved finger to her lips, reminding me to be quiet. "I don't plan to stay here any longer. We don't have time," she whispered. "Anyhow, we all need to wake up soon and plan our next move. We still don't have any rations, money, or horses, and we could use some better weapons."

"Good point." I started to reach for my own clothes, and then I asked (because a guy needs to know), "So, uh, was... was I... did I...?"

She just smiled at me and said, "You were wonderful. Now let's save the sweet talk for later when there're fewer people around, eh? Hurry and get dressed so I can wake the others."

When we got downstairs, the bartender was busy wiping down his counter. There were only a few patrons around, and one leftover drunk, collapsed at a table. A young man about Parkel's age was sweeping the floor.

The bartender glared angrily at us when he saw Shieda was with our group. "I see you'll be leaving then," he said.

Shieda approached him and said, "Thank you so much for all that you've done. I don't know what came over me yesterday. It was just so hot, and then..."

"Hmmm. Yes, well, that's fine..." the man said, ignoring her and going back to his cleaning. But then, he looked up again and addressed Therra. "There was a man here earlier asking for you, lady.

Told him you were asleep."

The color drained out of Therra's face. She seemed to have grown roots into the floor. "Wh-What? Wh-Who...? Where is he?"

"He went outside, 'bout fifteen minutes ago. Said he had to feed his horse. He should still be out there. Couldn't have got far."

With her jaw hanging open, she looked at all of us. Shieda said, "Go on out, Therra. We'll stay here awhile and make our plans." Finally, Therra nodded and walked outside. I noticed that Parkel looked a little dejected as he watched her leave.

When we were sitting down, Shieda mused, "Who do you suppose it could be? Who knows she's here?"

And then it hit all of us at once—Orlacc! He must've found us!

We all jumped to our feet and scrambled out the door after Therra. We soon found her, standing, talking to a man who most definitely was not Orlacc. He was about half a head taller than Therra, and he wore armor that was of the same color and that bore similar markings to hers. His long black hair was braided, and he had a huge, dark handlebar mustache. He seemed to be pleading with Therra. When we had caught up to her, we saw that there were tears streaming down her face. Parkel called to her, and she spoke, though she did not turn away from the mysterious stranger.

"My friends, this is Mik'kun of Ekhulta," she said, "my father."

Shieda and Domitrus had headed off to see if there was any place in this little town where we could trade for supplies and, possibly, horses (though what exactly we had that we could barter with I wasn't sure—perhaps some of Domitrus's trade secret healing elixirs?). If we could acquire a few steeds, we could chop several days—perhaps even a week—off our mission's duration, Parkel had told me. Plus, having horses would make us harder to catch if Orlacc or his men ever found us.

The rest of us had gone back into the tavern. The bartender took one look at us, let out a hiss, shrugged, and went back to his work. Therra and her father had sat at a corner table to talk things over. Shieda had asked me to keep an eye on our overwrought Amazon, and to keep Parkel by my side, in case a "situation" developed. We sat a few tables away from the two Ekhultans—far away enough to eavesdrop without appearing too obvious. It was just another little skill I had picked up from my days spent in the college cafeteria!

I wasn't sure if Parkel had picked up on my plan, but we didn't say all that much to each other when we'd sat down. I did ask him if Therra had ever told him anything about her father or her people.

96

"Aye," he said, nodding, but with his eyes glued on Therra's back. "That her father had arranged for her marriage to a man. That she defied his wishes and that he would have allowed her to be executed, but that she escaped. And that she had vowed to revenge herself on him, but that she was not certain whether she would have the strength and conviction to do so when the time came." He then turned towards me briefly, and added, "I would say that time appears to be at hand, does it not?" Then, his eyes went back to their "post."

"I guess," I answered, though I was hoping we'd be able to avoid another fight. We would have enough battling to do ahead of us already. On the other hand, I had a creeping feeling that there was little chance that Therra's reunion with her poppa would turn out amicably. At this point, I decided to listen in to their conversation.

"...is yet a place for you in our commune, girl," Mik'kun was saying apologetically. "The others in our village bear you no ill will. They will accept you back."

"There are other issues, Father. You know that," Therra answered. She had stopped crying, but she had seemed unsure of herself for the first time since I'd known her. "There is Uran, and Uran's family. What makes you think they will accept me again in Ekhulta? They could still prosecute their case against me! Then, too, there is the issue of my pride..."

"Of course!" Mik'kun responded, thumping his fist on the table. "Our family is the proudest in all of Ekhulta, in all of great Aeron itself! And that is one of the reasons I beg you to return: A proud father wishes to show off his daughter to his own people. A proud father wants his proudest achievement by his side for all to see. You must be able to understand that?"

Therra nodded, and then sighed. "Father...there is something more..." She put her hand on his and continued, "...when you allowed the Deathmen to take me... when I escaped them, I...I vowed that I would take...that I would take vengeance...upon you, Father."

He waved his other hand in the air, brushing aside her words. "I am an Ekhultan, girl, and yet I can forgive." Then, he leaned forward and looked into Therra's eyes. "Return, Daughter! You belong with me, with your people. Roving around the continent with these...these rogues is no life for you. Come home!"

Big surprise? Or not? Therra didn't defend us to her father! Instead she asked, "And what of Orlacc? I told you what he did to us...to me."

"That shall be your choice, Daughter. Forget him, if you will. I think that is the best choice, but, if you wish, you may raise an army and fight him."

Therra now put her head in her hands. "I am still uncertain. I...I must consider it."

Well, this certainly seemed to be going well! From their conversation, I was becoming convinced that Therra would decide to go with her father instead of with us. And we were already taking Domitrus home. Our chances of taking on Orlacc seemed to be getting lousier with each passing day. I was starting to think that maybe Shieda and I should just go off somewhere and live on our own. Just forget righteousness and all that stuff! So what if Orlacc overran Aeron?

I was just thinking of how much I was wishing for Shieda to get back, when another figure entered the tavern. He was Ekhultan too, judging by his outfit, but he also wore a black mask of cloth, wrapped around his head like a ninja hood. Parkel and I watched as he walked over to the table where Therra and her dad were conversing. Mik'kun looked up at the other man and nodded.

"I was just outside, with the horses," the man said, his voice slightly muffled. "A man and a woman were studying our mounts with great interest. When they saw me approach, they appeared nervous, but they asked me if I wanted to sell the animals. I drove them away, of course."

Therra had turned to look at the man when he had begun speaking. Now, she had a strange look of puzzlement on her face.

He father, meanwhile, addressed the other man, saying, "A fine job you did, I'm sure. Yes. As always." Then Mik'kun pointed to Therra. "Look who I have found! My lovely daughter has all but decided to return to our village. What say you to that?"

"I am pleased," said the man, his voice somewhat grim, "though she will have to work very hard to win back my good graces."

Therra's jaw dropped, and she let out a gasp of astonishment. "Wh-What is this...?"

But Mik'kun interrupted. "Go on—take off your mask, my friend, and reveal yourself to Therra. Offer her your hand in forgiveness."

The man's hand shot up to the edge of his face cloth, and he began to unwind the layers of the mask. When he stood revealed, Therra was as wide-eyed and blown away as anyone I've ever seen. The man, a younger Ekhultan with straight, unbraided ebony hair, no mustache, and a scarred, cruel face, leaned towards her and extended his hand. "You see, Therra—what has been broken can be mended. I do forgive you, and I offer you another chance."

Therra slowly rose from her chair and started backing away from the man. Surprisingly, she didn't automatically go for her sword like she usually did, but just kept inching backwards, which wasn't all that helpful a thing to do, since her table was in the corner of the room and she'd soon reached a wall. As she felt behind her, her hands gripped the cold stone, and she stood there, shaking with fear, rage, or maybe a sickening mixture of both.

"How dare you, Father!" she said, her voice quivering. "How dare you bring Uran here!"

At the mention of that name, Parkel leapt from his seat and drew his sword. Figuring that he might need some backup, I jumped off my barstool and followed him.

Uran and Mik'kun had cornered Therra, and they were closing in on her. "Daughter! Listen to reason! Marry Uran and all will be as it should be again, I swear it!" Mik'kun said.

Uran had his blade in front of him, and he was hissing at the older man. "I told you she would disobey! We should kill her and be done with this!" And to Therra, he said, "Hear that, woman? Make your decision! Marry me or die! You have no other choice!"

"You are wrong, brute!" Parkel suddenly shouted, his voice booming as I'd never heard it before. "She does yet have another choice!"

"Yeah!" I added, and I drew my own sword. With that, we charged the two Ekhultans.

Uran whirled and easily parried Parkel's onslaught. I had to veer aside myself to avoid stabbing Parkel in his leg. Then, Mik'kun unsheathed his sword and pointed it at Therra. "I had thought you would listen to me, girl, but I fear that I have misjudged you," he said. "You are not my daughter. She is lost to me. And now I shall do the work of the Deathmen myself." He raised his blade above Therra's head. I knew I had to move fast.

Running, I leaped up onto the table and aimed my strike for Mik'kun's swordhand. I was yelling all the while. My blade hit his handguard, knocking his arm back. Furiously, he turned to face me. Uh-oh!

I raised my weapon in defense, but I knew that if he managed to hit me with one good blow, he'd slice me to ribbons. He was a hell-of-a-lot bigger than I was! "C'mon, Therra!" I screeched. "Give me a hand here, willya?"

But she just stood there with her arms spread against the wall, and muttered, "I can't fight my own father, Morrelaine. I can't..."

I knew then that I was dogmeat. I started edging backwards, hoping to at least draw Mik'kun away from his terrified daughter. I glanced over to see how Parkel was doing. After nearly falling before, he'd recovered, and he'd brought his sword across Uran's face, slashing him a new scar. Enraged, Uran was hammering Parkel with blow after blow, forcing him slowly to the floor, where I knew he'd be an easy target for a fatal stab.

It was all falling apart, when something unusual happened—Parkel called out for Therra's help.

"Therra! I can't beat him! I need you!" he said, groaning beneath Uran's barrage.

And that was enough to wake her up. In one moment, she had been cowering against the wall, but in the next, she had whisked out her sword and snapped to attention, shouting, "I shall have no qualms about cutting you to shreds, Uran! You are most deserving of it! *Hai!*" With that, she lunged at him, and the two were soon locked in combat. With Uran out of the way, Parkel raced past me to take on Mik'kun. He nearly knocked over the table I was standing on, and I ended up vaulting to the floor to avoid Parkel's wildly arcing swordpoint. I watched as he forced Therra's father into the corner.

Well, with them all clanging away at each other, I decided I'd better try to find Shieda and Domitrus. Not only could we use the reinforcements, but I had a feeling that we'd need to leave town quickly. Once I was outside, I saw my two friends approaching the tavern. Shieda ran towards me when she saw how agitated I was.

"What's the matter?" she asked.

"Therra's father...betrayed her," I said, gasping for air. "He and this other guy...Uran...they're in there, fighting...I don't think our guys can win!"

Shieda, her face grim, scanned the area. Then she said, "I didn't want to do this, but..."

She started jogging towards the spot where the Ekhultans' horses were tethered, and she began loosening their restraints. "Go get them!" she shouted at us, pointing towards the tavern. "Tell them we're getting the hell out of here!" There were two other mounts waiting there, and Shieda freed them also.

Panicked, I cupped my hands to my face and yelled, "Parkel! Therra! Come quickly!" I was about to call for them again when they came charging through the front door of the tavern. Uran came running out after them, holding one hand over his face where Parkel had nicked him. Mik'kun soon followed him outside, limping. He had several gaping wounds on his shoulders, arms, and legs.

Therra and Parkel had suffered some cuts as well, but they didn't let that slow them down once they saw what we meant to do. Each leapt up onto one of the horses. I had jumped up behind Shieda, and Domitrus was already sitting tall in the fourth horse's saddle. With everyone mounted, we kicked our steeds' flanks and rode off. The Ekhultans' bellows died out behind us as we sped away from the little outpost on the plains, which, after a while, seemed to vanish in the midday haze, as if it had only been a mirage of some sort. I wanted to say something funny, to make light of the situation—it was, as I'm sure you've noticed, a nervous habit of mine. But I couldn't this time—I just couldn't think of anything.

Instead, it was Parkel who let out a shout. He seemed flushed with the fire of battle, the thrill of our narrow escape. We all followed suit, whooping it up, saying, "*Hyaah!*" in turn. All of us, that is, except Therra.

For once, she had nothing to say.

Chapter Seventeen

We rode for the rest of that day, camped, and then rode again for the first part of the next day. At about noon on the second day, we spied a town in the distance, and, beyond it, the sea. A cool ocean breeze rolled up to greet us, and it carried with it the smell of cooking food.

"That is Maggatti you see ahead of you, my friends," Domitrus said, letting out a sigh of relief. "It is the place where I was born."

Not too far off the coast an incredibly tall and narrow island—it looked almost more like a giant tree trunk than an island, actually—rose from out of the waters. Its summit had been leveled off, and there were a series of temple-like buildings arrayed at the top. I guessed that this must be Auriggido Mountain, the home of the sect Domitrus belonged to.

"Well, we made it," Shieda said. "We'll ride into town and sell these horses. We won't need them for our trip to the island, and we haven't got anyplace to house them in the meantime. And then? Well, we can use some of the profit to pay for a hearty meal."

"I was just going to ask about that," I said, my mouth suddenly watering. "I could really go for a nice, juicy burger or some crispy fried chicken."

"W-Will we not have to enlist a boat to carry us out to the island?" asked Parkel, who had, it seemed, given up on trying to analyze my bizarre outbursts. "That will cost us dearly. H-How can we...?"

"The Devoted have devised their own means for crossing the gulf between the shores of Aeron and Auriggido," said Domitrus. "Fear not, my friends—I shall guide you across when the time comes."

And with that, we galloped into town.

By late afternoon, we were feasting on some of the best chow I'd tasted since arriving in La-La Land. We'd managed to fetch a fair price for our mounts (or so Shieda told me), and then we'd followed Domitrus to a nice eatery near the waterfront. The place was a lot bigger and much more hospitable than Ye Olde Inne and Taverne at the Woodsyde had been. I'd even managed to get myself some chicken, though it had been slow-roasted on a spit and not deep-fried. Still, I wasn't about to complain—it was probably healthier, and it was highly munchable.

I had reduced my meal to a pile of bones and was working on my third beer when I remembered that Domitrus had said he'd been born in Maggatti. It occurred to me that I still knew very little about this man who was about to leave our group, and, all of a sudden, I found myself regretting that I wouldn't get a chance to know him any better.

Well, it seemed like we weren't going to be going anywhere in a hurry, so I nudged Domitrus with my elbow and asked, "Hey, you know, this place seems pretty nice and everything. So, why'd you end up leaving anyway?"

I realized after I'd spoken that I was slurring my words due to the beer and my low tolerance for alcohol. Still Domitrus, with his usual courteous demeanor, ignored my sorry state and said, "The story of the relationship between Maggatti and Auriggido is an old one, my friend, and it reaches back over many centuries. Do you wish to hear it?"

I glanced over at the others and noticed that Shieda and Parkel were busy discussing something about our travel plans, while Therra, who had become awfully quiet lately, was patiently listening in. They wouldn't miss me in their conversation for a while.

I turned back to Domitrus, looking at him through bleary eyes, and said, "You know what? I'd love to hear all about it!"

"Well, as I've learned it," Domitrus started, readjusting himself in his seat, adopting a more teacherly pose, "it goes something like this:

"The first people who occupied the land where Maggatti now stands were the Ordeks. They have been here for as long as our records go back and are part of all our ancient legends. The Ordeks are not quite human, but are descended from a race of beings who came from some distant place, out beyond the great Far Oceans. They are believed to have arrived here over ten thousand years ago.

"At one time, it is believed, the mysterious race ruled the entire continent of Aeron. Peace was maintained throughout the land for millennia, it is said. But then, the various human tribes began raising up their cities, forming distinct nations, and creating armies and weapons of destruction.

"Now it must be said that the Ordeks are not at all a warrior race—they brought Knowledge and Faith to the peoples and ruled with a firm benevolence and with fair and truthful justice. But, sadly, wherever the humans began fighting amongst themselves, the old Masters were driven out by the violent aggression. Eventually, they were forced back into this little corner of Aeron, Maggatti, the place where they had first established themselves.

"Over the centuries, the Ordeks had been interbreeding with the humans of Maggatti, and the two races were becoming almost indistinguishable from each other. Realizing that the humans were inherently banal and war-like creatures, the Masters began to fear that their achievements would be lost through such mixings. They decided to do something about it.

"Hundreds of years ago, the Ordek Masters—some two hundred of them who had remained pure— left Maggatti, and migrated to Auriggido island. Using giant and powerful mechanisms, they built great temples of Knowledge there, established new bylaws for their order, and carried on their pursuits of Science, Philosophy, and Transcendental Learning.

"But they did not wish to completely divorce themselves from their human brothers. The Ordeks believed that, by slowly disseminating their teaching throughout the Aeroni peoples, they could yet return a lasting peace to the continent. To accomplish this, the Masters founded a Seminary of Learning on the island. And, every year since the seminary's inception, the Order has recruited five promising students. Though the opportunity to enter the seminary is open to all the peoples of Aeron, the Masters tend to cull most of their candidates from right here in Maggatti.

"And that's how I came to be among them."

"So, with five people going over there every year, there must be a pretty large population out there on the island, huh?" I asked.

"No..." he answered, seeming somewhat unnerved by my slurred question. "Though five start each year, very few candidates progress very far through the training. Those who do not succeed are dropped from the rolls."

"So. . . what happens to them once they get 'dropped'?"

I noticed that Domitrus was really fretting over my inquiries—he kept wincing and shifting in his seat. "I-I have a difficult time discussing these aspects of the Order's training, Morrelaine, especially since my own studies are not yet completed, and there's still the chance I could fail. Still, I have made it farther than many others who have attempted the task. To answer your question, candidates who are deemed unsuitable have their minds cleansed. Then, they are returned to their people."

"Uh, 'cleansed?' I hate to ask, but what does that mean, exactly?"

Domitrus sighed, then said, "All Knowledge gleaned by them at the seminary is removed."

"But...why?" I asked. "I thought you said the Ordeks wanted to spread their knowledge throughout Aeron! Why not at least let these people go out into the world and share the stuff they have learned?"

"Well, this might be difficult for you to understand, but I shall try to explain it to you. You see, the Masters believe only in absolutes. To be useful, Knowledge must be perfect and pure, or, at least, very near to it. While the Masters do not say that they have yet attained absolute perfection, they demand that their teachings be understood at a certain level. Those who fall below that level of understanding are not allowed to disseminate grossly imperfect Knowledge around the world. That, the Masters say, would be blasphemous."

"Whew!" I said with a huff. And I said 'whew' as a way of avoiding all the things I really wanted to say. I have to admit that Domitrus had really let me down—I mean, there I was believing that he was this wonderful, saintly fellow, and yet it turns out he approves of—no, actually worships—these beings who are into racial superiority and mind control! It did occur to me that, by leaving the island in the first place to try to 'help the masses,' he had been starting to question his Masters' way of doing things. But then that made it seem all the more sad we were bringing him back to the place again—back to live with these spiritual and philosophical supremacists!

"Well, Domitrus—what makes you think your 'Masters' won't take some kind of action against you when you return? I mean, you did disobey them by leaving before your training was done, didn't you?"

"Th-They...the Masters, well they..." His brow furrowed, and he swallowed hard before continuing. "I...I may very well have to throw myself at their mercy. I can only hope..."

"You really don't sound too sure of yourself here, Domitrus," I said, trying not to let my frustrations show through. "And if you're not sure, why are you going back?"

"I-I must. It's the only home I have. And there are my studies..."

"Bull doo, Domitrus! You could always choose to come with us again. Or, if fighting battles bothers you, you could always stay here in Maggatti. Maybe you could teach people yourself? You said yourself that you wanted to bring some 'good' to the people of this world. Why go back to the island, and face having the knowledge you already have 'cleansed' from your mind?"

He raised his hands, gesturing as if trying to pull the right words to explain his feelings from out of the air, and then he dropped them to the table again, unable to find his answer. Finally, he said almost robotically, "I've had too much of Chaos, Morrelaine—it's made me weak, tired. I need their Order. The Masters' way will put me back on the right path."

I realized then that he was committed to his choice, and that I wouldn't be able to talk him out of it. Something that had happened during our quest had made him change his mind about helping the outside world—his world. Perhaps it was Orlacc's betrayal, and the fact that our group was now hunted fugitives. Or, maybe it was our imprisonment that got to him. Or the Sage's apparent death. For all I knew, it could have been something that happened to our group before I popped into Morrelaine's body. Anyhow, it didn't really matter what it was something had scared him. Something Chaotic, he'd said. And now he was running away from Chaos and towards Order, or, at least, that's how he saw it. I had a feeling that, if the Masters managed to 'cleanse' out the Chaos from inside of Domitrus, they'd take most of his compassion and free will along with it.

Our talk of Order vs. Chaos made me think of Argothrex and my visit to his underground world. What the hell was it he had said? Embrace the Chaos...Order needs to be met with Chaos. It made me wonder what that whole encounter would have done to Domitrus. Would it have changed his mind about seeking Order now?

Just as I was about to finish off my latest glass of beer, thereby wiping my mind clean of the whole discussion, I noticed that the room had fallen silent. I looked up and saw that Shieda, Parkel, and Therra were all staring at the door, where about a dozen gray-cloaked knights had just made their entrance. Oh crap!, thought I.

"They are here!" the knight standing at the front of the group said, and his astonished look turned to one of amusement. "Well, well. It seems Fate has given us the opportunity to recapture these would-be usurpers, thereby demonstrating our loyalty and love to our king. We shall all receive promotions!" Without taking his eyes off of us, he unhooked a small pouch from his belt and handed it to a stooped over old man who was standing nearby. "Your Ekhultan friends did you quite a favor when they told you which way this bunch was heading, citizen. Perhaps you should find them and give them half of that reward money. Now, stand aside."

The old man scurried off, and Therra cursed under her breath at her father's latest betrayal. As we stood preparing to fight, Domitrus leaned over the table and whispered to us all, "Escape. Head for the water's edge. I'll get us away from this place."

"Talk will not save you!" growled the lead knight as he approached with his sword drawn. "Do you surrender, or...?"

Therra had her hand on her sword's hilt, but Shieda put out an arm to keep her from drawing it. I had been wrong before when I'd imagined that our group was leaderless. And now, we were all watching our leader, waiting for her cue, as Shieda calmly spoke one word to all of us: "Windows."

"You choose not to fight then?" the knight said, letting down his guard, having mistaken our hesitation for surrender. "A wise decision. Now, you must..."

"Go!" Shieda shouted, and we all broke and headed for the windows. I could hear the knights, clattering to life behind me as their anguished leader exhorted them to action. It was a good plan Shieda had hastily conceived. There were so many people in the eatery that our pursuers were having a tough time getting at us through the crowd. And they were doing a pretty piss-poor job of it, as I saw when I turned my head back to see where my friends were. Two knights were lumbering towards me, but they were a good fifteen or so feet behind me. Still, the frightened townsfolk were doing their best to get out of the way, clearing a path for the knights, and hoping to avoid being caught in the middle of the fray.

I knew I had only seconds on them, so I made for the nearest window and dove through it.

Outside was a dark alley, running alongside the rear wall of the building. I knew that the way to the shore was out in front of the restaurant, so I turned to the right and jogged towards what I thought was the end of the alleyway. It was pitch black, though, and I couldn't see any lights up ahead. Nor, I discovered, could I see even the light from the window through which I'd just emerged. I was in complete darkness. I may have been in the alley, but, for all I knew, I might have been anywhere—maybe even in my own dorm room, with the shades drawn and the lights off.

"What the hell...?" I said out loud, slowing my pace. I tried to get my bearings again, but couldn't. And then a door opened up ahead, spilling light into the alleyway. A shadow moved within the radiance. The opening was in the wall where the back of the bar had been, so I assumed that the door was the bar's rear exit, and I guessed that the knights were about to come through it to get me.

"Oh shit!" I said.

"Such profanity," came a faintly familiar voice from within the light. "It's wonderful, coming from you, but you could be a bit more creative with it, Grant."

"Whaaa...?"

The figure stepped into the alley, and, from its tall, thin, long-haired outline, I guessed it was Argothrex himself. As I approached him, I was able to make out his features in the light emanating from the doorway. He was smiling. As usual.

"Hot damn, Argothrex, am I glad to see you," I said. "Hey, do you think you can get us out of here? Me and my friends are in a lot of trouble, and..."

He put up a hand to silence me, and he said, "Trust me: You can get yourselves out of here easily enough. I came here to give you this."

He held out some sort of necklace with a stone attached to it. It looked sort of like one of those weird crystal thingies that all the New Agers wear around their necks back home, except that this one gave off a little bit of light of its own. It was a blue light.

"I don't get it," I said. "What's it for?"

"Just take it and wear it. I don't have time to tell you all about it now, but I can tell you that you'll need it."

He put the necklace on me and then stood back. "When you're a hero, it pays to be properly attired," he said. I was still trying to figure the whole scene out when he pointed and said, "Now get going. Get outta here! Go find Domitrus and your other friends."

I was about to say something else, about to ask a million more questions, when he just fell backwards into the doorway. He and the door simply vanished into the shadows as if they were both sucked right into a black hole at the blink of an eye. And then I did blink, and everything just sort of came back on again, as if someone had flicked a switch: I heard the sound of voices, coming from inside the building, and I could see the stars above me, the lights coming from windows, and, best of all, I could see where the alleyway ended and the street began.

I ran in the direction Argothrex had pointed, and I soon came to one of the village streets. Turning right, I jogged a little ways down the street, and then I hung a left into another alley, and then trotted on down it. I figured I'd do well not to show up back in front of the bar, since that was where Orlacc's knights would almost certainly be.

After crossing a couple more streets, I made a right at a corner and headed towards the seashore. I could hear the waves washing against the beach. I could also hear angry bellowing in the distance—the lead knight, I assumed. I could only hope that the others had made it out okay.

When I reached the water's edge, I saw about a hundred boats in all different sizes and degrees of seaworthiness, tied up securely to the seawall. But I didn't see any of my companions. I listened, but I could only hear the shouts of the knights and the townsfolk, and then, not too far away, I saw them coming, carrying torches, heading down a pathway towards the beach. Great! I knew exactly where the enemy was—now if I could only find my friends!

I began to panic and to wonder if they'd left without me. After all, I had no way of knowing exactly how long I had been hanging out with Argothrex—the guy had a way of distorting time and space. I scanned the waters, but I only saw towering Auriggido in the distance, its temples illuminated by a few small fires. Sure that something had gone wrong, I furiously started untying one of the boats. And then, I heard a voice.

"Morrelaine," somebody whispered. It sounded like it had come from out on the water. Then, I heard a stirring of oars. "We're out here. Ten or fifteen feet out." It was Shieda. Peering through the night, I could see her and the others, crouched down low in a rowboat, just barely off shore.

"Don't take another boat, Morrelaine." This came from Domitrus.

"Why not?" I asked. "We could use two. That one looks a bit cramped, and we could move a lot faster if we spread out our weight."

I heard a flurry of clanging, and, turning, I saw that the knights were only a few hundred feet away. They hadn't spotted us yet, but they probably would in a matter of seconds. I gazed out at the rowboat.

"Just swim, Morrelaine," came Shieda's imploring voice. "Hurry!"

Something in her worried tone moved me to action. I ran into the water and paddled out to the boat. Therra and Shieda helped me get in. Parkel was manning the oars, and, once I was secure in the boat, he started rowing madly. The little boat seemed to jump with every stroke, and it turned, and we headed out to sea.

Meanwhile, back on the shore, the knights had spotted us and were hurriedly untying several boats. They would soon be after us.

"Wh-What're we going to do?" I asked, once I had caught my breath. "If they don't catch up to us at sea, they'll just come out to the island and slaughter us there! Either way, we're doomed!"

Shieda put a hand on my shoulder, and, when I turned to look at her, she was holding a finger to her lips. She pointed towards Domitrus, who was watching our pursuers intently. I followed his gaze. Indeed, they were all-out after us now in five boats. They had used my idea—by traveling two or three to a boat, they had distributed their weight among fewer craft. With each of their boats carrying a lighter load than ours, they were rapidly gaining on us.

I heard their leader shouting, "Faster! We're not there yet!" And then he bellowed another command: "Now! Weapons out!" The front man in each boat took out a bow and notched an arrow. Each archer then lit his arrow on fire and prepared to shoot. "Ready!"

"Oh crap, you guys!" I said. "If one of those hits us, we're all gonna drown! This little skiff's leaky enough as it..."

The air pinged, and a flaming arrow cut the water about six feet from us.

"Shit! Parkel! Row faster!" I screamed. "We've gotta...!"

"Silence, Morrelaine!" Domitrus hissed. He was standing up in the back of the boat, glowering at me, seemingly oblivious to the violent motion of the waves. He turned away from me again to watch our pursuers' progress. I could barely hear him when he muttered, "They should be gone by now."

No one else seemed especially worried, so I wondered if maybe they'd all agreed to some plan earlier while I was busy with Argothrex. I resigned myself to sinking as low in the boat as I could and watching and waiting. Still, Domitrus's remark had puzzled me. "Gone?" I said to myself.

Another volley of arrows fell on us, and one of the fiery shafts landed in our skiff. Springing to action like a cat, Shieda grabbed the arrow in her gloved hands and tossed it overboard, singeing her forearms in the process. "Domitrus!" she screamed. "This is cutting it a little close!"

"I don't understand it," he said, finally, looking a little worried. Then he craned his neck, spotted something, and yelled, "Ah! There!"

One of the closer boats was tipping up in the water, its bow raising in the air as the back of the craft slipped beneath the waves. As it sank, the surprised knights leaped into the water and began frantically shedding their bulky armor to keep from being drowned.

"What happened?" I asked. "Their boat seemed fine."

"Watch, Morrelaine," Domitrus said with glee. "Just watch the Masters' wisdom in action!"

As he was speaking, two more of the boats started sinking.

Domitrus turned to face me, and explained, "The Ordeks did not want just anyone to be able to make the journey to their sanctuary. Only a few of the hundred boats tied up at the shore are protected with the spell needed to gain access to the waters around Auriggido. All other crafts sink when they come too near to the island. The three crafts bear markings known only to the Masters and their top students. It's brilliant!"

He turned around, and we all watched as the lead knight's boat disappeared. The man's head was bobbing in the water about fifty feet behind us, and he was shouting something about how he and his men would be waiting for us when we left the island.

I watched Domitrus, who was almost crazy with joy and admiration at watching the whole incident. Well, I thought to myself, I don't know if I'd call the Masters' plan 'brilliant,' but, in this case, it sure was convenient!

Chapter Eighteen

The mountain-island towered above us as Domitrus steered our Parkel-driven boat into its safe harbor. The whole place looked kind of like a huge, lumpy block of ice: it was made almost entirely of a ghostly white stone, with veins of a quartzy gray rock spider webbed through it. As we made our way inland, the cliffs rose high on either side of us, prompting images of films I'd seen of Arctic voyages, where giant walls of ice kept collapsing into the sea, to run through my mind. We'll be there soon, and this'll be all over, I kept telling myself, over and over. Breathe in, breathe out. Don't hold it.

When we finally made it to a pebbly beach, Parkel hopped out of the boat and towed us to shore. With the boat secured, we all got out and stretched our cramped limbs. Domitrus grinned, and said, "My friends, welcome to the sanctuary at Auriggido."

Only the waves crashing against the rocks gave him any answer. The rest of us were all too tired to speak. When he noticed how bedraggled we all looked, Domitrus offered to lead us to the top of the island where there would be food and sleeping quarters. Grumbling, we all agreed. He brought us to an opening in the rock face that was at least twice the height of a person, and said, "Companions, I must warn you there will be no torches to light our way. We must clasp out hands while we ascend. Fear not, though, for I know the way well enough."

We did as he'd said, forming a human chain. Shieda took his hand, I grasped hers, and we were followed by Parkel and then Therra. I only hoped—for Therra's sake anyway—that the tunnel didn't get too narrow as we were making our way to the top. As we went on in the dark, I began losing my bearings. I couldn't have told you whether we were going up or down, or whether we had gone up and down. I knew we were moving away from the ocean

I could tell that much from the receding echoes of the breaking waves. Finally I asked Domitrus, "How much farther is it? Are we almost there?" I immediately wished I could have bitten back my words when I realized how much I'd sounded like a whiny child cooped up in the back seat of the car on a family vacation.

But Domitrus grunted and answered, "Only a little ways more, Morrelaine."

He wasn't lying. After a few more minutes, I noticed that a grayish light had filtered into the passageway, and, then, we rounded a bend and saw an opening ahead. Yahoo! thought the whiny child.

When we emerged from the tunnel, we were way, way above sea level. It was damp, windy, and chilly at that altitude, and it felt like there was a constant flume of salt water whipping through the air. When I looked out over the ocean, I could see the hearth fires of Maggatti burning in the distance. We must have been at least a couple of thousand feet up, I decided. Turning the other way, I noticed that most of the stone temples were still a ways up above us. There was, however, a long, low-roofed building flush up against the cliff face nearby.

Domitrus nodded his head towards the structure, and said, "That is the Hall of Welcoming. We must go there first. Come."

We did as he said, and soon we had stepped out of the elements and into, well, a hall. The only source of light came from a fireplace at one end of the building. There was a pair of benches beside it, and, in next to no time, we were all warming ourselves by the fire.

When she had caught her breath, Shieda asked, "Why are there no people around, Domitrus? They must have sensed our arrival."

"I am sure they did," Domitrus said, biting his lower lip nervously. "The Masters do carry on their activities at all hours, so perhaps they are involved in some contemplative ceremony. In truth, I do not know why no one has come to greet us. Perhaps I shall climb to the temples later and seek out..."

"You shall do no such thing, Domitrus. We are come to welcome you."

The voice was like flowing silk. It came from a man who had entered at the far end of the structure. As he approached us, I studied him, this supposed "Master" of the world. He was a good bit taller than I was, but not of inhuman proportions. He was thin, his head was shaved bald, and his feet were bare. He wore a simple white tunic, which fell to just below his knees, but which left his shoulders and arms naked.

I did notice one weird thing as he came into the firelight—his eyes were nearly shut, and they looked sort of bulgy, like a fetus's. He appeared to be able to walk around the place without having to see.

With a slight nod, he said, "I commend you all for returning our lost student to us."

Domitrus immediately prostrated himself before the man, lying flat on his stomach on the floor. Not to editorialize too much, but he looked completely ridiculous. From the ground, he whimpered, "Master Kaddavar...please forgive my impudence in choosing to leave the sanctuary! I-I beg you to restore my candidacy, and I...I shall endeavor to be as committed and obedient a student as any you have ever known!"

The corners of the Master's mouth quivered and dipped slightly, but he answered in the same muted tones he'd used before, and he said, "Domitrus...please. While your realization of your error does you credit, your shrill tones and obvious emotional turmoil do not. Remember, our sanctuary is about peace and balance, peace and balance...strength comes through silence and serenity." He inclined his head towards us (I can't say for sure that he looked at us, because I couldn't see his eyes) and continued, albeit somewhat distantly. "Still, the matter of his disobedience does demand our attentions. Therefore, we shall convene in one hour to discuss his trespasses against the code of our Order. Meantime...Domitrus, rouse yourself! Serve your friends! We would not have your companions go hungry while they are here, waiting for you!"

With that, Domitrus scrambled to his feet, and Master Kaddavar glided towards the door. He stopped near a protrusion, jutting out from one of the walls, that had what looked like a shaft of broken ice or crystal suspended from it, and he faced us again, saying, "When this device ceases to move, one hour shall have elapsed. You are all welcome to join us then to hear our council's decision."

Then, almost cryptically, he added, "We shall meet on the mountain." He started the shard swinging, like some sort of pendulum, and walked out of the room.

While we all looked somewhat cluelessly at each other, Domitrus began scurrying around the room, opening hidden cabinets in the rock walls and taking out various items. When he was done, he came and set a tray full of goodies down on a table near the fireplace and the benches where we were all sitting. From what I could see from where I was seated, the tray and bowls were made of a smoothly polished gray rock, while the pitcher and cups were made of a silver-like substance. The bowls contained a type of stew—a chili like paste—that smelled a bit like heated cooking oil. What was in the pitcher, I'm not sure, but it was thick and as white as chalk (Milk? Or Maalox? I don't know—I couldn't bring myself to try it). Domitrus knelt on the floor and held up the tray to each one of us in turn, averting his eyes from us like we were all royalty or something.

When he got to me, I grabbed the sides of the tray and said, "Here, Domitrus, let me."

But he held on to it tightly, and he gazed up at me with a defeated expression. "Please, Morrelaine," he said. "Allow me. I…I must make amends for my disobedience. I must work to repair the damage. Please. Please…I must…"

As he said this, he handed me my glass and bowl, and then went around the remainder of our circle, passing out food and muttering to himself. Finally, he ended up sitting on the floor with his back to the wall, eating fitfully out of his bowl, not looking at any of us, and still talking to himself.

Shieda and I regarded each other in the dull orange firelight, and she said, "This is not good."

A little more than an hour later, we were all standing at the highest point on Auriggido Mountain. Behind us, looming large, was a long, flat, rectangular building with columns and a sloping roof—the Temple of Depth, I was later told, where religious ceremonies were conducted. Before us stood a smaller, squatter, circular structure, also with columns, and with a translucent, domed roof. This one was reportedly called the Temple of Decision. We stood at the rear of a small crowd of Ordeks and human students, watching, while poor Domitrus knelt on the ground, hanging his head in shame.

We were assembled outside, I was later informed, because "only decisions of critical importance to the Order are delivered inside the Temple." Thanks to the wind and the sounds of the ocean below, I wasn't able to hear much of what the members of the tribunal were saying. After some discussion, a garment was brought out to the circle by two servants and was held out in front of Domitrus. I watched with some horror as Domitrus stood and the servants pulled the garment on over his head. It was a black robe, but with no sleeves and only eyeholes in the hood—a sort of medieval straitjacket or body bag, used to deny its wearer motion and identity. The frightening thing was that it looked like something a person might be forced to wear to their execution. Once our friend was incapacitated he looked something like a black sack with legs. Then, the two servants led him away, taking him around a corner and out of view.

Needless to say, our reaction was explosive: Parkel and Therra whipped out their swords, and I shouted, "Hey, wait a minute!" Shieda put up her hand to silence us, but we were all chomping at the bit. Master Kaddavar floated over and addressed us, fixing our group with his droopy-eyed gaze and speaking in lilting tones aimed at calming our obvious outrage.

"Domitrus is fortunate indeed," he said. "We have agreed to consider his case. And, in three day's time, we will deliver our final decision. He has been sequestered in the meantime to insure that he does not try to escape."

I blurted, "That's not fair! He didn't do anything to deser-"

But Shieda clamped her glove over my mouth, and asked, "May we see him?"

"Well, not tonight, certainly..." He seemed a little unsettled by her question. Then, he glanced over his shoulder as one of the other Masters, a mean looking one, who returned his gaze with an annoyed grimace. Master Kaddavar then faced us again and said, "Perhaps on the day of our decision...a few hours beforehand. That is the best I can offer, I'm afraid. We don't usually..."

By this time, the other, pissed-off looking Master had hovered over to where we were talking, and, ignoring us, he went ahead and shouted something in another language into Master Kaddavar's ear. Kaddavar jumped a little, but he didn't look at the other guy. Instead, he said—in English, for our benefit, I assume—"Yes, Master Fumoru. I know that we need not explain our ways to outsiders. But these four delivered our wayward student to us, and, for that, I thought..."

Master Fumoru simply hissed, and he fixed Kaddavar with a heavy lidded stare. But before their face-off could escalate further, Shieda said, "Thank you, Master Kaddavar, for doing all that you have for us. May we be shown to our quarters now?"

"Of...course," the Master answered, and he motioned for one of the servants to guide us. As we moved away from the temples, Shieda pulled us close and said, "Put your swords away, you two. We need to talk."

"About what?" Parkel asked.

"A plan to escape, I hope," said Therra, who then added with more gusto, "Or better yet, to fight!"

But the two sheathed their weapons while Shieda continued. "It won't be long before Orlacc's men on shore let him know we're out here. We have to decide whether we can stay here and wait for Domitrus's 'trial.' We may not have the time to spare."

I have to admit, this rankled me, and, before I knew what I was saying, I growled, "That's not right. It's just not! Domitrus came on our quest in good faith, and he did what he could to help us out! I don't know about the rest of you, but I'm staying here 'til I know what's going to happen to him!"

The air was pretty damn quiet after I said that. We had reached our accommodations— more rooms that were carved into the rock—and we were all bone tired. Shieda glared at me, smirking and shaking her head slightly. Finally, she said, "Fine. See you all tomorrow." And then she went inside.

Therra walked in without looking at me, but I could have sworn she had the Therra version of a grin on her face. Parkel patted me on the shoulder, and then he, too, retired for the night.

I stood there in the entryway for some time, gazing out over the endless ocean, smelling the salt air and listening to the rhythmic crashing and uncrashing of the clockwork sea of waves. It was beautiful—more beautiful than any place I'd been in a long time, back in my world, anyway. Still, for the first time in a while since I'd landed here, I found myself wishing I were somewhere else.

Anywhere but here.

Chapter Nineteen

I awoke the next morning to the sounds of clanging steel…a sword-fight!

Shieda and I sat up in bed simultaneously, looked at each other, and leapt out of bed and into our clothes. Whatever was going on outside, it had to be bad news!

By the time we'd reached the porch of our dwellings and were standing there out of breath and awestruck, we were certain we were witnessing the final act of a tragedy playing out before our eyes: Therra was standing with her back to us, raising and slamming down her sword, hacking away at poor Parkel. She was already much taller than he was, and now she was standing on higher ground too. It was all he could do to keep his sword arm raised to parry her blows. As we watched, Parkel dropped to one knee and gripped his sword's hilt with both hands, wincing, while his steel sang with Therra's every assault.

What the hell could have happened? I wondered as possible scenarios raced through my mind. Had Therra reverted to her bullying ways— after all she'd been through? She and Parkel had been getting along so well, but…could he have said something to her? Confessed his love for her, maybe? Lord, he couldn't have tried making a move on her last night, could he?

I turned to say something to Shieda, but she was just staring, red-faced, at the two. Before I could utter a word, she stepped down from the porch and yelled, "Therra! Parkel! Stop this ridiculous fighting before I…!"

But then the pair's reaction took us both by surprise; they turned to face us, and they were both grinning! Parkel got to his feet and said, "I am unharmed, as you can see. There's no need to worry."

Therra nodded and added, "Aye. You see, we made a pact, he and I. I want to learn the shipman's craft, and he the swordfighter's ways."

They both sheathed their swords and stood there, looking at Shieda, blinking innocuously.

"Right, well…well, just try not to attract too much attention," Shieda finally muttered after Therra and Parkel's explanation had sunk in. "You two were creating quite a row out here. And, um, try not to disturb any of the Masters either, okay?"

They both nodded their assent, and Parkel asked, "Will you be needing either of us for anything today?"

"N-No, probably not," said Shieda. "Why?"

"We were thinking of exploring the island," he answered.

"Perhaps we might find a...a more isolated spot for our sword training," Therra added hopefully.

"Sure, that sounds fine," Shieda said, her brow furrowing as she, like me, wondered what exactly was going on between these two. "Just...just be careful. And don't stray too far—in case something does happen."

The pair nodded, smiled, grabbed their supply sacks, and trotted off. Shieda returned to our porch, where I was still standing, gripping the railing. "It sometimes feels like I'm watching over small children," she said with a bewildered look on her face as she passed me and headed for our room.

"Yeah, I suppose," I answered, turning to follow her. "But these 'children'—especially Therra—they're so big, it makes them very dangerous!"

We stayed inside for a time, sitting on our bed, talking. I brought up the subject of my little outburst from the night before—my "heroic" tirade about wanting to stay on the island while Domitrus awaited his trial. I wanted to know if she'd been upset with me for getting in her face during a "leadership moment," but she told me she hadn't been, and that, in fact, she had agreed with me, but had wanted to make sure we all knew what we'd be up against once we'd left Auriggido.

"Orlacc's men will be out there, and they'll have all our escape routes blocked. We'll have to keep that in mind," she said, looking deeply into my eyes.

"I know, you're right," I answered, wondering if she was just worried and in need of consoling or if she wanted something more. "I'm sure we'll think of something. I just wanted to make sure you knew I wasn't trying to undermine your leadership of our group or anything, 'cause..."

"Well, that's good," she quipped, "because leadership is what I've had in mind all along." She turned away from me and began to play with the laces on one of her boots, tightening them from the bottom up.

"Uh, what are you talking about?"

"Well, it's what I've sought all along—almost since I arrived in this strange land—a chance to lead. To effect change." She finished the first boot and was re-tying the top laces before starting on the next.

I wondered if she was maybe toying with me—making fun of me or trying to upset the "fragile male ego" she probably supposed I had. I decided to probe further, and said, "Well, I should have guessed that! Nice plan you had for it too: getting yourself turned into a cat and letting yourself be treated like a house pet."

She glowered at me over one knee. "That was supposed to be temporary! And anyhow I was planning to escape at some point and to lead a revolt against Orlacc and his kind one day!"

"Now you're starting to sound like Therra!" I huffed.

"Not really. Therra fights for vengeance. I do it for different reasons."

"Such as?"

"Well, what do you think? To free those people from tyranny, of course!" She seemed to get a little dreamy, and she forgot her boot-lace-tightening project for a moment. "The people here don't know there are other ways to live besides in warring tribes and under Absolute Monarchy..."

"Oh, give me a break!" I said. "You can't mean you're fighting to make this world 'safe for democracy' and all that crap, can you? Democracy's got its problems, you know? Besides, didn't you have better things to do with your time, like trying to get back to your own world?"

"Back to what? The England or America of 1906? Do you know what it was like to be a woman—even a wealthy one—back then? Perhaps things are different where you come from, but in my time and place, it's awfully hard for a woman to make a difference—or to be recognized for doing so!"

"So, okay...so you replace everything they've got here with what we have at home, right? And 'if you don't like the person who is leading you, you can just vote them out of office,' right? That's what they tell you, but all that really matters is who owes whom a favor, and who's holding the most money. What we need is something new, not some woman trying to play the John Wayne Army hero!"

"Well, at least the women of your time can vote—or so you told me!" she said, exasperated. "So! What you are saying is you'd rather we condemn these people to lives of drudgery when we might offer them a better way? Is that it?"

"I don't know! But you sound like you want to play God with this world! How can you be so sure we have the right to 'offer' them anything? To come here from some other planet and try to change this one to meet some...some idealized version of our 'civilization?'"

"Well, why else do you think we were brought here?"

"I..."

At that moment, our eyes locked. We were staring at each other, both of us dreaming up comebacks, readying ourselves to parry each other's next statements, when, all of a sudden, it all seemed...really funny. Making noises like sputtering balloons, we let our angry masks dissolve into laughing faces, and, within moments, we were both heaving and moaning so loudly with laughter that it was all we could do to keep from rolling off of the bed.

Finally, breathlessly, she asked me, "Wh-What was it I said that made you laugh so much?"

"Oh, nothing you said, really," I answered, calming my own urge to giggle again. "I just can't believe that the two of us came across all these dimensions of time and space, and we've made it through all these...adventures, only to end up arguing about politics. It's crazy."

"Perhaps it is," she said sweetly (though not sounding convinced), and we kissed.

But a guttural sound tore us from our quiet moment together. When we looked up, we saw Kaddavar, standing in our doorway. Without attempting to apologize for his interrupting us, he said, "I thought you two might enjoy a tour of our Sanctuary."

We nodded, and, as we followed him out of our room, Shieda whispered, "By the way, who's John Wayne?"

Well, I'll spare you most of the details of our tour, since most of the stuff we saw was pretty much what you'd expect, considering what I've described so far. The living quarters were all squarish rooms, carved out of the rock. None had any windows and all were Spartan in décor. The dining hall was pretty much the same, but long and rectangular, and with a large table running down its center with benches for seating. I never saw any kitchen, so I don't know for certain how they prepared the meals they served—whatever they were comprised of. Master Kaddavar never made mention of any livestock or gardening facilities, so I'm not even sure how they got their food. Who knows? Maybe the Masters themselves didn't need to eat, and maybe they created food for their disciples out of thin air?

The Temple of Depth was, as I've said, a long, flat building with columns. But there was nothing inside of it. According to our tour guide, the place was used for ceremonies, general meetings, and for meditation. For those purposes, I guess, it was perfect: there wasn't anything there to distract them—nothing at all but the whistling wind.

The Temple of Decision was another matter entirely. There was no furniture inside, but the walls and ceiling were splashed with ornate hieroglyphics and designs. The pictures on the rounded walls seemed to depict events from the Ordeks' history—I assumed this because there were several drawings of bald, round-faced men in robes, running around, doing things, and there were also a few clear representations of Auriggido Mountain. The pictures on the ceiling—which, like I said before, was made of a translucent rock that seemed to be able to attract and hold the light—looked more like constellations, like on the roof of a planetarium or something. At the apex of the dome, there was an opening, about seven feet in diameter (must've sucked during a rainstorm!), and, filling up the center of the room was a raised, circular pool, surrounded by a waist-high railing.

One other thing made this particular structure stand out from all the others: while it seemed to be made of the same white rock that covered the entire island, the walls here had a slightly brownish hue to them—not an overly obvious discoloration, but something you could notice when the light hit just right.

Master Kaddavar rattled off a list of some of the past decisions that had been made in the temple—things with names like the (something-or-other) Compromise and the (blah-blah-blah) Edict— before he finally realized that we had no idea what he was talking about. He leaned against the railing, sighed, and said, "But, of course, you have no interest in such things right now. You are worried about your friend, Domitrus. Well, suffice it to say that this very chamber is where the High Council will meet to decide his fate."

"Y-You almost make it sound like you're putting him on trial for his life," I said. "Like he might get the death penalty or something."

Kaddavar smiled in his thin-lipped way at me, and answered, "Of course...I forget myself. Although you might say that, to us, at least, a life without our Knowledge is equivalent to a living death." He crinkled his already almost closed eyes even further, so that he looked somewhat like somebody's 90-year-old grandmother, but, with the way he'd just spoken about Domitrus, the last thing I felt like doing was running over and giving him a hug.

He seemed to sense our discomfort, and he quickly moved on to the next subject.

"One last thing I will show you—something very great. In fact, it is so great that it can be called the Heart of our Order, our *raison d'être*, if you will."

Ooh, French! How hoity toity! How high falutin! "Your...reason for existence?" I asked.

"*Oui!*" he answered, affecting the closest thing he had to a glare, and, gesturing, he added, "that too. Very clever."

He took a candle from a hidden drawer, and, somehow, he made a door open in the floor just outside of the pool and railing. As we moved towards it, I saw there were stairs leading down. Kaddavar stopped, and put up his hand dramatically.

"What I am about to show you many of our students will never see, for it is not to be looked upon lightly. I would not normally allow outsiders to view it, but...as you are somewhat...special..."

Shieda and I exchanged quizzical glances. "By 'special,' you mean...?" she asked.

"I shall explain momentarily," he said, grinning again. "Come."

We followed him down into the opening. The staircase wound around the outside of the pool's outer walls, which seemed to continue down for hundreds of feet below the temple itself. As we left the light behind, I noticed that Master Kaddavar's candle was lit, though I never so much as saw him strike a match. The temperature dropped as we went further and further down, and, soon, I could see the ghosts of my own breath, congealing in front of my face. I also noted that the brown discoloration in the walls that I had perceived when we were above continued down here, and, in fact, it got more intense as we descended. By the time we had gone down nearly 1,000 feet, the walls were completely brown—there was nothing of the shiny white substance left in them.

Just when I began to wonder just how far down this pool went, and how much water there must be contained within it (could the Ordeks have somehow forced the seawater to rise up through a shaft drilled into the center of the mountain all the way down to the ocean?), we came to an opening in the walls.

"This is it," Master Kaddavar said.

Shieda and I peered through what I at first took to be a large pane of glass, but what turned out to be a polished slab of the purest crystal, carved into the side of the pool's walls. I say "purest" to contrast the portal from what lay inside the great rounded chamber where I'd assumed water would be. But there was no water inside this section of the shaft, as I had called it. Instead, the entire inside of the chamber was filled with fractured crystal, gleaming and clear in some areas, clouded in others. The crystal's cracks made it seem that giant, silvery cobwebs were draped throughout the entire glassy maze. My fingers brushed against the window's surface, and I found it to be ice-cold, yet dry to the touch.

I was starting to wonder how the whole thing was being lit, when I noticed a light source coming from somewhere near the center of the chamber. If I shifted back and forth a little, I could just make out a round, glowing ball of luminescence.

"Ahh, you see it?" the Master said.

Shieda answered, dreamily, off to my right, "Yes."

Then I said, "I see it too, but...what is it?"

We both turned to look at the Master when he didn't answer right away, and we saw that there were dried tears staining his cheeks. He looked like a priest who had just seen God.

"That, my young guests, is our Perfect Star, our Jewel of the Utmost. It is, in microcosm, a representation of the perfected universe—the way it once was, and the way it should be again. It is the Faultless All."

He stood there with his arms upraised, as if awaiting a thunderclap. Instead, he got more of my questions.

"That?" I asked, pointing to the globe of light. "But you can't even get to it! How are you supposed to do anything with it? Or even examine it up close?"

I sensed that Master Kaddavar was starting to speak again, but then another voice boomed down at us from above, drowning out our guide's.

"Go ahead, Kaddavar!" it said. "Tell them everything! Explain it all to them even before you've heard their decision!"

It was Master Fumoru. He was descending the stairs above us, coming into our view around the bend. Uh oh, I thought, he looks mad! I began to wonder if we, too, would soon be on trial, maybe for defiling the temple or some such "crime of imperfection." Well, he was mad all right, but not for the reasons I originally suspected.

"What decision?" blurted Shieda, exasperated. "Why do you keep talking in riddles?"

Master Fumoru smiled, and then he nudged Kaddavar. "Tell them," he said.

Sheepishly, Master Kaddavar half-heartedly grinned, and said, "There is something that I've been meaning to tell you...or ask you, as the case may be." He glanced at Fumoru, who nodded, and continued.

"What your befuddled guide is trying to explain is that we have a little proposal..."

Chapter Twenty

Shieda and I spent most of the rest of that day and nearly all of the next not talking to each other. Instead, we wandered hypnotically past each other when we were each following our own paths to various isolated spots around the island. Sometimes we acknowledged each other's presence, other times we didn't. When we did manage to get a few words out to each other, the exchange usually went something like this:

"Have you decided?"

"No."

"Neither have I. I'm still...thinking."

Throughout this time, I'd find myself sitting at the peak of some promontory on the island, gazing out over the swirling seas, and then I'd move to some higher spot, and then I'd look for someplace where the jutting rocks shut out the winds so that maybe I could hear myself think. None of it helped.

When we'd gone to bed that second night on the island, we'd barely said "good night" to each other. We didn't cuddle up with each other, like we usually did, but went to sleep facing in opposite directions. The next day, it was more of the same. We both drifted silently across Auriggido's surface, looking for places where we could contemplate, ruminate, reflect, consider ...

Why this strange state of affairs, you wonder?

Well, it had to do with the Masters' proposal. Needless to say, we found out why Master Kaddavar had earlier deemed us "somewhat special." It all goes back to what they—Kaddavar and Fumoru—said that night in the space below the Temple of Decision, in front of their "Perfect Star," their "Jewel of the Utmost."

Here's my play-by-play:

"We want you to join our Order," Fumoru had said, and Kaddavar had nodded in agreement, smiling.

"What? Are you crazy?" I said. "After seeing the way you've treated Domitrus?"

"You are not like Domitrus! The two of you are Outkind!" Fumoru bellowed.

Kaddavar smiled benevolently, and, in his silky voice explained,

"All those who come to us seeking Truth are welcomed here, and some will find what they seek through years and years of training. You two, however, are a different story. You have traveled between worlds, and you have knowledge and experiences to offer us. We would like to make a study of your...we wish you to stay here and share your learning with us."

Shieda had stepped in front of me, and now she said, "That's just boffo, but you still failed to answer his question: Why? What, pray tell, do we stand to gain from this 'opportunity?'"

Fumoru 'ha-rumphed,' but Kaddavar went on. "Why, answers to all your questions, of course. And to all the questions that you will ever ask. Everything that you could ever hope to know and more. Limitless facts and truths, all yours, should you agree to share what you know with us."

"Ha!" I spat. "What could you possibly teach us that we'd want to know, eh?"

Master Fumoru came over to where I was standing, bent, and looked directly into my eyes. For the first time, he fully opened his eyelids, and I got to see what these guys' soul-windows looked like. And it was scary.

His eyes were impossibly dark and endless, purpleblack, but flecked with glowing white shards. I had the feeling that I was standing at the edge of some yawning abyss, about to topple into endless space-time, about to hurtle like a mindless, entranced comet into Forever. Then, he spoke, and I nearly jumped when his voice shattered my trance.

"What could we teach you human? We could tell you why you were brought here, for example. Or we could explain how the Universe is constructed, and what 'Life' and 'Death' truly are. We could share with you the secret methods for traveling between the Worlds. We might even be able to help you shape your destinies. All these secrets and more, open to you, if you join us. What say you?"

Then, I felt Shieda's arm around me, pulling me close to her. I felt like I had snapped back to that room, and I sucked in a breath of air. It was as if I had just broken the surface after nearly drowning under ice in a frozen lake. I heard Shieda ask, "And if we were to stay...what about our friends? What of Domitrus? Would you release him?"

Fumoru was standing about five feet away from me now. I was wondering how he had moved away so fast. Master Kaddavar said, "Your two warrior friends, and yes, perhaps even pitiful Domitrus, would be allowed to leave Auriggido. We could even help them escape in such a manner as to evade your enemy's forces. We have that capability."

"Should Domitrus decide to remain among our Order, however, he would still have to stand trial," Fumoru said. "His breaching of our Protocol would still need to be addressed."

"However," added Kaddavar, "the members of the Council might look more favorably upon Domitrus should you decide to stay. They might consider his act of leading you to our Sanctuary a 'high deed' on his part. Such things are not unheard of."

"Perhaps he might earn his way back into his former educational circle—his status restored," said Fumoru, smiling. "Yes, even that is possible, I suppose, should you agree to remain here."

They were both just standing there, grinning at us. I was unsure, so I looked over at Shieda, but she, like me, seemed to be in a bit of a daze. Just as I felt doubt welling up inside of me, I peered through the glass at the Jewel. It pulsed, and grew brilliant for a moment, filling my mind with a strange, comforting warmth, almost as if it was telling me it wanted us to stay, to be near it. My head began to swim.

"You both must deliberate. We can see that," Kaddavar said.

"Yes," assented Fumoru. "Take your time. Consider it fully."

That night—the night before Domitrus's trial, we were getting ready to go to bed when we finally spoke to each other at length again.

Shieda had undressed and was wearing one of the soft cloth nightgowns that the Ordeks had provided us. She was playing with the collar, eyeing it with a mildly disgusted expression on her face.

"I really wish I could take a bath," she said, still fiddling with the garment. "I mean a real bath. That mist spray thing they have here that comes out of the rocks—well, it isn't very refreshing. In fact it's chilly and it doesn't last anywhere near long enough."

I was sitting on the bed, undoing the ties on my vest. "That's wonderful. You finally say something to me, and it's got nothing to do with the real issue at hand."

Now she glared at me. "That sounded like an accusation."

"Not really," I said. "I've avoided talking about their proposal as much as you have. It's just that now that Domitrus's trial is so close, well, we have to make a decision."

Shieda hopped on the bed, knee-walked over to me, and peeled off my vest. I looked up at her. From the look on her face it was obvious she was as torn as I was by the Masters' offer. She managed a half-hearted smile, and said, "Well, you brought it up, sweetie: You go first. What's your feeling?"

I let out a self-mocking huff of air. "Feelings, you mean! I hate the thought of splitting with Therra and Parkel—and maybe even Domitrus as well. But I'm dying to know some of the things the Masters talked about the other night. Like the reason I was brought to this world. Although Argothrex sort of explained..."

"Who?"

Ah, yes—I decided I'd better tell her about Argothrex, about my meetings with him, both in his underground world and outside the Maggatti tavern. I did my best to explain the cryptic things he had said about Order and Chaos, and about how it was his job to "turn the jewel."

"My guess is that these 'Masters,' the Ordeks, or whatever you want to call them, are the caretakers of Order in the way that Argothrex and his buddies are in charge of Chaos," I said once I'd finished my tale. "I haven't been able to get ahold of Argothrex whenever I've wanted to so far, but these Masters are right here, available to answer my questions whenever I want. I dunno. I figure I've learned a little about Chaos—maybe I should try to learn more about the Order side of things. I mean, isn't Order supposed to be preferable...?"

"I don't know—Chaos has its place," Shieda mumbled. "After all, it played a hefty part in bringing us together."

She had been massaging my shoulders, but now she leaned back on the bed and gazed at the ceiling dreamily. "Wow. I suppose I've always assumed we were in some sort of underworld here—a sort of 'lower' or 'middle' Earth (I gave here a raised-eyebrow look here, but she didn't seem to notice), and that I'd fallen through some crack in the ground. I had no idea there were all these parallel dimensions and timelines!" She looked at me again, and said, "Well, it certainly sounds as if you've made up your mind to stay here."

"No, not really... not for sure," I answered, shrugging. I stood and removed the last of my leather armor. I then paced around the room, looking for the nightshirt I'd probably misplaced. "I mean, like I said, I'd be concerned about what would happen to the others. I know the Masters promised they'd be safe, and we could maybe avoid going to war against Orlacc by staying here. But I don't know. I'm not sure whether I like or trust the Ordeks. They're a little...off-putting."

"We're agreed there. And what do you suppose would happen to Parkel and Therra? Do you think they'd still try to oppose Orlacc? I can't imagine Therra giving up that fight."

"Well...I don't think they'd have much of a chance against his forces, unless they could somehow raise an army, and, like they said earlier, they're both outlaws among their peoples." I'd found my nightshirt, pulled it on, and returned to our bed. I hopped in, and continued: "I guess that's what they needed me for, right? To help recruit the Grimnells, my, uh, people."

"So, in other words, you still haven't decided yet. Is that what you're saying?"

"That's exactly what I'm saying, though I hate to admit it: Saving our friends and staying here with regular doses of cold, hard knowledge and power? Or friendship, adventure on the trail, and the likelihood of facing certain death? What a choice!" I groaned and let my head crash into the pillows. "So, what about you?"

She grimaced and said, "I haven't decided either. But there is one decision I've made that I would like to share with you, if I might?"

I lay down next to her and said, "Go 'head."

"I feel that we've become... very close with each other. We have a good relationship, and I don't want to see that end." She looked into my eyes, searching, and said, "I guess what I'm proposing is that we should stick together, no matter what happens. Whichever one of us makes up his mind first, well, the other should go along with that choice...so we can remain together. How do you feel?"

I reached out and pulled her close to me. "I agree with all my heart. I...I love you, Shieda."

I felt her arms grip me, and she snuggled her face against my chest. "And I, you, my Morrelaine."

I was so glad she'd said what she had. As we were falling asleep, I thought, now, at least, I knew that, no matter what kind of mess we found ourselves in during the coming days, we wouldn't have to face it alone.

As Master Kaddavar had promised, we were allowed to see Domitrus for a couple of hours on the day of his trial. The poor guy was cooped up in an icy cave—small, and rough-walled, with no furniture but a stone bench, and with a sliding, polished-crystal door for entry and egress. And the man looked like someone had reached right into his chest and yanked his heart out: he was pale, starved-looking, and shivering.

"M-My f-friends-s-s," he said through chattering teeth once the guards had left, "y-you didn't come t-to c-c-come to see me."

"Domitrus... never mind that," Shieda said. "It's no problem. You didn't think we'd forget you now, did you?"

"I did n-not want y-y-you to s-s-see me this way." He bundled his arms and clothes around himself more tightly, and he would not meet any of our gazes with his eyes. "I...I am ashamed."

Therra spat, and she came forward, looming over Domitrus, Shieda, and I. "I've heard enough such talk from you, mystic! Straighten up your back and show some dignity! You've done nothing to earn the least bit of shame!"

But Domitrus simply continued staring at the ground.

Therra let out a frustrated growl.

"Therra," Shieda said in a calming tone, "thank you for your encouragement, but now isn't the time. Could the two of you wait outside for a few moments so Morrelaine and I can speak with Domitrus?"

Parkel nodded solemnly, and, when he saw that Therra was still hesitating, he put his hand on her arm. "Come...we've things to discuss as well," he said, and they departed.

Shieda said, "Domitrus, move closer..."

And she proceeded to tell him all about the choice that the Masters had offered us. When she had finished, Domitrus was no longer staring at the floor; instead, he was rapt. Of course she had to explain the part about us being from another world or time or whatever to make it all fit, but I guess she figured that we knew the guy well enough by now to be able to trust him not to blow our cover with anyone else who didn't already know. Besides, this was kinda do-or-die time for ol' Domitrus.

"My friends, I admit, I am astonished at your revelations!" Domitrus said, his eyes wide. "I knew there were great forces at work in our universe, but I never..."

"We can discuss that later, Domitrus," Shieda interrupted. "Right now, we need to find out something from you."

Domitrus managed to regain some of his former composure, and said, "Of course. Go on."

"Well, as I've said, the Masters have given us a couple of options. They told us that, if we choose to stay here at Auriggido, they will set you and the others free, and that they'd even make it possible for you to evade Orlacc's forces, at least for a time."

Domitrus's brow furrowed. "I sense there is more to your question."

Shieda sighed and then looked at me for support. Okay, it was my turn to talk, I figured—time for me to help out with this decision-making thing. "Here's the deal," I said. "You have to want to leave the island. If you still insist on staying here, the Masters are going to put you on trial, no matter what." I stopped, but nobody said anything, so I added, "So the best thing for you to do would be to tell 'em that you want a ticket outta here. Then, Shieda and I will stay here, pick up a few tips about manipulating the nature of the universe—an' stuff like that—and you guys can go on about your business. A happy ending for everyone!"

But I could tell right away from the look on Domitrus's face that I'd lost him. He saddened again, and shuffled off to his seat against the back wall of his cell. Finally, he looked up and said, "I wish it were that simple, Morrelaine. I must confess that a part of me now yearns to rejoin the four of you on the trail of adventure on the mainland, so that portion of my spirit has not completely disappeared. But, in coming here, I did make my choice, and I must go through with this trial to see whether the Masters will accept me here in their sanctuary again. I must see this through to the end!"

Shieda gazed at me again with pleading eyes. "Well," I said to her, "I mean, what's the worst that'll happen? If he loses his trial, he'll have his mind wiped and he'll be sent back to the mainland anyway. Maybe he could join up with us then?"

But she was glaring at me, steaming. "What?" I asked.

"You don't know how traumatic that 'mind wipe' can be for a person," she answered. "I have heard stories…people are never the same…"

"My friends, please don't argue on my account," Domitrus said. "I…I am prepared to meet my fate, whatever it shall be. Do not make your choices based upon what shall happen to me. I could not bear that responsibility."

Shieda and I looked knowingly at each other then—we both knew that there would be no convincing Domitrus. He seemed resigned to hearing the Masters' "justice."

"Domitrus…you've been a wonderful friend and companion on the trail," Shieda said, about to cry, it appeared. "I hope this goes well for you. I wish you only the best."

He placed his hand up to the glass near where Shieda was sitting, and said, "Mistress…I know that I was not always the bravest of warriors during our quest. B-But I shall make you proud of me today. I shall face my fate with the bravest of faces. You will see."

It was time to get in my blessings, so I said, "Hey, pal, remember that, no matter how many people are standing against you out there, you've got at least the four of us pulling for you. You'll never be alone."

I saw a tear run down Domitrus's cheek, and I thought, Oh no! Now here I go! But then Shieda put a hand on my back and pulled me away, saying, "Come on, we have to go. We've...we've still got some decisions of our own to make. Farewell, Domitrus."

We said our good-byes and exited the chamber. "Now I'm more confused than ever!" Shieda said to me when we were outside.

"You mean you don't want to stay here anymore? But I thought you wanted to learn all those secrets and stuff?"

"Did you see the way Domitrus looked in that cell?" she said. "I don't know if I can live among the Masters when that's how they treat people!"

"I dunno," I answered. "Where I come from, some people are treated a lot worse than that."

She thought for a moment, then said, "True, but still... "

"Well, we don't need to argue the point—I feel just as confused as you do. But, what do we do? Leave Domitrus to be mindwiped? Even if we stay, he's going to go through with the trial. We can maybe ensure Parkel's and Therra's safety, but...there's no real way to win here!"

"I know, I know..." she answered, but she had nothing else to add.

"Well, we'd better decide now—time's running out," I said, trying to sound decisive. "We agreed that we'd both go with whatever the first person who came to a decision chose, and I'm pretty sure what I want to do is..."

Just then, Parkel and Therra came charging toward us.

"We must talk, we must talk before the Masters begin the trial," Parkel shouted.

"Which should be any moment," Therra, out of breath, added. They were practically falling all over each other, each trying to get our attention. As they crowded us, Shieda glared, and said, "Well, what is it?"

"We have planned an escape route," Therra began. "And we've got our boat ready!" Parkel went on. "All we need do is..."

Shieda interrupted them, saying, "Please, you two! We can't throw together some ill-conceived plan when Domitrus will go on trial for his life any moment. Leave me be to think!"

But Therra ignored her, and said, "Look, here, I will make a map." She drew a circle in the snow with her swordpoint, and said, "This is the island, and we are here." With that, she made a dot on one side of the circle. Then, she drew another dot near the first one. "This is where the trial shall be taking place, and here..." She made another dot, this time on the opposite side of the circle. "...this is where we shall go to escape."

"It's a small cove," Parkel enthused. "Therra and I have already moved our boat there. We need only to free Domitrus, and we can make our getaway."

Shieda thought for a moment, and then looked at me. "Well, they're right. We could..."

"So this is your decision? We rescue Domitrus and leave?" I asked, looking into her eyes. "Because, if it is, well, you know what we said."

And then, a voice boomed, "Hear ye, hear ye! All who would witnesseth the trial of our former student, Domitrus Secundus, will now meet with us on the Mountain."

We all turned to see the small crowd that had emerged from the holding chambers. Domitrus was there, again wearing the strange hooded outfit. Leading the procession was Master Kaddavar (he was also the one who had made the announcement). He was surrounded by other Masters, ones we did not recognize.

Before we could move or say anything more about our plans, Master Fumoru popped up next to us.

"Come, my guests. I believe you will not want to miss this event," he said with a smug grin on his face.

As we headed up the side of the mountain, following the procession, Shieda whispered to me, "Well?"

But I just shrugged. I had no idea what to say or do other than to follow.

Chapter Twenty-One

We seemed to be the only ones in any hurry, fighting, as we were, to get to the front of the crowd. Everyone else walking up to the crest of the mountain looked like they were sleepwalking. Maybe we were the only ones that really cared what became of ol' Domitrus. Or, maybe this was just how these people were—zoned-out zombies, completely self-absorbed, lost in the droning routine.

It was a mighty cold day, but the sun was forcefully beaming down upon the icy summit from a blue-gray sky. Still, from somewhere far away, I thought I heard a low rumble, like the sound of a distant storm, gathering force. Swell! A day of extremes for an extremely nervewracking day!

Everyone on the whole island must have come out to see the trial: there were people standing shoulder to shoulder for as far as I could see. Not a good sign, I was thinking. It may have meant these people were expecting to see something drastic happen—probably something bad (for Domitrus, anyway). And what if we do have to make a run for it? I thought.

Parkel, behind me, tugged on my sleeve. As if in answer to my silent question, he said, "We did not finish telling you of our escape plan. We..."

"Parkel, please! I have enough on my mind already without you..."

"But I must tell you how we are going to get ourselves back to the boat we sequestered! If I don't, we might..." Just then Shieda reached back and silenced us with a wave of her hand. We had reached the front of the crowd and were now facing the spot where the action would take place. On a sort of stage or podium made out of rock, three of the Masters were standing, surrounded by four guards, waiting. Then Domitrus was ushered up some steps and foisted onto the stage by his captors. They were followed by Fumoru and Kaddavar. A hush fell over the audience.

"In the name of our Shining Star of Wisdom, itself the living symbol of all that is Good, Pure, and Orderly, and in the name of our Ordek Order and the Council of Five, which here represents it, I

137

call this trial into session," Kaddavar said, his voice echoing over the
icy landscape. Briefly, he glanced in our direction, and then he
continued.

"For the benefit of our guests, I will explain a bit about how we
conduct these proceedings. Prior to coming here, our council met in our
Temple of Decision. There, we debated Domitrus's fate. We chose
advocates both for and against his cause—I myself acted as
prosecutor, while my esteemed and knowledgeable colleague, Master
Fumoru, argued fervently in Domitrus's behalf."

"Boy, now that's comforting," I whispered to Shieda. She nodded
and let out a sigh, but continued listening.

"After five hours, the meeting was brought to a close, and the
question of Domitrus's future was decided. As soon as that was
completed, we had our guard fetch him, and we called you all here.
We believe in bestowing a swift and fair justice, you see." He paused
for a moment, as if to make sure all he'd said had sunk in. Then,
he turned towards Domitrus and the other members of the council,
and said, "Now we are ready. Master Fumoru shall issue the
Council's proclamation."

Fumoru stepped forward. The four of us shifted uncomfortably in
our spots as we waited for The Big Moment. Once this was all over,
this chapter of our journey would be ended, and we'd have to move on
to something else, no matter what became of Domitrus. I stole a glance
down at Argothrex's jewel, which I was wearing at my throat, and
wished that Argothrex could somehow be here to protect us.
'Course even if he were here, he might not help us out in the way we'd
like, knowing him. He'd be just as likely to throw us off the
mountain's highest peak into the cold sea. "So swim! Swim, you're
free!" he'd probably say. That's Chaos for you!

Fumoru was clearing his throat.

"We, the members of the Council of Five, decree the
following." As he spoke, the guard pulled Domitrus's hood back so
he could hear the verdict. "The subject, Domitrus Secundus,
willingly disobeyed the code of our Order by straying from the
sanctuary before his teaching was completed. Further, the subject
has been heard to state that he 'could accomplish more by...fighting
the oppressor powers than...through the continuation of...priestly
studies at Auriggido Mountain...removed from the affairs of the
world.' And that he 'felt that our Order was intended to foster good
amongst the peoples of this world, and that perhaps we needed to do
our service amongst these selfsame peoples.'"

As he read these statements, an astonished murmur rippled through the crowd. Fumoru paused and shook his head, looking disgusted. I, meanwhile, wondered how the hell he was able to quote what Domitrus had said to us out on the trail verbatim—the words were from the speech Domitrus had given us when he'd announced that he wanted to return to the sanctuary. I began to get a sick feeling in my stomach as the thought that the Masters of Order and Chaos were watching us at all times—perhaps even controlling our decisions and actions—gripped me. I pawed at my jewel again, disdainfully, pondering whether I should just hurl it into the sea or not. I didn't want to be some kind of gamepiece in a cosmic battle between Argothrex and the Ordeks!

But then I felt a twinge of pain shoot through my temples, and a thought whooshed into my mind as quick as a lightning strike. The words (though I wasn't sure there were actual words) were: No, throw yourself into the sea! It was enough to knock me off guard, and I almost fell over where I was standing. But then I caught a glimpse of Fumoru's face, and he was smiling, ever so slightly. A swift and fair justice! Puh-leeze!

"The errors that these words show in Domitrus's way of thinking," Fumoru continued, "considered with his actions before and after he uttered them, proved to our Council that our wayward student is not a candidate for our usual corrective procedures."

The four of us exchanged glances, our faces showing our relief at the Council's ruling. Thank God! No mindwipe for Domitrus! But Fumoru put up his hand for silence—he had more to say.

"Indeed, we have decided that Domitrus may stay and live among us, and may again seek to learn our teachings."

Hallelujah! Shieda reached back and put her arm around me, pulling me up next to her, and we sat there embracing. I looked at Domitrus and thought I could make out the cautious beginnings of a smile forming on his lips. We had all gotten so worried over nothing! Even the people in the crowd seemed pleased by the unusual ruling.

"However," continued Fumoru, and it felt like something in the air fell, "a thorough examination has revealed to us that there is a basic flaw in Domitrus's personality, an imperfection so deep and pervasive that it will be impossible for him to forget these silly, rebellious notions which occur to him from time to time. And since we are the Masters here, and it is up to us to decide what is to become of our teachings, we must not allow such an out-of-control element as Domitrus's wanderlust to interfere with our world-plan."

Far away I heard a toll of thunder, and, below, waves were crashing angrily against the foot of the island-mountain. I began to shiver.

"Therefore," Fumoru said, walking over to the kneeling Domitrus and putting his hand on Domitrus's head, "we have elected to perform a far rarer procedure upon our 'devoted' student." Fumoru's smile broadened as he glared into Domitrus's eyes, then swept his gaze out over the crowd, finally settling his eyes upon our group.

"For the first time in long, long years, we Ordeks are going to perform a complete cleansing. We will empty out Domitrus's flawed personality entirely and begin teaching him from a tabula rasa stage, so to speak. He will truly be a new Domitrus."

For a moment, I could hear nothing. The Masters looked at each other and nodded, and the guards approached Domitrus. I looked closer at my condemned friend's face, wondering what he could be thinking, wondering if he could have imagined that this would come to pass. He'd said he would take whatever the Masters gave him, but could he have known he'd lose everything? It was an execution! Not of body, but of mind, of identity! I was wondering what we should do. Could we just leave? What else could we do? Everything seemed to be cracking apart in slow motion.

And then I noticed a tremor distorting Domitrus's face. His jaw fell, and he began to shake violently. As the guards were pulling him to his feet, he started struggling against them and against his bonds. And he finally found his voice.

"*Nnnnnooooooooooo!* This isn't what I wanted! Let me go! I won't do it! I won't submit!!!" His words rang out, strangely hoarse, but also full of life.

Chaos had arrived!

Therra and Parkel flew past us, their steel already bared, and rushed towards Domitrus's guards. As Shieda and I drew our weapons, she looked at me and said, "What the hell were we thinking?"

"Well, we didn't know," I said. "We do now. Let's just get the five of us the hell out of here."

As we leapt onto the stage, we had to contend with people running in every direction. The unarmed acolytes were busy falling all over each other, trying to get away, while armed guards and others, trained in hand-to-hand combat, were closing in on our little group. The Masters were reeling, and they seemed to be busy assessing the situation.

I noticed Shieda was hitting people only with the flat of her sword, and I followed suit. No need to kill if we didn't have to. Therra and Parkel had managed to knock out the guards and free Domitrus from his straitjacketlike restraints, and now they were throwing, kicking, and shoving back the fighters who were trying to contain them. Even Domitrus was slinging punches, pounding on the people who had tried to deny him his identity. I'd never seen the man so fired up!

I plowed someone off the stage to my right, and then spun round to try to get my bearings. Shieda ducked a blow from one of the guards and swept his feet out from under him. He landed on his back with a "Whoop!" Then she caught her breath and turned toward me.

"The point is, we have to get out of here!" she said.

I looked around and saw dozens of Ordek students and attendants streaming towards us from every direction save one: they weren't going anywhere near the slope that fell off into the sea. I remembered what the voice I'd heard in my head had said—Throw yourself into the sea! That was where we had to go—I knew it.

"We have to head for that slope," I said.

"What? Are you joking? We're too high up!"

"The only way we're gonna get outta here is by jumping into the ocean."

Shieda bit her lip, and considered my words for a moment. Then, she nodded her head. I had been learning to trust the voices in my head, and Shieda seemed to be learning to trust me.

"We could hit the rocks on the way down," she said apprehensively.

"We'll be all right," I said. "Trust me. You go on ahead, and I'll snag the others."

She still looked worried, but she leaped off the stage and headed towards the cliff. I turned, and saw Therra, about to slash an enemy with her blade. And I ran.

"Therra, no! We've gotta get out..."

I'm sure she didn't know why I was yelling at her, but she pulled back on her swing. Still, her sword cut across the cheek of one of the guards, drawing blood. Something made me look towards the Masters.

They had been watching silently, standing stock-still, as if in shock, until now. As if scenting the guard's wound, Fumoru turned to Kaddavar, and said, "Kaddavar, this must not be. If they escape..."

And the first Ordek we had met upon arriving on the island raised his hands forcefully, and shouted, "There will be no more violence done here! No blood may be spilt on our island! Masters, join with

141

me!" And the assembled lifted their hands in unison, and all opened their mouths and uttered a short, melodic moan, a shock-burst of tone. The tuneful sound seemed to travel out from their group, and to head out towards the sea. It only took me a moment to see where it was really going. Shieda, running, was hit in the back and knocked over. As she struggled to her feet, winds from the sky came down and surrounded her. She was buffeted about for a few moments, and then a sort of a glass casing formed around her. And then I realized—it was ice!

I let out an unrecognizable noise, a cry of anguish. Then, I charged them, screaming for all I was worth, "Goddamn you, you Goddamn bastards! If you killed her, I'll..."

But they faced me calmly, their bodies moving fluidly, and fired their bubble of sound at me. I was caught by the blow and thrown off the stage, and I landed on my back on the ground. I waited for the winds to surround me, waited as I looked up at the sky. I did feel something, but no ice crystallized around me. I was unharmed. What the hell?

I heard Parkel shout, and, as I sat up, I saw his ice-encased form slump to the ground. A berserk Therra rushed the Masters, but she too was downed in seconds flat. Domitrus and I were the only ones left who hadn't been flash-frozen.

"Crap!" I said. "I've gotta get us out of here!"

I ran to where Shieda lay—she looked okay within the ice. Her eyes were open, and her skin was pale, but she appeared to be still in one piece and probably still alive. I tapped my knuckles on the shell, yep, it was solid enough. I knew what I had to do. I got behind Shieda, and started pushing her frozen form like a sled across the icy ground. When I got near the cliff, I stopped, but Shieda in her ice sheath continued on, and went flying over the edge. She was gone.

Holding my breath, I stepped closer to the precipice. Closer, closer. I looked down, flinching as I gauged the distance. I couldn't see her anywhere below, but the good news was that it was a straight fall all the way down: there were no rocks she could have hit! Now I prayed that she wouldn't sink, that she'd float like a big ice cube. I turned to get the others.

As I ran to where Therra lay, I watched the Masters on stage, their eyes and motions following me in synch. They looked like some sort of alien dance troupe. Then, they loosed their tonal assault on me again—I could hear the ring of the note and feel the vibration around me. But nothing was happening to me for some reason. Then, I realized—it was the jewel Argothrex had given me. Somehow, it was keeping me protected. I glanced down at it, and, sure enough, it was lit up like a Christmas bulb. I had Chaos to thank once again!

But I knew it couldn't save me forever. The Masters would figure something out. As I grabbed Therra, I called to Domitrus, "Help me! Get Parkel!"

He had been standing there, agape, probably wondering what the hell I was doing, whisking our buddies around like toboggans, but my cries brought him out of it. He sprinted off the stage, and started shoving Parkel along.

Meanwhile, the Masters must have realized that they weren't going to be able to stop me by freezing me. Kaddavar called out angrily over the din, "Guards! Acolytes! Students! Stop them! Don't let them get away!" And everybody who was anybody (or nobody) came running towards us.

"Get away?" Domitrus said, puffing, as he came up beside me. "Surely no one is escaping here? We're merely saving our companions from a life of captivity by giving them a quick death, are we not? I am certain they will die in the fall...won't they?"

"If they do, we're dying with them," I answered. The assembled hordes of Auriggido were crowding around us, but no one wanted to get in our way. The few who tried were cruelly thumped aside by the hurtling ice barges we were pushing along. But some of them had begun running alongside us, hacking at us with swords and gauntleted fists. I felt a sword swoosh over my head—I was sure I'd just lost a few hairs from the top of my skull.

Poor Domitrus, being a bigger target, fared less well. I saw him take a hit in his thigh, and a slash across his arm.

As he cried out in pain, I called to him, "Domitrus! When I give the word, jump up on top of Parkel! Okay?"

"I don't under..."

"We can ride them into the sea. You'll see! Watch me, and do what I do!" Thanks again to the real Morrelaine's agile body, I was able to mount Therra's ice casing. With a little more effort, Domitrus was able to follow my lead, and soon we were scooting along speedily. No one was daring enough to try getting in our way.

However, the Masters had one final card to deal: Domitrus and I both heard the deadly tone cleave through the air towards us at the same time. They knew they couldn't get me, but they were easily able to flash-freeze their one-time student. But, luckily for us, Domitrus's frosty sheath bonded to Parkel's, and we were all headed to the same place anyway. It did mean I'd have to take care of everybody by myself when we landed—assuming we lived through the experience, that is.

I watched the last of the Ordek-followers' dumbfounded faces go by as I came to the edge. I was sure glad to finally be leaving this place behind, though I would not have minded a more conventional—or comfortable mode of exit!

And so, I shot over the side. Immediately I wished I'd remembered to close my eyes, because the glimpse I caught of the drop before I did shut them nearly made me puke. I screamed and screamed all the way down, and, boy, did it seem to take forever. But finally, kerrsploosh! We all met the ocean rather abruptly.

If there had been any danger of my resting on my laurels (which there hadn't been), the frigid waters took care of it quickly. I bobbed back to the surface and looked around. First, up the side of the mountain. I saw the ridge we had fallen from, and, sure enough, it was obscenely high up there. Next, I gazed around me to see if my friends were all there. One, two, three...and farther away, Shieda. They had made it! Sure, they looked like ice cubes, floating in a big cocktail; but at least they had gotten off of the island.

Now, how to get us all away from here safely? Parkel had told us where he'd hidden our boat, but I'd have to grab it fast before the Masters sent someone to intercept us. I began to swim around the base of the mountain.

I'd gotten about half of the way to where I was going when the mountain itself attacked me. I heard a series of booms, and then big splashes in the sea around me. One of the splashes was very near. I looked up and saw several chunks of rock falling towards me. A small piece hit me in the forehead, scratching me and drawing blood. I was just happy that it missed both of my eyes! I didn't want to believe that it was possible the Masters were causing this—I mean, no one can move a mountain, right? But I had to admit, I couldn't be certain what I believed. Anyhow, I kept going, but a lot faster than I had been before the rocks fell.

About twenty minutes later, I found the little inlet where Therra and Parkel had parked the magic boat. By the way it was floundering against the shoreline, I could tell that the waves were getting bigger. It looked like a storm was coming after all.

When I got back to where everyone was floating, I saw more rocks falling from Auriggido's high cliffs, and some of them were coming down pretty near my friends. I had to act fast—odds were that it was only a matter of time before one of the boulders hit its target. Since none of them seemed to be thawing out on their own, I figured I'd have to get them away from the frigid island and into (hopefully) warmer waters. I began paddling up to each one of them, and gently shoving each along with one of my oars. It was a slow process, especially since the waves were working against me.

I kept at it for what seemed like an hour. When I looked behind me, I saw that I'd put about fifty feet of distance between the island and us—not too great, but at least we were out of range of the falling rocks. I noticed that the sky had turned the color of an upset stomach, while the waves were lifting and dropping the boat dramatically. I could allow myself no more time to rest.

I glanced back one more time, oh, maybe an hour or two later. We'd made it a safe distance from the island, but it had started to pour rain on us, and I'd begun to see flashes of lightning. As I was pushing Shieda with my oar, I saw that she had finally started to thaw a little. Her limbs were still encased, but most of the outer ice sheath had melted away. I decided it was time to try to get everyone into the boat. Shieda and Parkel (now that he'd split apart from Domitrus) were easy to manage, but I had a little more trouble pulling Domitrus over the side of the craft. I had to jump into the sea to get Therra aboard. I nearly gave up, but I was finally able to push her up and over the side. We were all aboard.

As I was grabbing the oar, I realized with horror that we were only about twenty feet from some jagged rocks along the continental shore. Great! I thought. I can't even relax and let us drift! If I do, the waves will smash us against those rocks! Just then, as if to drive the point home, a bolt of lightning struck not far from us, lighting up the water and sending up a plume of orange sparks. Death in all directions, I mused.

Resigned to my task, I grabbed both oars and began rowing away. I had to keep rowing, non-stop, to keep us away from the shore. I have no idea how much time went by: I was conscious only of the spray getting in my eyes and streaming down my face; of the overcast day turning into a black, windy night, split with staccato bursts of thunder and lightning; and of the roller coaster rising and falling of the sea. But I kept rowing, every now and then letting out an unintelligible groan as I felt a muscle strain.

Much later, I could barely feel the oars for the pains in my arms and shoulders. My throat was raw, and my nose and brow felt like they were packed with ice cubes. A flash of lightning showed me that Auriggido was now just a small, jagged tooth on the horizon. I had no idea what time it was, but I felt like I couldn't go on.

Then, I felt a hand on my back. I turned, and there was Parkel. He was shivering, and his hair and clothes were plastered to his body from the rain. Through trembling lips, he spoke.

"I can take over now, Morrelaine."

I moved aside, and mumbled, "No problem." I saw him slide into the seat and take up the oars. We're safe, I thought to myself. And that was my last waking thought.

Chapter Twenty-Two

At first I thought I was a child again. I was rocking, swaying back and forth, up and down gently. And a soft, sweet hand was stroking my hair. The air smelled of moisture and salt. A seagull's song echoed on the breeze. "It's all right, my love," a voice said quietly. "Everything's okay now."

I opened my eyes. I was reclining in Shieda's lap in the back of our magic dinghy. Her upside-down face came into my field of vision, and I reached back, pulled her close, and kissed her. She tasted like life to me, sweet, precious, tingling life. When we parted lips again, I felt revived.

Straight ahead of me was Parkel, seated and rowing, steadily driving us forward. He smiled when he saw me awake. To my left, Domitrus was slumped against the side of the boat. Therra was dressing his wounds with bandages made of torn cloth and dipped in the sea for salt-sterilization.

"Okay, now what..." I said, starting to rise, but Shieda held me back.

"Take it easy, you," she said. "You're exhausted, and you may even be sick. Why not rest a spell?"

She was right, and, anyhow, I'm no hero. Plus, she was comfortable to lean against. "Can I at least sit up a little?" I asked. "I want to see where we are."

Not that I really had any way of telling, of course. There was the same, continuous shoreline off to our left, um, port side. The rocky coast seemed to be getting a little steeper, though—the banks were turning into cliffs. At least the sea had calmed and the sky was filled only with high, white clouds. Auriggido had completely disappeared behind us.

"So where are we?" I asked.

"We don't know, exactly," said Shieda.

"Heading North," Parkel interjected, "away from that hellish island and those monstrous devils."

"Aye," added Therra, tearing another cloth into bandages with her teeth. "North. And straight on, straight into the dung heap kingdom of that mongrel, Orlacc."

Now I had to sit up. "Wait a minute! Why are we ...? Why didn't we turn and go the other way?"

"Because, darling," said Shieda, moving behind me to support me, "we have no food and no water, and, anyway, we're near the domain of, um, your people."

For a moment, there was silence, and I realized she was talking about the Grimnells. That was where we had been intending to go next anyway, but I wasn't sure I was ready to masquerade as one of them—a leader even! Sure, my disguise was perfect, but, otherwise, I was in the dark.

"Shieda, I..."

"Shh. Don't worry. It'll be fine."

With her eyes, she let me know she'd do her best to help me, and that we couldn't talk anymore about it now. I had to calm down and wait to see what would happen.

I lay back again for a while and watched the sky. The others spoke every now and then, mostly about what to do once we had reached safe haven and perhaps had recruited a Grimnell army. After almost an hour, Parkel asked me, "How will I know where I should put us ashore to be nearest your people, Morrelaine? Is there a beach? Or a cove, say?"

"Um, ah...!"

As I scrambled to sit up, Domitrus interrupted, "Look, my friends! Ships!"

We all looked. Coming around the cliffs furthest from us were three huge sailing vessels. They all had the same symbol—a gold lion—emblazoned on their green mainsails. And, as we watched, a fourth ship came into view.

Parkel turned to face us. "Damn. They're Orlacc's warcraft!"

Therra immediately drew her sword, while the rest of us waited on the edges of our seats, so to speak. Three more ships came around the cliffs, and the first four we'd seen were bearing down on us. Finally, Shieda blurted, "Parkel, put us ashore immediately!"

"Where, milady?" He was right: The cliffs along the shore had become too high. There was no place to park the boat, and not enough time for us to try to scale the rock walls. If we tried it, Orlacc's men would probably pick us off with their arrows like we were ducks in a shooting gallery. And, of course, there would be no point to turning the boat around—we could never hope to outrun those ships!

Speaking of arrows, a few of them began splooshing into the

water near us. Shieda shoved me aside and said,

"Shit! Morrelaine, get off of me!" She scrambled towards the front of our boat.

"What are you doing?" I screamed.

"I'm going to try to whip up some magic—a mental shield—to stop those things from hitting us!" She raised her arms, and began speaking softly to herself. Domitrus, to my left, mimicked her words, trying to add his strength to their effect. It was working! Arrows, falling out of the sky right towards us were being flung to either side of the boat.

But just then, the first two of Orlacc's ships swept past on either side of us, sending powerful waves in our direction. We were tossed about, and I worried that Shieda and Domitrus might lose their concentration.

Now, the third ship was heading straight for us. I saw good ol' Orlacc, peering at us from the prow. "Ready to be crushed at last, insects?" he shouted.

"Parkel...!" I yelled, but he was already rowing furiously. We made it out of Orlacc's way with seconds to spare. The huge warship surged past us, and we heard its master bellow, "Come about! Quickly!"

"That was lucky. Damn lucky," I said.

"Nay," Parkel answered, grunting, "as Domitrus earlier stated, this craft has had powerful magicks placed upon it to keep it afloat. If I can keep us out of the ships' direct path, they should not be able to sink us."

"Great. That won't be easy. There's gotta be some way we can fight back!"

"Aye, there is," Therra said as she stood and sheathed her sword. "I'll climb aboard that lead ship and slit Orlacc's throat. That'll put an end to this!"

But as she moved to dive, Parkel stopped her: "Try that, and you'll be filled full of arrows before you reach his vessel. Once you leave our boat, you leave its protection. His men will be able to strike at you."

"He's right," I added. "We'll have to think of something else."

She sat down again after a moment, and muttered, "Yes, I see." No one else had any suggestions. I grabbed my jewel and thought, Damn it, Argothrex! Where are you now?!?!?

The four ships that had been at the rear of Orlacc's charge broke off their attack, and the three that had passed us had turned around, so that we were now surrounded by enemy ships. Orlacc pulled his ship up alongside us. We had nowhere to go.

"I think you can see that we have you outnumbered, renegade scum," Orlacc called down to us. "You have no choice but to surrender. Do so quickly, and perhaps I shall spare those among you of the female persuasion. I may be able to find some use for any females you have."

Therra jumped to her feet. "How dare you underestimate...!"

"I wasn't speaking of you, of course," interrupted Orlacc, sneering. "I hardly consider you female or persuasive, and certainly not useful. Nay, I plan to torture and kill you first of all, Therra, to help get me in the mood for the real killings."

This time, it took both Parkel and me to keep Therra from trying to jump ship and take on Orlacc's armada single-handedly. I was attempting to think of something clever to say to disrupt the mood of futility that was settling over us, but nothing was coming to mind. But then Shieda spoke up.

"We don't need to surrender to you, Orlacc. Our boat is protected by magic. Domitrus and I are working a spell to keep your swords and arrows from us, so you can't get at us from up there. You can't sink our boat either, so that's out. If you send your men down here in armor, they'll sink under the weight of it; but if you send them down without it, we'll cut them to ribbons. We may not be able to outrun you, but we can try to wait you out. We're staying put."

While she was talking, Orlacc's self-satisfied grin fell, and he motioned for one of his guard captains to come over. "What is she telling me, man?" he asked the captain. "She can't be serious!"

"It's true, sir—we couldn't hit them with our arrows before."

Orlacc thought for a moment, then commanded, "Bring me a lance, soldier. Quickly!"

The man disappeared, then reappeared with the weapon. Orlacc grabbed it, and held it aloft. "I think you'll find this a bit heavier than an arrow, sorceress!" And he flung it towards us. But, just as the arrows had done earlier, the lance swerved in mid-air and crashed into the sea. Shieda let out a groan when the weapon glanced off her invisible shield: apparently the extra weight did make a difference. Still, we were safe for the moment.

"Weeooo!" I yelled. "How you like them apples, Orlacc?"

The angry king practically growled at me. Then he shouted, "Bring me more men and weapons! And my sorcerer—summon him here!"

Meanwhile, we used the time to hold sort of a conference. Parkel began by asking if we should try to get away. "I know how to row rhythmically, with great speed. We could try..."

"If the wind dies down, it might work, but as it is now, we can't hope to outrun them," Shieda said. "But there are other problems. For example..."

Just then, Orlacc reappeared above us, this time with Frouder, his court wizard, and Kryfalikk, his second-incommand, at his side. We knew these were the men Orlacc thought of as his "best people." Frouder seemed to be concentrating, and when Shieda saw this, she closed her eyes and went back to chanting to herself. It looked like some sort of magical face-off was brewing.

"It is of no use, my lord," Frouder said a few minutes later. "The woman is no sorceress of any expertise. Nor is the old man a threat. But the craft and its crew are under the protection of some powerful spells, placed upon them by superior mages, perhaps even by gods. I could defeat the woman easily if her power were not being reinforced by these other magicks, but as it stands, I can do nothing."

Orlacc turned to Kryfalikk, and spat, "Well, it's up to you then. You had better think of something, Kryfalikk."

I've got to hand it to the guy: he tried. First, he had men from several of the ships hurl their weapons at us, and fire at us with arrows simultaneously. I guess he figured maybe Shieda couldn't handle an all-out assault. She winced again with the effort, but her shield held. Next, he tried pelting us with heavy objects—rocks, a full wooden chest, and some other furniture were all heaved onto us. Again, the strain showed on Shieda's face as the items thudded in midair and fell into the sea, but her shield held.

Finally, Kryfalikk tried a head-on attack. We heard the squeaky sounds of a winch being operated, and then a *ploosh*, as a small but sturdy-looking landing boat was lowered into the water from Orlacc's ship. Nine men, including Kryfalikk himself, climbed down a rope ladder and into the craft. When all were aboard, they cast off and headed towards us with swords and teeth bared. It was obvious from the expression on Kryfalikk's face that he was down to his last plan. If this didn't work, he might lose face with Orlacc.

"Ack!" Parkel groaned. "Their weapons can't get through, but can they?"

Therra stood up again, and jeered at the oncoming horde: "Come on, dogs! Come my way, and I'll slice your ears off!"

Then, Shieda, through clenched teeth said, "Let them get close to us."

"What?" I said. "You mean they can get past your shield?"

"Yes. It's meant to keep out hurled objects—lifeless objects. People can pass through. I'm not strong enough to keep nine heavily armed men out. But don't worry. I've got other tricks..."

Their boat was drawing near. By now, Kryfalikk must have figured out that he'd made it past the shield, and he was exhorting his men to row faster. The few in the front of their craft would be within striking distance momentarily.

"This...is going to take some effort," Shieda said, and she raised her hands and muttered something. Suddenly, there was a flash, and bright object shot through the air towards Kryfalikk's boat. By the time I uncovered my eyes and looked up, Kryfalikk's boat was engulfed in hissing flames. Some of the cloth parts of his men's clothing had caught fire, and they were jumping into the sea, while the rest of the soldiers were fast going down with their ship. The ones who couldn't think quickly enough started drowning under the weight of their armor, as Shieda had predicted they would earlier. Meanwhile, Orlacc had directed his men to throw ropes over the side of his ship, and three of the soldiers—including Kryfalikk—managed to pull themselves back up to the deck. The other six disappeared below the waves within minutes. It was grim, but an effective demonstration, and it clearly rattled Orlacc.

"Tell me, mage!" he screamed, his face reddening. "Can the bitch do that to all my ships?"

"Nay, liege," Frouder answered, "I believe she cannot produce enough of that daemonic fire to harm any of our larger warcraft. And if she were to go on the offensive, she would soon have to give up her protective measures. Nay, I think we are safe here from her fire magicks. But, pray... listen a moment to me, for I've a thought." Now, he spoke loudly, I assume, so we could hear. "If the woman were to let down her guard for even a moment, I believe I could undo all her protective workings and could cast a spell that would prevent her from creating any further, ah, problems for us. It has occurred to me that she must sleep eventually. Though I am older than she, I believe I can stay awake longer, especially considering she has neither food to eat nor water to drink."

"You're suggesting we...wait them out?" Orlacc asked.

"Precisely, my lord."

Orlacc sighed, and said, "Very well, we wait. Kryfalikk, post a guard to watch our captives and join us inside."

A bedraggled-looking Kryfalikk stuck his face over the ship's rail and spat at us. "When we've dragged you aboard, I swear I'll hack off a limb from each one of you and pour salt in the holes, you maggots." Then, he left. A stoic soldier moved to the railing and watched us.

Things had calmed down for now, but only for now, I mused. I turned to look at Shieda, to see whether she had some plan in mind or some clever words to say. But all she could manage was this:

"It's going to be a long day, everyone, and an even longer night."

Sure enough, we spent a lot of time just sitting and waiting for something to happen. For a few hours, we tried to come up with an escape plan, but nothing we dreamed up seemed feasible. If the wind had let up enough for even a few minutes, we might have made a break for it—Orlacc might not have been able to catch us if he didn't have the wind to power his ships. But the sea breeze kept right on puffing all day.

"Damn. I can't believe we managed to get away from the Ordeks only to die here at Orlacc's hands!" I said, breaking a long silence. "We've been through so much already! Why can't we catch a break?"

"Don't worry," said Shieda. "We'll think of something. I mean, we've made it through every other bloody situation so far, right?"

"I cannot speak for any of you, but I will not allow myself to die 'til I've had my revenge," Therra said.

"Hmm," Parkel interrupted, and we all turned towards him.

"What is it, Parkel?" I asked.

"I was just thinking…if we had a sail of our own, we could escape. Perhaps if we used one of the oars for a mast…"

"And for a sail?" queried Therra.

"Why, we could use our clothes, of course!"

It was dead quiet for several seconds, as the picture formed in all our minds. There we were, skipping across the wave crests, rocketing ahead of Orlacc's ships, all of us naked as jaybirds. The image was just too much, and each one of us broke into laughter, even poor Domitrus, whose wounds had kept him miserable and silent for the past few hours.

When we had all regained our composure, Shieda said, "I don't think we have near enough fabric, let alone a way to stitch it together, Parkel, but it was a wonderfully pleasant thought."

Parkel turned a little red, but he shrugged and said, "In my time at sea, I've seen and done many strange things. I shall have to tell you about some of them sometime."

"Something amusing, eh?" came a voice from above us. It was

Orlacc, peering over his ship's rail. "Well laugh while you can. Soon it will grow cold as night falls. You'll be cold, hungry, and tired. Your wants will gnaw at you until you beg me to give you death's release. We shall see who laughs then!"

I felt a pang in my stomach when he mentioned hunger. As he strode away snickering, I turned to my friends and asked, "Doesn't that guy have anything to do besides bothering us?" But no one had an answer.

And, sure enough, once the sun had set, we began shivering. The ocean's damp air didn't help any. Just as I was wondering if it could get any worse, Orlacc decided to toy with us some more. He had his men move some dining tables out on the deck, and he threw a banquet for several of his top captains. They drank beer and wine, listened to court musicians' melodies, and roared with laughter until they fell out of their chairs. Occasionally, Orlacc's soldiers would toss gnawed bones, pieces of gristle, and bread crusts over the side to mock us in our hunger. When it was over, a drunken and food-spattered Orlacc stood looking down at us with Kryfalikk at his side as his servants cleaned up the mess.

"I've worked hard to entertain you my friends, and now I must retire," he said, staggering. "I can keep this up for days, swine. Can you?"

And, with that, Orlacc and Kryfalikk disappeared from the deck, their laughter trailing after them. Two sentries were left behind to keep watch over us.

"Well, that was a truly hideous experience," Shieda said when they had gone.

"Yeah. After listening to them eat, I don't know whether I have more or less of an appetite than I had before," I said. "So, um, what now?"

"Now, you all concentrate on keeping me awake so I can maintain my spells."

"What would you have us do, milady?" Domitrus asked.

"You should get some sleep, Domitrus, if you can. You've been through a lot. We're going to have to get you back to full strength as soon as possible. As for the rest of you...talk to me, sing to me, dance with me...I don't care what you do or how you do it, but you have to keep me awake."

After a short, clueless pause, Parkel piped up: "Perhaps I could tell you a story of the sea? It would seem appropriate, considering our location."

Shieda, smiling, settled into her "seat" on the boat, adjusting her position, and then looked up at Parkel. "Very well, Parkel. Tell me a tale."

"It was about eight years ago when first I learned to love the sea.

"I had grown up in a small seaside village called Oph'met in the nation of Ruzal. I had been orphaned at the age of three, and had found my way into the care of a generous but gruff blacksmith named Borpha Vorr.

"I spent my youth learning Borpha's trade, also keeping Borpha's house and preparing Borpha's meals (alas, Borpha had no wife). It was a meager living with little changing from day to day. And soon I realized I had no taste for metal or for metalworking.

"When I started becoming a man, I knew that I had to find a way to leave Borpha. But it would not be easy. Business had been bad for a few years, and Borpha's strength was fading as he aged. I did not know what to do.

"In the meantime, I had met a man who became an inspiration to me while I was out running errands for my master. He was an old salt by the name of Sischwa. He would spend his days whittling down by the ports, and when I'd pass him on my way to the shops of the town, he would stop me and tell me stories.

"And what tales he told! Stories of pirates—'gangs of the high seas,' he called them. Tales of adventure, of battles, of scrapes with death. Tales of freedom, most of all. After listening to Sischwa's stories, I began to gaze out at the sea with the same longing and love for it in my heart that I knew he had in his. I dreamt of the ocean, carrying me away from my humble existence on its wave crests, opening up the world to me as I wanted myself to be in it. If only I could sail the seas!

"I had heard of pirates throughout my life. Most were long dead legends, but I had heard one pirate's name whispered by frightened tongues. He was perhaps the greatest, most ruthless of all pirates—Hanez-Ka. Why, only a few months prior to my first meeting with Sischwa he had raided a village just up the coast from ours. Perhaps he was still not far from Oph'met.

"One day, after talking again for a few hours with Sischwa, I decided it was time for me to leave the village, and Borpha, and set out on my own. I made my way to the docks with a small packet containing my few worldly possessions, and stole a rickety skiff (tinier, but not much different than the one we are in right now). I rowed a ways out to sea, and prepared to fashion a sail out of cloth. I was so intent in my work that I failed to notice the approach of several ships until they were practically on top of me.

"They weren't over large, and they appeared battered by the ravages of battle and years spent at sea, but they still were sleek and colorful—the masts and structures were decorated with cloths of many colors, more than I could hope to name! These were not the ships of any one nation. These belonged to outsiders, rogues...pirates!

"I tried at first to paddle out of their way. But they soon raced past me, ignoring me completely. I realized they were on their way to raid Oph'met! I immediately turned my craft about, and rowed towards shore, excited by the pirates' presence, but also worried for Sischwa, Borpha, and the other townsfolk.

"When I reached shore, the invaders had already landed, and were busy raping, pillaging and looting the town. Oph'met was too small to have a fleet or an army of its own. We had a volunteer corps, but this was not easy to mobilize, since many of its members were old mercenary soldiers with a penchant for drink. The pirates might slash their throats before they had even stood up from their barstools.

"Hacking, slashing, groping, and laughing, the pirates made their way through town. I grabbed a sword from a corpse, and made ready to defend my homeland. An old woman I knew saw me, and thought I had joined the interlopers. 'Traitor!' she cried. 'The blacksmith's boy is one of 'em!'

"Just as I was about to protest, a large rogue came lumbering towards me. 'A wannabe, eh?' he said. 'Ye might prove useful.' And he clunked me on the head with the pommel of his sword.

"When I awoke, I was on board one of their ships. Kneeling, I looked around me. Several of my fellow villagers—mostly young women—were roped together and strewn about the deck. The rogues were all around, perched above my people, laughing and disparaging them. As I started to rise, one of the pirates kicked my feet out from under me. I sat up and looked at him.

"One of the imprisoned women called out, 'Do away wit' 'im first. No one likes a traitor!' Then, to me, she added, 'Hope you're happy, boy—they kilt yer master.'"

"I couldn't believe it! Borpha was dead! And I had wished for these savages to arrive! I cursed myself, and hoped for a quick death. But then, the pirate who had struck me with his sword in the village stepped in front of me, smiling, as he gazed down at me. 'Hear that, son?

"They want me to do ya in! Perhaps I ought to... though I do need me a new serving boy..."

"The cries rose from the captured villagers and the pirates alike: 'Kill! Kill! Kill!' Everyone, it seemed, wanted me dead! But just then, a hunched figure approached the pirate who stood over me. It was Sischwa! He was alive! 'Bah! Ignore 'em, I say! The boy's a good one—paid me mind when all others shooed me on. He'll make a good man one day, sir.'"

"The pirate smiled at me again, and motioned for me to stand. As I rose to my feet, I felt my bonds being loosed from behind me. I was being freed. But why? Then, the pirate addressed me again. 'Sischwa's one to trust boy. If he vouches for ya, it's good enough for me. You've just got yerself a job as my serving boy. Me? I'm Hanez-Ka, the leader of everyone you see here. Come with me.'"

"I served him for nearly six years, moving up slowly from servant to trusted assistant. I spent my days learning to use a sword (though only passably) and dagger, how to fight 'dirty,' and how to outthink a foe. I became comfortable swinging about in the ship's rigging, high above the decks. We maneuvered through battles, narrow escapes, and through violent sea storms. After I'd gained some experience, the other pirates began taking a liking to me. But with Hanez-Ka...it was different. He treated me like a son almost, sharing stories and ideas with me that he never told the other men. He told me even of his own childhood, scavenging in the streets of Terasskos—his story was similar to my own. He, too, had dreamed of a way out. A chance trip to the coast during a pirate invasion led to his capture. He was taken on by the head pirate, and had been taught the ways of the sea. When the old pirate retired, Hanez-Ka—already a terror in his own right—took over as leader of the bandits.

"It was discussions like these that led me to believe Hanez-Ka might also be grooming me as a successor. My heart leaped at the thought! I still needed to learn to lead, but the idea of becoming a leader of men filled me with joy. Not at all bad a station in life for one who had been merely an orphaned street urchin!

"Then came the day we were overtaken by Terasskossian warships. (I did not know it then, but these were King Orlacc's men we were facing.) They outnumbered us, 12 ships to our seven, and they had far more men than we. Their captain, DeVissk, was determined to catch us and put an end to our raiding.

"When the battle was finished, and more than half our men lay dead or dying, Captain DeVissk came face to face with Hanez-Ka.

'No last minute bribe to try to save your life?' he asked our leader. 'No offer of treasure? Well, I'm disappointed, Hanez-Ka!'

"The once mighty-seeming pirate dropped to his knees, and begged DeVissk to spare him. 'All my treasure, my ships, and my slaves, great captain! All these I offer you. Just allow me one small boat for escape, and a few of my trusted cohorts. I promise on my life that we shall leave these waters and never return.' Then, he looked at me, and pointed. 'Why, right here, I have a well-trained cabin boy. I've groomed him for service myself. And he's yours for the taking, captain. Yours!'

"This was almost too much for me to bear! Hanez-Ka had fallen unbelievably in my estimation in just a few moments. I realized then that I'd been a fool to trust him, a fool to believe his fatherly overtures, and a fool to think that my salvation lay in piracy. I struggled against my captors, hoping to break free and slit Hanez-Ka's throat myself, but they held me tight.

"Meanwhile, the Terasskossians were mocking him, laughing at his groveling. Finally, the captain said, 'Your kind never fails to disgust me. Take care of him.' And as the captain turned and walked away, his mate unsheathed a sword, and hacked Hanez-Ka's head right off. It was a dismal end to his once legendary career. Now, his name and his deeds would be forgotten (except by those who despised him).

"They executed or imprisoned the rest of the pirates, but they put the slaves, including myself, ashore upon a nameless, rocky beach. From there, we each wandered in our separate directions. I had nowhere to go—I was considered a traitor in my village. I made my way from town to town for a few years. Then, when I was seeking my fortune in the village of Eyoki when I heard that Orlacc was recruiting warriors for a special campaign. I decided to try my hand at mercenary soldiering, and, besides, a part of me felt it would be right for me to fight on the side of the Terasskossians, as DeVissk had spared my life.

"I could not have imagined that joining with Orlacc would bring me to where I am this moment."

I was so tired that I barely heard his final words. No one seemed eager to speak, to tell the next tale, so I snuggled into Shieda's bosom and fell asleep, cold and wet though I was. Silly me: I neglected to check whether she was awake or not.

Chapter Twenty-Three

I felt like I was in some sort of drug-induced dream state when I awoke that morning. Thoughts were coming to me slowly, like they were in bubbles, floating through the damp air: Look, there's Parkel, asleep. He looks so comfortable. And Therra—who knew she could snore soooo loudly! Domitrus—I don't think he's dead, but he's awfully quiet. Shieda? Where are you, Shieda?

I sat up uneasily, and turned to look behind me for my mate. *Siiigh.* There you are, resting comfortably, serenely asleep. Asleep? Asleep!

The memory of our predicament came flooding back to me, and woke me from my stupor. If Orlacc caught us now, we were as good as dead.

"Shieda! Wake up honey! C'mon!" I was shaking her, but she was so drained that it was having little effect. Finally, she came around.

"Mmmm... God, I...I'm sorry, I..."

The others were stirring now, jostled awake by the commotion I was making.

"It's okay. You just gotta wake up and get that spell working again before..."

And then, thwssskkk! An arrow slashed the air and planted itself firmly in the bow of our boat, right near Shieda's head. We looked up and saw the archers, lining the decks of the nearest warships. The man who had fired the arrow called out, "M'Lord! Come quick! We've broken through their shield! They are defenseless!!!"

Bleary-eyed but anxious, Orlacc appeared on-deck in his robes, followed closely by a staggering Kryfalikk. "What are you saying? Tell me again, soldier, quickly!" he snapped.

"W-We saw they were asleep," the archer stammered, "so we fired one upon them, and it struck their craft. Look! There t'is!"

"Crap, we've gotta get rowing!" I said.

"We can't outrun..." Parkel started, but he reached for the oars anyway. As he stumbled, the boat rocked violently, and we all grabbed hold of its edges, trying to keep it from capsizing. Shieda shot Parkel a harsh look, and said, "If you don't mind terribly, I need to concentrate. It'll take me a minute to re-weave the spell."

"Try that, and I'll put an arrow through you!" It was Orlacc, calling down from above. He had taken a bow from one of his men, and had drawn it taut with an arrow notched and aimed at my beloved's heart. The other archers were also poised, with bows drawn, ready to let fire. One word from their commander, and we would disappear under a hail of arrows. I couldn't see any way that we would survive. There were too many projectiles for just the five of us to escape unscathed!

"Oh, I have tasted this moment so many times in the recent days, my foolish adversaries," Orlacc mused, his voice the only sound besides the lapping waves and the creaking ships. "And now that it is finally here, I almost hate to let it pass. There will be other moments to savor, of course—it won't be ended when the arrows strike you. You will squirm and writhe about for a time, and then I will have the pleasure of removing your battered and fatally wounded bodies, and disposing of them as I see fit, as well as the satisfaction of knowing that I have rid myself of the primary obstacles to my plans. But it will not be the same without the thrill of the hunt, the uncertainty over how it all will end. Nevertheless..."

"...On my mark, men: Ready, aim..." He squinted his eye and drew back his bow string just a little bit more...

And something huge, and I mean gigantic, hit the water. None of us saw it coming because we were so intent on the situation, so I couldn't tell you what it was. All I knew was that there was a magnificent splash, and then the boat rocked about so much that I was sure we would flip over. Miraculously, we remained upright.

We heard a guttural noise escape Orlacc's throat. He had fired just as the object hit, but his aim had been thrown off. The archers let the tension out of their bows, as they all looked skyward to see where the object had come from.

"What the hell was that?" I asked no one in particular.

"I'm not su..." Shieda started, but then a collective gasp arose from within Orlacc's ranks. Another black shape was falling from the sky. The second meteor found one of the ships this time. Moments after the object had smashed into its side, the ship listed, and began to sink as water poured through the gaping hole in its flank. Men screamed, and the armored soldiers leapt off the doomed warcraft as it disappeared into the sea.

"What madness is this?" Orlacc screeched. His men were panicking now, rushing all over the decks, wondering if they might be the next to be drowned.

"From the clifftops!" Kryfalikk said. "Someone's dropping rocks on us from up there!"

Orlacc shielded his eyes from the sunlight and gazed upwards. I followed his line of sight, and then we saw them at the same instant: tiny silhouettes, moving around at the cliff's edge.

"Ho! Strangers...!" Orlacc called, but before he could finish, another boulder was flung in our direction. This one came down at a weird angle. It glanced off of one of the ships nearest us, and plunged into the water just yards from our boat. Still we did not capsize. The ship's side was damaged, but not enough to cause it to take on water.

"Why are you shooting at us?" yelled Orlacc, trying again to get a word in before another rock fell from above. After a few moments, about twenty of the silhouetted figures appeared.

"You will leave our area now, King Orlacc," shouted a voice from the clifftop. It sounded like an old man's voice, dry and weathered. "Allow the five adventurers to go free, or we will send down more rocks to sink your ships."

"Our area! And just who are you, stranger, that you would dare command me from the open seas?" Orlacc responded.

After a pause, the voice from above answered, "I am Obishku, war-chief of the Grimnells."

"Grimnells!" Parkel said, throwing me a knowing glance.

Therra, too, turned to face me, actually smiling. "They're your people, Morrelaine! We're saved! Say something to them! Tell them you are with us!"

But I just wanted to curl up in the bottom of the boat and hide. So what if they rescued us? What then? "I thought you hated my people," I muttered to Therra.

"How could I hate anyone who would free us from this dark situation?" she asked. Then, she looked to the cliffs and shouted, "Ho, Obishku! One of your finest warriors—Morrelaine—is with us! Save us, and he shall walk among you again. What say you?"

But there was no answer. Instead, Orlacc returned to ranting. He called again for his wizard, Frouder.

"Mage, I will not be beaten by a Grimnell! Tell me there is something you can do."

"I can think of nothing, my king. I..."

"Blast the cliff out from under them," said Orlacc, waving his arms. "Surely you can do that much!"

"Yes, my lord, but the stones from the explosion would fall

161

upon us, and sink us as readily as their projectiles could. I would recommend against it."

"Set them afire then! Or deflect their boulders!"

"I-I cannot burn what I cannot see, majesty. And their rocks are too big, and they come too quickly, for me to work a spell against them. I'm afraid..."

"You're afraid? You're afraid?!?!? You have no idea how afraid you shall be. What good have you been to me lately, wizard?" And he shoved Frouder towards the ship's rail. The magician crumpled to the deck.

"I-I'll remember that, lord," Frouder muttered.

"We have the next stone ready," came Obishku's voice again. "You have only moments to decide."

Orlacc's fury was boiling now, but he refused to give up. In the midst of his rage, one more idea occurred to him. "Move our ships closer in—close the circle around our captives," he commanded his men. And then, he shouted, "We are surrounding our prisoners, Grimnell chief! We will come so near to them that you cannot strike at us without hitting them. Are you willing, chief, to sacrifice them to destroy us?"

"Are you willing," Obishku countered, "to risk your remaining ships, and all your many men aboard them?"

Orlacc sighed. Clearly, he'd hoped his threat would have a more immediate and powerful effect. But he stood firm, and said, "Yes."

Nothing moved for about half a minute. The wind, the waves, and the rocking ships were the only sounds. Then, Obishku, with a chilling confidence in his voice, spoke again: "I must warn you, O king, you should not waste you energy in this pursuit. Your quarry are protected by a power far greater than any you possess."

Orlacc puffed up his chest a few more times, trying to think of some threat to hurl back at Obishku, but apparently he could not find any words. He stopped, and stood there with his shoulders dropped, not moving a muscle. His face was impassive. Only his eyes moved, circling, darting around, searching the ships, the sky, for an answer. Or for a way out.

He scowled at the fallen Frouder, and said, "I suppose I needn't even ask you whether what he says is correct, for I know it to be true: I've seen that boat remain upright through everything." Then, with a single nod to himself, he chose his course. "Turn our ships around," he shouted. "Set a course for home. We are finished here."

But he strode over to the rail and looked down at us with a cold fire in his gaze. "But we are not finished, enemies! You may think you've won here today, but you've only raised the stakes. Oh, I'll return to my kingdom, all right, but once I'm home, I'll muster the most powerful army this land has ever seen. Then I'll come for you." He pointed directly at me, and added, "I'll burn down your Grimnell forests to get to you if I have to, and, what's more, I'll enjoy doing it!"

I could tell that each of us wanted to say something, to challenge him, but we all remained silent. I think each one of us realized we had been incredibly lucky. We stood, afraid to move, solemnly watching as his ships moved away. Ironically, the wind had finally died down. It would take them a long time to reach Terasskos.

Finally, one of us moved. Shieda slumped down in the boat, breaking the spell of mopiness.

"I told you it would be a long day," she said.

"Aye, you did," answered Parkel. "I am pleased that we survived it."

"Well, it's not over yet," I said. "We've got to figure out what to do next, and I, for one, am sick of sitting in this boat. Where are we gonna go?"

As if in answer, Obishku called again from above. "Ho, down there! We are preparing the ladder, and, when we have it properly anchored, we shall lower it to you."

"Ladder? What ladder?" I asked, but no one had a reply, except Therra, who said, "Your people came to save you, Morrelaine, don't you see? I think they mean to pull us from this boat."

She was right, for the next thing that happened was that a huge rope ladder unfurled itself down the side of the cliff like a giant banner. It was made of rope that was as thick as my arm and its fist-sized knots looked secure, but I still wasn't too pleased with the idea of having to climb up the sheer cliff face, which rose at least a few hundred feet above the ocean. I could feel my stomach twisting into knots.

"So, um, who wants to go first?" I asked.

"Why, you must go," Therra said, earnestly. Parkel had started rowing us towards the spot where the ladder touched the water's surface. "They will want to be sure that you are indeed among us. If one of us were to go first, they might assume we were holding you as prisoner, or even that we had done away with you. They have no cause to trust us. For those reasons, and to show respect for your people, we must let you lead us."

163

My heart sank. "What do you mean by 'lead'?" We were getting quite close to the ladder now. "I-I mean, shouldn't I stay behind to, um, y'know, make sure you guys get up safely first?"

"No, she's right, Morrelaine," Shieda said. "You should go first." She stroked my hair with her hand and pulled me close to her. "Don't worry," she said in a tired yet loving whisper, "I'll be right behind you."

Something in her voice and her touch lifted my spirits and warmed my heart enough so that I was able to take hold of the ladder and begin climbing. Okay, just get it over with, I thought. Once we've all made it to the top, we can finally grab some downtime.

"Here I go. Wish me luck." And so, I climbed, looking straight ahead of me for the first ten minutes or so. I was definitely afraid to look down—they always say that's a surefire way to scare yourself into paralysis. After a short while, I did look up. I'd hoped to be able to measure my progress, but the cliff top seemed just as far away as when I'd started.

Wonderful, I thought. And I thought sitting in the boat was tedious!

Left arm up, right arm, then legs, then arms, again and again. I could feel some extra weight pulling on the ladder below me, so I figured that the others had started climbing up behind me. I had to keep moving, but my joints were aching, especially my shoulders, since they were supporting a great deal of my body weight. Still, I figured I should keep moving so we could all get up before the winds started up again.

I heard a cawing sound, and I made the mistake of trying to locate its source. I turned my head and saw a seagull float by me in the air, looking at me. "Oh God, oh Jesus!" I said, facing forward again, closing my eyes tight. Oh well, I thought, now I've done it—I really am scared. I figured it couldn't get much worse, so, slowly, I looked down and saw the sea far below me, and our boat, which now looked like a child's toy, bobbing in the waves. Twenty-or-so feet down on the ladder, I could see Parkel climbing. Behind him was Therra, and I could not see beyond her, but I assumed the others were following. I began to wonder how poor Domitrus was going to make it—he wasn't all that strong anyway, and he was suffering from injuries and exhaustion. I shifted my gaze skyward again, and saw that there was still a ways to go before I would reach the top. I paused, in limbo, barely able to breathe, let alone climb.

"Morrelaine! Rest if you must, but keep going if you can!" It was Parkel, shouting up from below. He sounded desperate. "You have made it half of the way, Morrelaine! You've done well!"

Halfway? I mused. That's not so bad. Maybe I can do this. I can do this! I turned my head up and began climbing again, hand over hand, from one rope-rung to the next, moving like a machine in high gear. I felt like a train, tearing up the tracks, racing along with one goal in mind: GET THERE! They're all depending on you!

The next thing I knew, I had made it to the top. Two pairs of arms reached down to pull me over the lip and set me down on the grass. I was so out of breath, and so bleary-eyed, that I could barely make out the other Grimnells, moving about all around me. I merely sat there for a time, sucking in the wind. By the time I was recovered, Parkel was being helped over the edge.

An old Grimnell, about my height but with a wide, bearded face, snow-white hair, and thin limbs dangling from his torso, approached me, nodding. "O-Obishku?" I asked.

"Aye, honored one, it is I," answered the wizened man. "How are you feeling at present, might I ask?"

My whole body was sore, and my entire form seemed to be throbbing—pulsing—with every heartbeat. But, I started climbing to my feet anyways, saying, "Just glad to be alive, sir. And ready to help rescue my friends, if you don't mind."

"'Sir?' 'If I don't mind?' Hmm... " he said, arching an eyebrow, and then stealing a knowing look at his men. "Truly your time away has changed you. The Morrelaine we knew would never have... would have been unlikely to have accorded me such... well, open respect."

Oy! What was that all about? I wondered.

"Anyhow, I think you can see we have matters well in hand," he continued, pointing to the cliff's edge, where six well-muscled Grimnells were poised. Parkel was sprawled on the grass nearby, gasping for air.

He added, "You are, of course, free to inspect our efforts."

As he was speaking, Therra's gloved hand appeared at the clifftop. Two of the Grimnells immediately reached to help her. "I need no aid to make my way," came her voice from below, but, as she came over the top, she smiled, and added, "though I certainly appreciate your overtures."

Parkel and I each patted her on the back, welcoming her, and then I went to the edge to check on Domitrus and Shieda. To my horror, they were still a long way from the top of the ladder. The wind had picked up again, and they seemed to be having trouble. They were just hanging there, barely moving, as the ladder began to sway in the rising gale.

"What's the matter you guys?" I called down to them. "You've just gotta keep climbing. You'll make it."

Domitrus's strained voice came up from below, saying, "My wounds, they are too much for me! I fear I cannot hang on much longer!"

"Domitrus, listen to me!" It was Shieda. She muttered something I couldn't hear from that great distance, and then Domitrus looked back up at the clifftop, and started climbing again. It was as if he'd been recharged. He flew up the rock face like a spider, and, soon, he was over the top and on the ground beside us. Smiling, I turned to look below again, expecting to see Shieda working her way towards the top of the ladder. Instead, she was still about a hundred feet from the top, and she had her head down. She was just hanging there, cringing, as the ladder lurched from side to side in the wind like a huge pendulum.

"What's wrong, Shieda?" I shouted. "It's only a little further. You've got to make it! What? I can't quite hear... "

She turned her face up towards me, and I could see she was as pale as bone. Something had gone awfully awry. "I s-said I used too much energy helping Domitrus! Already tired. I-I can't climb..."

I saw her go limp, and I knew I had to move. She was moments away from passing out. I wasn't about to lose her, not her—the one person I had ever really touched in this universe or any other. All I could think to do was to grab the ropes and start yanking them with all my strength. "Help me!" I screeched to the others, and the two nearest Grimnells started pulling with me. "C'mon, damn it!" I ordered, and Therra and Parkel joined in the task.

I was worried we were taking too long, that, no matter what, we'd get to the end of the ladder and find that Shieda was gone, fallen to her death. I tried to push the image out of my mind. Unfortunately, I was too intent on my task to be able to look over the edge to reassure myself that she was still there. So I kept pulling and pulling, for what seemed like too long. My mind seemed to come unlatched from time, and pictures from our recent adventures flashed before me. I could feel the ocean's mist on my face; no, I was crying. "Shieda!!!" I could feel my muscles melting, as resignation stabbed my heart. I was about to crumble into a heap, when I saw her head and shoulders appear. We'd saved her!

They laid her across my lap, and I cradled her in my arms, thinking of nothing but her, feeling her chilly skin and her heartbeat. Finally, when she opened her eyes, I whispered, "Don't ever do that again."

She smiled and touched my cheek.

With my sanity now somewhat restored, I again turned my attention to the world around me. Everyone—our group and about twenty Grimnells—was standing around, watching me care for Shieda. They seemed relieved, and yet there was also a look of expectancy on all their faces. What next?, they seemed to be asking. Since I didn't know, I asked them.

"What next, guys?"

Obishku cleared his throat, and said, "We will escort you and your guests back to our village, glorious one. There, after you have rested, we shall call a war council, and hear how you wish to lead us against King Orlacc. He has, after all, promised to seek you out, and we must prepare."

I nodded grimly. I still didn't know how I was going to be able to fool these people, let alone lead them, but I wasn't ready to worry about that now. And then, something occurred to me out of the blue.

"Obishku? Tell me...how did you know when we'd be sailing by these cliffs, and that we'd need to be rescued from Orlacc's navy?"

The old Grimnell smiled, and answered, "A little old man told us."

I looked down to see Shieda's reaction, but she had a faraway look in her eyes.

Chapter Twenty-Four

We barely had any time to rest. Our group was exhausted, but Obishku insisted that we hurry back to "our" village, which was called Nornlunn, he said. We were given some dried fruits to eat and a root beer-like beverage to drink, and then we were helped up and on our way.

Not far from the cliff's edge the treeline began, and it was into this forest that our party plunged. Here, the trees and vines were thick, and the terrain was rough. I already felt pretty disgusting—my body had been covered in sweat, blood, and salt water, and I hadn't had a chance to wash in days. Now, thorny branches were whipping my face, leaving little welts that stung and throbbed with warmth. And this place was supposed to be home to me?

I looked to see how the others were faring. Domitrus, who had hardly spoken at all for the past 48 hours, seemed like a walking dead man. His normally ruddy complexion had gone ashen, and his eyes and mouth drooped. Was he dying? I had no idea just how bad his wounds were under his bandages, and it had been a while since Therra had checked them. My poor Shieda looked almost as pale as Domitrus, but she seemed more present, more determined to keep moving. Parkel and Therra? They were young and strong, but even they seemed a little less sturdy on their feet than usual.

I thought about all of us, and of how we'd all changed in the course of our many adventures. Orlacc, of course, was gone, and now we had Shieda as our leader. Her father, the Sage, had disappeared, though we didn't know for sure whether he was alive or dead. Parkel had become more assertive—he was no longer the whiny boy I had counseled on the ways of love way back when. Therra had finally let down her guard somewhat, and she was more willing to cooperate, to work as part of a team. Hell, she and Parkel had even become friends, though I wasn't sure whether there was any more to it than that. Who could have imagined that a few short weeks ago?

And now that I had time to think, I began again to wonder about my role in all this. I'd changed a bit too, of course. I had accepted that this was no dream almost as soon as I'd arrived here, but I still had no idea what was really going on. Why was I sent here? What was the universe trying to teach me by putting me into this body and making me participate in this adventure? And what would happen to me when it was all over, assuming we survived Orlacc's onslaught?

I remembered the day that I'd come to this world. I had been typing up some homework on my computer, thinking about how mediocre my life was. I'd been so scared about my future, and yet so resigned to it: life was going to continue to be boring—there was just no way to rise above it, or so it had seemed. And then, I'd felt called out of my room; called to that little brick building; called into this world. Was that it? Was the universe trying to save me from a life of boredom? It couldn't be that simple! Could it?

And yet, even here, in this land of great adventure, I still seemed to be at the mercy of events. I still didn't seem to have any control over my own destiny. I still did not feel like I fit in, and I was still sometimes surprised that the others put up with me. What did I contribute? I was only a four-foot tall, cowardly Grimnell with a so-so sense of humor. What was so great about that? I looked at my tiny, gloved hands, which had often seemed so useless, and sighed.

Then, I felt Shieda's hand caress my back. She asked me if I was okay in a tired and parched-sounding voice. I nodded, and we smiled at each other with our lips and our eyes. Could that be it? Was love the reason I had traveled to this strange and beautiful land?

It wasn't a bad reason, if it was the reason.

We stopped once by a stream for some rest and some drinks, but we were soon on our way again. We reached Nornlunn nearly six hours after we'd left the cliffs by the sea. It was late afternoon, maybe an hour before suppertime. We were all about ready to collapse.

Nornlunn was in an area where the vegetation had been thinned out. Obviously, the Grimnells had made use of the forest's natural features when they'd designed their dwellings—houses were built high up using trees for fortification, and a few multi-storied homes rose high above the ground. There were walkways suspended from the taller trees around the village perimeter. I gathered these were used for defense. Ropes and pulleys seemed to be everywhere. It appeared that people could hoist things into the treetops and even across the entire village. A river, running through the center of town, was used to provide drinking water, for washing, and to power rudimentary machines. Scads of people, all as short as I was, were milling about, going about their business, when we arrived.

As we entered the town, the other Grimnells stopped what they were doing and stared at our party. Some even averted their eyes when they saw me.

Obishku seemed to sense my discomfort, and he said, "We have prepared rooms for your friends near to your home, my leader. And we...we took great care to keep your dwelling the same as when you left it. Come, follow me, and I will show your friends where they will be staying."

But, just as he said that, several men—I took them to be soldiers, since they wore elaborate armor and had swords, bows, and clubs strapped to their belts and backs—rushed to greet, er, to greet me.

"Do you know yet where King Orlacc will strike, sir?" one began.

"Where should we concentrate our perimeter defenses, leader?" asked another.

"You know me well, Morrelaine," said a third, and, indeed, I felt as if I did recognize him, as if maybe I had met him once, long ago. He wore an ornate suit of molded leather armor, which curled and twisted into a series of sharp points on his chest and shoulders, and which was painted red, brown, and black. His face was wide, like many of the Grimnells', and it looked like it laughed a lot. "Morrelaine," he repeated. "I could lead a preemptive strike against their forces, if you would but command it!"

I seemed to recall his name was..."Trolcott?"

"Yes, my friend," he answered, drawing closer to me. "What is it?"

"I...you...how do I...?" Oh no! I was faltering.

Badly!

Luckily, Shieda came to my aid. "Please! You will have to excuse him. We're all quite tired from our long journey and our many adventures, and we'd like some rest, if you please."

The soldiers bit their lips and backed away sullenly. Perhaps they were not used to being given orders by such a tall person as Shieda.

"Obishku?" she said.

"Yes, of course," the old man answered. "She's right, men. I was about to show them to their quarters." Turning to us he said, "Come this way, please."

The part of Nornlunn where we were to be staying was in an elevated section of town. The houses here were built some thirty feet off of the ground, and they had ladders leading up to a wood-plank walkway that surrounded them. The raised complex contained six dwellings, and there were other such groupings of houses in the nearby trees.

"Uptown, eh?" I joked, but nobody was listening.

Domitrus groaned as he was being helped up the ladder, but, soon, we were all clustered at the top. We dropped Therra, Parkel, and Domitrus off at a rather large treehouse. Parkel and Domitrus quickly bid their goodbyes and retired, but Therra remained outside.

"Perhaps I should go with you and Trolcott," she said eagerly, addressing Obishku. "We could eat something, and discuss war strategies."

"Nay, mighty one," he responded. "The woman was right when she said you needed to rest. Fear not. We shall talk soon." With that, Therra nodded, and skulked into her dwelling.

When we got to our, er, my place, Obishku followed us in, but stayed near the door. "In three hours we shall come for you. Shortly before that, someone will bring you some water for bathing and some fresh clothes. Then, we will dine, and convene our council." We thanked him, and he bowed and backed out through the door. At last! We were alone!

"C'mere!" I said to Shieda, and we hugged. "You don't know how afraid I was that I'd lost you on that ladder!"

"No more afraid than I've been for you several times, I'm sure," she answered. "But we're here, safe, now, and you can relax."

"Relax? Are you kidding?" I asked as we pulled apart. "There's a few hundred people out there who are gonna expect me to lead them into battle! And I've got no idea what I should say or do!" We both began undressing. "I thought you said you were gonna help me handle this part! Whatever happened to that?"

"I'll tell you what I know, and that should help some. It won't be easy, though. But I'll stand by you, no matter what happens. Does that make you feel any better?"

"Some," I said. We had stripped off our battered armor, and were both now in our underclothes. I gazed at Shieda in the fading daylight, and suddenly felt that I'd been a little harsh with her. I also felt the urge to make love to her again—it had been a while since that first time—but I knew we were both probably too tired for that. She must have guessed my mood, because she sauntered over to where I was standing and wrapped her arms around me. I put my hands on her waist and gazed into her beautiful green eyes. "Actually," I said, "having you with me is the best thing I could hope for in life."

But, as she stooped to kiss me, someone pulled aside the curtain-door of the dwelling and entered. As she stepped into the room, I saw that she was a young, Grimnell woman, with long, red-and-gold streaked hair and large, chocolate-brown eyes. When she saw me, she froze, and our eyes locked. For a few moments, we stood there like that, and my heart stirred, moved by distinct feeling of recognition and, and...What else?

Then, our eyes unlocked. Hers darted from me to Shieda and back again. Then, her eyes brimmed over with tears, and she started shaking. She let out a tiny cry, turned, and fled our treehouse.

"What was that about?" Shieda said after the little woman had gone.

"I-I'm not sure," I said. "I think I...I think I know her, somehow."

"Hmmmph!" Shieda said. "I'll just bet!" And she strolled away and climbed into bed.

We dozed off-and-on for a while, and we cuddled, and talked.

She told me what she knew about Morrelaine and the Grimnells. She'd heard of the Grimnells when she was living with the Sage in West Serra Land. They were always referred to in a derogatory way: "'Oh, those Grimnells, they eat wood and bugs, and they never bathe!'" she explained, mocking her former townspeople. Every so often, a small band of Grimnells would pass through West Serra Land, and she'd had occasion to speak to them a few times. "They seemed fine to me, though they kept to themselves, mostly," Shieda said. "They acted like they were accustomed to being treated poorly."

She added that she had actually heard of Obishku before, "for he was their highest war-chief." And then, one time, she overheard some Grimnells talking about Morrelaine. "He was a rising star," she explained. "He had successfully led his people in defending their land from several raiding parties. Apparently, rogue bands of ex-soldiers and village outcasts often attempted to steal from the Grimnells, because they were so small, and were considered weak. Also, they said, Morrelaine had repelled an invasion from Terasskos, led by a young prince named Orlacc. Interesting, eh? He was out, trying to prove his manhood to his father by capturing the Grimnell's forests for the kingdom!"

"Me? I did that?"

"Er, well, not you exactly. It was the old Morrelaine, remember?"

"Oh...right." My heart sank.

"They said he was a great thinker, that he defeated his enemies, not by hitting them with an all-out assault, but by outwitting them. He was said to be a great designer and architect, and it was thought that he would one day rise to lead his people into a new age of prosperity. But, then he disappeared for a time before resurfacing as a member of Orlacc's quest, which must have seemed strange to the Grimnells!"

I missed out almost entirely on the last part of what she'd said, because I was so preoccupied with her descriptions of Morrelaine's achievements. "Oh God!" I stammered, turning my head to face her. "How am I ever going to live up to all that?"

She reached up her hand and stroked my cheek. "You're smart too, and you've got a good, strong heart. If you can find the courage that I know is there inside that heart, I'm sure you'll be able to lead these people as well as Morrelaine ever could. Even better, perhaps."

Lord, it was so wonderful to have her there, believing in me! It was almost enough to make me start believing in myself. But still, it was only almost enough. But, I looked her in the eyes, and said, "And you'll be there to help me?"

"As much as I can."

"Thank God. Maybe it'll be all right, then," I murmured, not really convinced.

"One thing you told me struck me as odd, though," I said, sweeping the previous topic under the rug. "You mentioned that the real Morrelaine fought a battle against Orlacc way back when, and your father said in his story that he defied Orlacc when he came to West Serra Land, looking to capture you. What I don't get is, if the Sage and Morrelaine had been Orlacc's enemies before, what made him so sure they'd join up with his phony quest to retake his kingdom? And, like, why would the real Morrelaine sign on with someone who had once tried to conquer his own people?"

Her brow furrowed—clearly neither of us had all the answers.

"Well, you heard Orlacc himself say he had forgotten meeting my father. Of course, who knows when anything he says can be believed," she reasoned. "As for my father, knowing him as I do, I'm pretty sure he knew where this 'quest' would lead when he attached himself to it. And the real Morrelaine? I can only speculate, but Orlacc was practically a boy when he led his attempted invasion—perhaps Morrelaine believed he had changed over the years. Then again, as I said before, Morrelaine vanished from the Allarraban woods some time ago. Who's to say he hadn't changed in the intervening years?"

"Hmm. Makes me wonder why Morrelaine cut out of here..." I mused. "Y'know, Obishku said this weird thing before... "

Just then, there was a knock outside our door, and then a man appeared carrying two steaming buckets of water. "I was asked to

174

bring you these," he said, and then he set the buckets down, bowed, and left.

"Ah, relief!" I said. "Relief from thinking about this stuff!"

We eagerly doffed our dirty underclothes, and began bathing each other's bodies with the water and a sponge. Soon, we were clean and refreshed again for the first time in half a week. While we were washing up, someone else had knocked without entering. We noticed some fresh clothes piled up neatly just outside the doorway. There were two robes—a black one for me and a taller, white one for Shieda—and brand new set of armor for me. "Look at this!" I said, examining the armor. It was striking—freshly painted and a lot more elaborate than my old set. I couldn't wait to try it on.

Unfortunately, Fate, in the form of Obishku, had other plans. The old man entered our treehouse without knocking, looking quite perturbed. He sat on our bed and glowered at us. Finally, I had to ask, "What's wrong?"

"I have seen Liassa," he answered, nodding grimly, as if he'd explained everything. "I have called off the council for tonight. We must discuss this matter first."

"Wait a minute!" I said. Now I was getting kind of pissed. Every move I was making seemed to be the wrong one, and I was getting tired of it. "What the hell are you talking about? Who's Liassa?"

"What!?" he exclaimed, squinting at me in disbelief. "You claim not to know? What is the meaning of this, Morrelaine? You left your betrothed here, waiting patiently for you, and then disappeared for years! And then, when you return, you parade this human woman around Nornlunn for all to see! My niece is crushed, Morrelaine, and what for? Why are you not acting like yourself, my friend?"

My mind had jumped over several speed bumps and skidded into the answer. Liassa...the woman who had walked in on us before...my betrothed...his niece...oh no!

"That woman who came in here before," I asked in a humble voice, "we were supposed to get m-married?"

"Of course!" Obishku answered, crossing his arms.

I looked to Shieda for help, but she was just standing there with her hand over her open mouth. I decided there was only one course for me to take: the truth. Letting out a huge sigh, I said, "Obishku, my friend, why don't you bring Liassa here, and I'll try to explain everything to you."

He looked at me quizzically, but he went to go get Liassa.

Shieda put her hand on my shoulder and said, "I hope you know what you're doing."

I shuddered a little, but answered, "I do. I'm putting an end to this charade."

When they returned, I sat them down on the bed, and did my best to explain how I had entered Morrelaine's body and how I'd ended up with Shieda in Nornlunn. I watched them as their expressions changed from anger (Obishku) and hurt (Liassa) to confusion and awe. By the time I was finished, Liassa was on the verge of tears again.

"I find all this very hard to accept, yet I cannot fathom another explanation, and all my senses tell me that you are not lying," Obishku said finally, though he shook his head as if not fully convinced. "Truly, it is amazing that you have come this far."

Liassa looked at him, then at me, let out a yelp, and ran away crying. I guess I hadn't exactly won her over with my story.

"I'm sorry about her," I said to Obishku. "I wish she'd let me talk to her. Maybe we'd both feel better."

"Liassa will understand eventually, and I don't blame you for taking up with the human woman," replied the old man, shrugging. "After all, you are not the Morrelaine who promised his heart to her, and, inside, you are indeed a human. I only wish we had known this before we risked so many men rescuing you from Orlacc. He's never liked our kind, but when we saved your group, we stirred his hunger for our blood. We have provoked him, and now we will pay the price."

Ouch! That wasn't exactly a vote of confidence!

"I, um, I'd still like to be involved with the battle planning," I said. "We came to you because you were our last hope for raising an army to oppose Orlacc. I mean, what about the war council? You're not just going to forget that?"

Obishku frowned, and avoided making eye contact with me or Shieda. "Perhaps you are correct: if the others do not know you are not Morrelaine, your presence will inspire them. We must still call the council either way, for we'll need a plan to counteract Orlacc. I only wish I could feel more confident about the outcome. Even if we had the real Morrelaine here, this would be a difficult fight. But without him..."

"Maybe you should give me a chance before you count me out!" I blurted angrily, almost before I knew what I was saying. "I've learned a lot since I came to this world, and, well, you said yourself that we had some powerful magic on our side!"

He smiled at me, but his eyes were weary. "I did not mean to upset you. Perhaps I spoke too harshly. Maybe your learning and your magic and your spirit will be enough. Maybe.... " He stood, and ambled toward the door. "Well, I shall leave you two alone now. We shall eat a large meal for breakfast, and then we shall talk of war. Until then..." And he left.

"Well, that went over miserably!" I said once he was out of earshot. I plodded over to the bed and threw myself onto it.

Shieda sat beside and massaged my back. After a few minutes, she said, "You did the right thing. You listened to your heart."

"Yeah, and look where it got me! Nowhere! No one's gonna listen to me or follow me! I'm just as much of a loser here as I was back home! Almost makes me wish I was back there! At least no one expected anything from me!"

Shieda stopped rubbing and she pulled away from me. Maybe I had hurt her, but for the moment, at least, I didn't much care. I was busy wallowing in my frustration. She stood up and paced around the room for a while. Finally, she said, "We could still go down below. Get something to eat."

"Nah," I answered, burying my face in the pillow. "I'd rather just sleep."

And after that, I did. But I was not at peace.

Chapter Twenty-Five

Early the next morning, before dawn, I awoke with my stomach growling. The night's events came flooding back into my mind, and I sat up in bed, already in a bad mood. I didn't know what I was going to do, but just then a strange smell wafted through the room and drew me to the window.

I looked out the window and saw a figure, standing among the trees below. It was short and squat, but too tall to be a Grimnell. It wore a white robe that seemed almost to glow in the moonlight, and it carried a staff topped by a glittering jewel. And in one hand, the figure held a lit pipe that looked much like the one the Sage had smoked.

An owl hooted, making its customary noise, but I understood it to say *Let us go for a walk in the woods, my son.*

I resolved to go find out what this person wanted, so I climbed down the ladder from the treehouse, and walked over to where the figure had been standing. It was gone, but I saw it, off in the woods about a hundred feet away from me, lit by a shaft of moonlight. Determined, I trudged into the forest.

But when I reached the spot where the figure had been, it was gone. There was only the shaft of light. The owl cried again: Over here! I looked around, and saw another shaft of light knifing through the trees in the distance, and, standing within it, the figure. It shimmered as a breeze blew the canopy of leaves overhead. Again, I hurried towards the light, and again I was disappointed. Again, the owl spoke, and again I spied another ray, piercing the darkness. I ran after it again.

I was getting a little tired! I still hadn't had much rest, and now my legs felt heavy like iron, and my eyelids drooped. Still, I kept on, faltering as I went, with the bushes thwapping me in the legs and face. At one point, I heard a rustling in the forest beside me. I turned to look, but saw nothing, only the leaves and branches. I went on.

This time, when I approached the light, the figure was still in it. Its back was to me. I could see it was hunched over, and its long hair was gathered into a ponytail. As I reached the area, the figure turned to face me, and I saw at long last that it was, indeed, the Sage.

"You're alive!" I said, as soon as I stopped panting enough to be able to speak.

Before I could say more, the Sage bowed slightly and said, "I am here. And I must tell you..."

"How did you get out of Orlacc's castle? I thought for sure you..."

"Listen to me!" he said, waving a cautionary finger. "Your battle with Orlacc will go badly for you, unless you look elsewhere for a solution. Seek it outside of the Grimnells. Search for it inside of yourself. And search for it outside of yourself."

"Yeah. But, but now that you're here you can help us," I enthused. "We can slam 'em with magic! Freak 'em out with your spells, and then...oh, I don't know. Teleport Orlacc to some other plane or something!" I wanted to rush forward and hug him, but something about his unearthly glow and his rigid, urgent manner unnerved me.

"Magic is but one part of the equation," he said, frowning. "You must not rely upon it."

I was about to say something more, but, just then, Shieda leaped out of the bushes. Besides being surprised to see her, I was wowed by the fact that she was stark naked. She was also crying.

"A-ha!" she shouted, her voice quivering. "That's just wonderful, father! All this time, we thought you were dead, and now when you come back, the first thing you do is call Morrelaine out for a moonlight meeting! What about me, father? Why not me?"

Now, the Sage finally smiled his old smile. "How do you know I did not call both of you here?"

"But I'm your daughter!"

"Shieda?" I asked, unable to contain my curiosity. "Why are you naked?"

"Oh, come on, Morrelaine!" she said, wiping her eyes and sniffling. "I'm used to sneaking through the forest at night without any clothes on! I was a cat for several years, remember?"

Crossing his hands atop his staff, and with his pipe hanging out of his mouth, the Sage grinned again, this time more broadly, and said, "I am pleased you two have found each other. You will get along beautifully, I think. I give your relationship my blessing." He chuckled, as he eyed both of us.

But then, his mood shifted again. He shuffled closer to us, but seemed reluctant to leave the light, and we could see, as he moved, that he was not altogether... solid. "Listen, please, for I don't have much time." When he saw we were rapt, he continued: "If you must know, I did not escape Orlacc's castle. His men tried to kill me, and his sorcerer tried to bind me. But, pshaw, I outwitted them. Now, I am in another realm of existence, and I have many things to do here. I serve a new master now.

"As I was saying before, Morrelaine, you will not win the war with Orlacc by depending on either the Grimnells or magic. The answers are within and without. Look in every corner, every crack, every crevice. Find the unlikeliest places. What appears to be the least in strength and importance will, in truth, be the greatest.

"And I will say this also: Something from your world, Grant—I cannot tell you what—will be the key to your victory."

When he'd finished, he let his reed pipe fall to the ground, and he put it out with his foot. Shieda and I stood there with our mouths hanging open for a few moments, watching him, waiting. Then, he put up a hand and said, "Now go. Return!"

Words poured out of our mouths. "Wait a minute—"

"Father—"

"—what about—"

"—when will I see you—"

"—so many questions—"

"—again?"

The Sage looked skyward, and the light intensified. At the same time, the forest came alive, almost violently. The leaves shook, the tree trunks creaked as they swayed back and forth, and the voices of crickets, owls, birds, and other animals echoed all around us, shouting, calling us to madness. Just then, I heard the wind rushing, and we both collapsed to the ground, the air torn from our chests, our screams drowned out by the deafening gulf between worlds which was now opening before us. As I lost consciousness, I gazed upward.

The Sage was glowing in the sky like a star.

It was bright all around us, as Shieda and I sat up in bed. The night was gone, and sunlight was pouring through our windows. We were back in our treehouse. Morning was upon us.

After we both came somewhat to our senses, we looked at each other. We were both naked and sweating. Finally, she said, "I-I think we just had a vision!"

I swallowed, remembering what the Sage had said. "I know," I answered.

We bathed again after an attendant brought us another sponge and more water, and then we donned our armor—me, my new set, and Shieda, that little black leather number she'd be wearing since she'd stopped being a cat. As soon as we were both looking ASAP (As Snazzy As Possible), we climbed the ladder down to the village, and had breakfast (a cooked meal, finally!) with Parkel, Therra, and Domitrus. All three of them looked much improved. It's wondrous what a good night's rest can do for a person, especially one who does not experience pre-dawn visions!

"You're looking a lot better this morning, Domitrus," I said between bites of some kind of egg and bread mixture.

"Aye. I am feeling more my old self today. That ordeal at Auriggido took much out of me, my friend. I-I wish to thank you all again for saving my life."

"You're part of our family," Shieda said, putting a reassuring hand on his knee.

"Aye, and we need you among us to fight Orlacc," Therra said, poking the air with her fork, flinging bits of food into the cooking fire. "I hope now you see that battling alongside us is a much better lot in life than wasting your days away on that frigid rock of an island, studying under those diseased, maniacal priests!"

"They're not priests," I mumbled. "They're something more." Oops! They were all staring at me now. I quickly shoveled another forkful into my mouth. "Mmmm! This is great stuff, eh guys?" I asked, talking through food. Luckily, Domitrus spoke up.

"While I agree that the Sanctuary was no place for me," he said, avoiding everyone's gaze by staring at his meal, "I am not yet sure where my destiny lies. Again, I find that I am of little help to you. In fact, I have been a burden from the start. That is no life for me either."

Shieda and Therra were both about to protest, but just then Obishku arrived. He nodded, and said, "I do not wish to interrupt you, but our war council is ready. If you will join us?"

He was looking straight at me, treating me like I was the leader of our group. "Uh, of course," I said. We got up, dusted ourselves off, and followed him.

Soon, we reached another part of the Grimnell settlement, away from the main village. There was another campfire here, and around it were gathered about thirty soldiers, each clad in black armor, trimmed with red, gold, brown, or green paint—the colors of the forest. As soon as we approached, all eyes were on us. I immediately recognized Trolcott, the soldier whose name I had remembered the day before, sitting on a log. Obishku motioned for us to sit next to him, and we complied. Obishku remained standing, and addressed us in a commanding voice:

"As a war-chief of the Grimnell tribe, I officially call this council to order. As one of our brightest lights has finally returned to us, I now defer to him. Morrelaine?"

Damn it! He knew the whole story about me! Why was he doing this? Putting me on the spot?

"Uh, well, okay. T-Trolcott, you…you seem to be pretty on top of things. C-Can you tell us what we're up against?"

His brow furrowed, but he said, "Y-Yes, of course, great one, I'll do my best, but…" and he gazed over at the other men "…some time ago, Belgear was assigned the task of scouting the enemy's forces. Perhaps he…?"

"…would be better suited to answer the question? Of course," I said, trying to sound relaxed. "How silly of me! Belgear, come forward, please!" Hmmm. This isn't so hard after all, I thought.

A sprightly, fresh-faced Grimnell leaped forward, practically tripping over his gold cape. He was skinnier and shorter than the others, perhaps a foot shorter than I was. He smiled, and bowed before me—a bit goofy, like a court jester. "It is an honor to serve you, mighty leader! Of the enemy, I can tell you this: he has an army of nearly one thousand men. However, he has only six hundred horses, so, um, if he wishes to move quickly against us, he will only have that many men to dispatch. Two hundred of his men are skilled archers. The rest are proficient with either sword, mace, or lance."

"And, um, might I ask how many men we have?" I asked.

"Soldiers at the ready?" He rolled his eyes skyward, and counted on his fingers. Finally, he answered, "Two hundred and ninety-two. Er, two ninety-three, now that you have returned, sir."

"Shit!" I said, momentarily forgetting myself. "Not even half as many? How the hell are we going to take him on?!?!?"

Everyone was silent for a while, and I began to wonder whether I had already let them all down. But then Trolcott said, "It is true, Morrelaine, that it was once estimated we would have to have three times as many men as an invading human army to be able to match them in sheer strength. But we have always relied on our leaders' cleverness to triumph in the past."

"He is right," said Obishku, regarding me with squinted eyes. "And you were one of our most masterful strategists when you were last with us, those many years ago. What do you say we should do in this situation?"

Damn him! He was at it again! Why does he seem to have it in for me? I wondered. "Well, um, from what I, uh, remember, you were pretty good with the battle planning yourself, Obishku. I-I defer to you in this matter."

Uh-oh! That was a dumb move! A collective gasp went around the group, and they began muttering amongst themselves and eyeing me suspiciously. Apparently, I'd made some major faux pas. I had no idea what to say or do next—I wanted to get up and run away into the forest, but of course I couldn't do that. I was about to put my head in my hands when Parkel, of all people, spoke up.

"Excuse me?" he said. "If I may be allowed to speak?"

"Of course! Certainly!" I chirped, relieved. The assembly quieted down as Parkel stood.

"Therra and I spent some time discussing battle strategies last night, and we believe we have devised a satisfactory plan of action."

"Continue," I said, afraid to let the awkward silence return.

"Well," he said, and he began pacing as he spoke. "I mentioned to Therra that we have had quite a bit of luck using fire in the past. This woman, Shieda, is a sorceress of some skill, and she has successfully woven fire spells to save us twice in the course of our adventures together—once in Orlacc's castle, and once against his ships. It occurred to me that, if she could produce true fire from out of thin air, certainly she could create also the illusion of fire. I merely mentioned this to Therra as an aside, as a tactic we might be able to use.

"She then told me of an attack on her village that was thwarted. Her people were outnumbered, so rather than charge blindly into battle, they laid a trap for their enemy. They built a duplicate of their village some miles away from the real village. The attackers did not discern the ploy. They invaded the false village. Therra's people had placed incendiary fluids all about the place, and they set fire to the trap from without. Most of the enemy fighters were consumed in the inferno. The rest were cut down as they attempted to flee.

"We shared these stories, and then talked some more, and thought awhile, and then Therra conceived a plan, which, er, well, perhaps she should explain it to you. Therra?"

He sat, and Therra got up. She reached overhead, and broke a small branch off of a tree. The assembly gasped again, either because of her sudden movement or because of her height. She drew a curved line in the dirt, and said, "This line represents the edge of your forest. This is where Orlacc will make his first approach."

"How can you be sure?" Trolcott asked.

She flashed him a slightly irritated look. "You are aware we've fought him on several occasions?!?!?" She huffed and blustered energetically, but she quickly tempered her anger and pressed on. "Though he can, at times, be clever, we know Orlacc is not patient when he believes his goal is within sight. If he does not use the pass through the mountains to stage his campaign, he will be forced to take a far more roundabout land or sea route to reach the Allarraban. He won't want to wait for his 'revenge.' That is why he will engage you where the pass opens onto your homeland—here."

When no one disagreed with her, she went on. She drew a short line behind the first. "Here, we will have our first firewall. Only it will not be made of real fire, but of illusion. While his men are stalled in front of this apparent inferno, our archers will attack them from these trees here."

She poked dots in the ground with her stick, indicating several spots along the rim of the forest.

"Madame, we have only forty-seven trained archers," Belgear interrupted. "How can they...?"

"It will be enough," Therra replied. "The archers' arrows will do no real harm to Orlacc's forces, but they will make them angry. This will draw them closer to the false firewall.

"When they feel no heat coming from the fire, they will realize it is a trick, and they will charge through the illusion at Orlacc's command." She next scratched another shape into the dirt, a sort of "U" shape, beneath the firewall line. "Around this curve, we will have placed wood and other burning materials. Domitrus, who is educated in the properties of fluids, will concoct a mixture that encourages fires to grow. We will douse the woodpiles with this potion, light them, and raise a blazing wall that will surround them on these three sides.

"Now, some of Orlacc's men—the less intelligent ones—will assume this blaze to also be a trick. These fools, I believe, will charge into the wall, and will be burnt. The rest will turn and try to go back the way they came." Her eyes simmered with vengeance as she described the next phase of her plan: "By the time the retreating dogs get back to the magic firewall, we will have played another trick on them. Shieda will use her sorcery to replace the false with the true—she will weave another fire spell—and the fools will be trapped inside a blazing box. We shall let the flames take care of our enemies!"

Everyone looked perplexed for a few moments. Then, Obishku broke the silence.

"Fire is a very dangerous force of nature. How can we be sure the blaze will not consume our forest?"

"We can dig trenches at the rear of the firewall," Therra answered. "I have seen trenches used before to control a fire's direction."

"We're, um, kind of relying on a lot of magic here, aren't we?" I asked.

"As the other one stated before, we must rely on cleverness when facing superior numbers," said Therra, confidently. "I would venture that this plan could be deemed clever. And what other choices do we have?"

Now everyone's gaze turned upon me. This leadership stuff was crap!

"Of course, if our esteemed leader has an alternate plan, we would dearly love to hear it," Trolcott said deferentially.

"Yes, please!" Obishku added. "Do dazzle us with your wisdom, Morrelaine!"

"Um, well, no, I don't really have any ideas right now." Unless maybe you want to bring in some tanks and stealth bombers, I thought. Damn! I'd taken my first leadership test among my "own people," and I'd failed miserably. What the hell am I even doing here? I wondered, asking myself, and, in a way, Argothrex, though I knew he'd probably lost interest in my well being by now. I was nothing more than clutter—someone who gets in the way of everything. I'd quickly blown the trust of Obishku, and I figured I was well on my way to losing the faith of the other Grimnells as well. Thank you so much for putting me here and letting me screw things up, Argothrex!

"I-I'll try to think of something," I said, shaking my head helplessly.

"Don't worry, Morrelaine," Parkel said, trying, I knew, to bolster my ego. "I believe in this plan. I know it will work."

I shrugged, and the others soon lost interest in me. As we all went off in our own directions, I shuffled back to my tree house with Shieda. "You did the best you could," she said.

"Which isn't saying much," I moaned. "But it's not just that. I was just remembering what your father said last night, and it has me worried. He said we shouldn't depend on magic, which is what this plan is all about."

Shieda thought for a moment, but couldn't think of much to say, other than, "Well, I just hope I'm up to it."

When we had climbed up the ladder and into our house, we saw that Liassa, the Grimnell woman Morrelaine had been engaged to, was waiting for us. She still appeared melancholy, as she watched us enter, but at least she wasn't crying this time.

"Uh, hi. What are you doing here?" I asked.

"I came to speak with you," she answered, in a voice as sweet as honey.

Shieda put her hand on her hip, and swaggered towards the little woman, looming over her. "Look, sweetheart, he's very tired and concerned about the upcoming battle. I think maybe you should just leave us both alone for a while."

Something about Liassa's face, her expression, touched me and softened my heavy heart. I couldn't know whether it was something I was really feeling or some left over part of Morrelaine asserting itself, but it didn't matter. I figured this woman had gone through enough pain since I'd come here. There was no reason for me to be mean to her or to push her away.

"Didn't you hear me?" Shieda was saying to the frightened little Grimnell.

"Shieda, hold on," I interrupted. "Let's...let's let her stay. I don't think she's here to get all over my back like the others. What's the harm?"

"No harm," Shieda answered in a fierce but muted tone. "As long as you don't mind it."

"Please, it's true," Liassa pleaded. "I've seen what a difficult time you've been having, and I wouldn't dream of making things worse for you. I truly wish only to speak with you." Then, she eyed Shieda, and added, "Alone, if possible."

Shieda's mouth fell open, but before she could say anything, I spoke. "It'll be okay, Shieda. Just let her talk to me for a little while, and that'll be it. You know you can trust me."

"Oh, I know I can trust you," she answered, as she ambled towards the door. "I also know you know what'll happen if you betray that trust. I'll be back in fifteen minutes." And, with that, she bolted through the door.

"S-Sorry about that," I said, turning back to Liassa, who was now sitting on our bed, looking up at me. "I guess I can understand how she feels. I mean, I'd probably be the same way if..."

"Obishku loves you... Morrelaine... very much," she said, cutting me off, but gazing at me so earnestly, it was almost scary.

"Morrelaine disappointed him, though. My uncle wanted Morrelaine as his successor. He has no children of his own, which is one reason we have become like father and daughter. But Morrelaine rejected his offer in favor of quests and a life of exploration and adventure, much of it away from our tribe. I thought it might help you to know this. It has been hard for him, seeing 'Morrelaine' again, without a reconciliation."

"Hmm. That explains a lot," I said. "I thought I was going to lose it out there today, what with.... But what am I supposed to do? I'm not..."

"Please," Liassa interrupted, as she pulled me by my arm towards the bed, "sit with me."

I was a little nervous, but I complied. I sat, while she looked me over. "W-What are you doing?" I asked, but she didn't answer. There was still a sadness in her eyes, and a hint of resignation, but there was also a tenderness, a quiet fire, burning just below the surface. What did she want from me?

Finally, she took a deep breath, and said, "It has been difficult for me to accept that you are now Morrelaine, the...the only Morrelaine, and that my beloved is lost to me forever."

"You don't know that," I said, trying to sound comforting and hopeful. "He could come back someday, maybe even in this body if I end up going home somehow."

Her brow furrowed. Clearly, she did not care for talk of other worlds and body-switching. I couldn't blame her for that: those subjects, after all, had made both our lives a lot more complicated! "Nevertheless, I have decided I must accept this turn of events, and...and I must accept you."

"Well, thank you," I said, moved to have at least one of the Grimnells willing to give me a chance.

"I ask only one last boon from you," she continued, facing me square on. "I-I want you to try to let him come through one last time. I want you to close your eyes, and to silence your thoughts, and, if there is any portion of his spirit still within you, I want you to allow it to step forward. And I-I need you to kiss me."

"W-Wait. I don't know if I can..." I started, but I saw the hope, the sincerity, the need in her eyes, and I felt the warmth of her love for Morrelaine emanating from her entire being.

"Okay," I answered, at last.

And then we kissed. I have to admit, it felt like something did happen. I closed my eyes, but I saw starlight dancing behind my eyelids, the world spinning round, a hundred times a second, day into night and back again. I felt a pull on my heart, and throughout the very fibers of my being, almost like something was separating inside me. Suddenly, I needed her too. I pulled her close, and we let the passion flow electrically between us. I have no idea how long it lasted, but then, like a storm receding, the feeling passed, and we were back, sitting there on the bed, looking at each other.

Finally, after what seemed like several minutes had passed, she whispered, "Thank you."

Not immediately knowing what to say, I simply smiled. Then, I did say, dreamily, "You know, you Grimnells are fascinating people."

She giggled as she blushed. "I'm sure your people are fascinating too!" Then, her expression became serious, and she said, "Actually, I have met others like you before. Well, not like you truly."

"What do you mean?" I asked, lurching forward. She'd said it off the cuff, but her remark had certainly grabbed my attention.

"Well, they are insane. At least...that is what Obishku deemed them."

"Them? Them who?"

"Oh dear. Perhaps I should explain," she said, seeming a little flustered. "One of my duties is bringing food to prisoners of our tribe. A few years ago, two old Grimnells arrived, spouting nonsense about having come from another world...only, perhaps it wasn't nonsense. I didn't know that then."

"Y-You mean they were locked up because no one believed them?"

"Well, some Grimnells in the past have become so violently insane that they have hurt others. Our leaders decided they should be kept away from the rest of the tribe, and that is why we set aside room for them in our prison. Do they not do this in your world?"

"Well..." She had a point there. "Liassa, this is important. Where did these men say they were from?"

"They only told their stories for a while after they first came here. After that, they seemed to give up, and to accept their fate." She searched her mind for a moment, and then said, "I believe they said it was a world called Ert, or Erth. I don't remember all that well."

I wasn't sure exactly why, but I knew I needed to talk with them. They were from home! And maybe, just maybe, they would have another piece of the puzzle.

"I must speak with them, Liassa, right away. Can you get me inside to see them?"

"Why, yes, but... shouldn't you be resting for the battle?"

"No. This is more important. Please, if you can get me in..."

She considered for a moment. She didn't look happy, but she answered, "Yes. It could be very dangerous. Obishku won't like it if he discovers us. But you were kind to me. I will take you there."

I had Shieda round up Domitrus, Parkel, and Therra, and then we all headed for the stockade. The place was a series of large dugouts, carved into the earth and covered over with bars made of logs, which were lashed together with rope. The prisoners below us seemed to brighten up a little when they saw Liassa coming.

"Now, now, quiet down, all of you," she said, like a scolding parent. "I bring not food or drink at this hour, but visitors."

"Who is't?" said one, an old man, reaching up through the bars. "Is't me brother, Kahmil, returning from battle at last? It has been so long since I've seen 'im!"

"Ach, you are wrong, Torrma!" exclaimed a mudcaked woman to the first prisoner. "It is my husband, Stolth, come back from adventuring in Corgorarr near Ekhulta! Come home to fetch me at last!"

"Neither one of you is right, I'm afraid," said Liassa, bending to unlock the trap door that led down into the stockade. "These people are here to see Bock and Bakkle."

"Why them?" screeched the disheveled woman below. "They never did no one any good! Even claim they're from the sky, they do!"

"Now, now, step away from the ladder, all of you," Liassa was saying. The female prisoner kept arguing, but the others did as Liassa had asked. The man who had spoken before muttered something to the others about how kind Liassa had been to them. "Carries the food down herself, she does. Not just throw it down like the others do."

"Remind me why we are here again," Shieda whispered to me as we climbed down into the filthy pit of the jail.

"Well, besides the fact that these two are the only known Earthlings we've met here besides each other, there's what your father said: 'Something from your world will be your key to victory.' Maybe these guys fit in with that somehow."

"Sort of a longshot, don't you think?" she asked.

"Still worth a try," I answered.

We had passed through two doors, and now we stood before a third. As Liassa moved to unlock it, she said, "This is where we keep the crazy ones. Keeps them from being tormented by the others." We went in, and she locked the door behind us. She waved her hand, indicating a darkened corner of the room where several figures were huddled. As we approached, she called out, "Bock! Bakkle! You have visitors."

Two craggy heads slowly emerged from the shadows. Their eyes were wide and watery, their hair matted and steely gray, and they were covered in stubble, dirt, and sweat. They both wore tattered clothes, which hung damply on their yellow-white hides. The one on the left, who turned out to be Bock, appeared to be built fairly sturdily. Even though he was pretty old—in his midsixties was my guess—he was still trim and well-muscled. The other one was a different story. He was flabby, sagging, and balding, and his teeth were encrusted in black. This second one, Bakkle, started to cry when he saw us.

"Oh no! More of zem brother!" he wailed. "Zey vill fight me for my food! Vhat am I going to do?"

"Ve shall be fine. I alvays protect you, do I not?" Then, Bock turned to us and said, "Vhat do you vant vit us?"

"Hmmmm. I detect a distinct accent," Shieda whispered to me. "German maybe?"

"Sounds like it. How 'bout it? Are you guys from Germany?" I asked them.

Now the tall one also had tears in his eyes, but he was smiling. He approached me, gesticulating, and said, "Yes! Yes! How did you know zat? I have been trying to tell zeese others zat for years, but zey do not listen!"

"That's because most of these people know nothing about Earth. But we do. Shieda here is a native of England, but she was in San Francisco in 1906 when she was transported here. And I am from Boston. I was attending college there in 2014 when I fell through a hole and arrived in this world."

Bock and Bakkle both looked bewildered. Maybe it was the years I'd mentioned. After all, they could be from another time themselves.

"He said 2014, brother," said Bakkle. "Have ve been here dat long?"

"I think there's some sort of time distortion when you pass through the portal into this reality," I explained, sounding surprisingly scientific. "Otherwise, Shieda, who ought to be old enough to be my great-grandmother, would look like an old woman." She nudged me in my side with her elbow, but I continued. "It may have something to do with the body you transport into, too. I don't know. But I take it your names aren't really Bock and Bakkle, right?"

A look passed between them, and they seemed to agree to trust us. Then, they faced us again, and Bakkle said, "His name is Otto and I am Helmut Hunsvang."

"Ve tried telling zeese people dat, but zey vould not believe us," Bock/Otto added. "Ve have been so tormented by ze other inmates, ve had begun to doubt our own stories. But now you...you believe us!"

Shieda and I both nodded, and I said, "Of course. Uh, now why don't you tell us your 'stories?' Like, how did you guys get here?"

"Velllll..." Otto began. "You see, Helmut and I are zee flight mechanics in Germany. Ve build ze flying machines, like Herr von Zeppelin, only ve build zem even better!

"Vun day, ve vere test-flying our airship around in zee clouds, vhen zuddenly, zee vinds began to howl, and zee thunder and lightning started. Ve tried to zave ourselves, to come in for a zafe landing, but zee storm vas too ztrong. Ve knew zat ve vould zoon crash. Zuddenly, zee lightning ztruck our ship, and ve vere on fire! As ve fell out of zee sky, ve both lost consciousness.

"Ve expected ve vould never vake up, but vhen ve did, ve found ourselves here, in zeese strange little bodies, is zis bizarre land. Zeese people discovered us and called us Bock and Bakkle, and vhen ve tried to explain our story, zhey locked us up!"

It sounded no more fantastic than Shieda's story, or my own. Actually, mine was probably the weirdest of the lot, since there was no real disaster involved. Hearing their story also made me wonder just how many Earth people might be stuck here in other bodies on this world.

"Well, you're lucky, actually," I said somewhat unfeelingly. An image of the Hindenburg engulfed in flames had shot through my mind. "Those early Zeppelins really didn't work out. Their creators soon found out that the hydrogen they were using to fly was too unstable—and too flammable—for them to depend on. Nowadays, they use helium."

"Funny you should zay dat," said Otto. "You zee, ve vere ze only vuns who figured out zat zee hydrogen vould not vork. And ze helium—ve could not get our hands on very much of it. But ve had discovered a new zubstance, vhich ve called 'Hunsvang Negative X2 Gas.' It vas perfectly zafe, easy to zynthesize, and ve vere having much luck vit it. Ve vere planning to unveil it to zee vorld, but zen ve vere caught in zee storm und ended up here."

"Hmmmm," I said. The wheels of my mind were whirring. "Easy to synthesize, you say?"

"Vhy yes!" answered Otto. "As a matter of fact, ve vere planning to repair our airship vhen ve first arrived here. Hunsvang Negative X2 Gas is very easy to create vrom naturally occurring elements. In time, ve could haff restored our vessel and flown home. But zeese people zaw fit to hide our vreckage and lock us up virst!"

"You mean to say you could reconstruct your Zeppelin out of materials you can get here, in the forest?" When they both nodded, I turned to the others and said, "Holy Moley! Well, that's it then! I think I know how we can defeat Orlacc and his men!"

"By building balloons?" Shieda asked.

"Think about it," I said. "If we could fix this thing, we could fly over Orlacc's armies. We could storm his castle from the air! I know it'll work!"

"I am sorry I must interrupt," Liassa said, "but if Obishku learns that I've brought you here, I will face grim consequences. I must ask that we go now."

"Honey, you don't understand!" I said, grabbing her by the shoulders. "I'm going to tell your uncle to free Otto and Helmut! Then we're going to build a blimp and win this war! Let's get going right now!" I turned to the Hunsvangs, and said, "Don't worry you guys. You'll be free soon. Then, we can get to work."

Determined, I wheeled around and marched out of there. It all made sense to me now, and maybe I was finally going to get my chance to play the effective leader! I had found the solution the Sage had told me about—I was sure of it! Now I only needed enough time to put it into play.

The others were not as clear about things as I was, though. As I was leaving, I heard Parkel say, "I must say I understood little of what transpired here just now. Shieda?"

"I'm not quite sure either, Parkel," Shieda answered, "but if he's found something he's this certain about, then I suppose we'd better follow him,"

"Strange," Liassa mused. "A moment ago, he sounded almost like the old Morrelaine."

Chapter Twenty-Six

The next day was a blur—we were all caught up in a flurry of work. Things started out well. I went to visit Obishku first thing in the morning to talk to him about releasing Otto and Helmut and helping them dig up and repair their craft. He seemed to be in a somewhat regretful mood.

"I have spoken with my niece, Morrelaine, and she told me that she has forgiven you for...well, for this situation," he said after motioning for me to take a seat. He offered me a cup of root tea. "She said she has decided she can accept you. If she can do that, I can do no less. I am sorry for my earlier behavior."

We shook hands. It felt like a heavy weight had been lifted from my shoulders. But I wasn't about to rest on my laurels. I told him about my plan, and pleaded with him to release my fellow Earthmen.

He sighed, and said, "I find it incredible that you believe you will be able to create a flying machine. That is something I doubt even the old Morrelaine, with all his great faculties, could accomplish. But I see no harm in trying. Very well. You may instruct Liassa to release the two prisoners. I shall order some workers to salvage their machine, though I warn you, it is in poor condition."

Once I'd gotten his approval, I didn't sit around for long. Helmut and Otto were freed, and allowed to clean up, eat a decent meal, and change clothes. After that, they were immediately put to work on assembling this world's first fully functional airship.

I got my first look at their wreck once it had been mostly dug out from under the dirt, twigs, and pine needles it had been buried under. It looked like the worst broken child's toy I'd ever seen, only much bigger.

"Maybe I shouldn't have asked to see it," I muttered. "Don't vorry," said Helmut, noticing my dismay. "If zere is vun zing my brother und I are good at, it is making zings fly!"

Liassa, Domitrus, and about thirty Grimnell women and non-warrior men were put at the Hunsvangs' disposal. They set about collecting the raw materials they needed to make their 'safe fuel,' and the cloth and wood they would use to build the body of the skycraft.

Unlike me, they seemed to slip easily into their leadership roles, but, well, that's what they had done back home, so they were probably more used to it. At least that's what I kept telling myself!

The rest of us got started on preparing the designated 'battle zone.' With an army of Grimnells helping us, we chose spots for the illusory and the real firewalls, gathered wood and scrub brush to ignite, dug a trench to keep the fire from setting ablaze the entire forest, and planned where we and the other soldiers would take up positions. The archers, meanwhile, selected the trees they would shoot from and attached ropes to them so they would be able to climb up or down them as needed. That afternoon, we called Domitrus and Shieda away from their balloon-building jobs, and had them help prepare for the impending firefight.

"I must tell you, sir, that I am enjoying working with those Grimnell scientists you discovered," Domitrus told me, as he went about dabbing a gummy substance he'd created all over the pieces of wood we intended to set fire to. "Their knowledge of chemicals is...vast. And to imagine that they have actually soared above the clouds!" His brow wrinkled, and he added, "Strange...they say they don't believe in magic. They seem so sophisticated in some ways, and yet..."

I had to admit, it was wonderful to see him feeling good about himself again. For a while there, it seemed like he had been about ready to give up on life. Now, he was getting a chance to put his talents to work, and a chance to see that he really did have something to offer the world. I patted him on the back and said, "Just you keep working with them, and I'm sure something really amazing will come out of it."

It was late evening—about 8:30, I'd guess—when we'd finished preparing for battle. I had hoped against hope that the Hunsvangs might have their airship completed in time to use against Orlacc tomorrow, but the two men were still not in the best of shape after spending almost three years in prison, and they had worn themselves out earlier in the day. They were both sleeping in their own tree house while the rest of us gathered around the central fire and ate.

After the meal, most of the soldiers—the smart ones, anyway—went off to bed. A few diehards remained out by the fire, and, of course, so did our little group. I guess maybe we all wanted a little more time together before the next day's Main Event.

"Well, it is getting late," Parkel said after we'd been talking awhile. "Perhaps we'd better get some sleep as well. Therra, are you coming?"

"I may have decided I can tolerate your existence, whelp," she growled back at him, "but you're still not fit to give me orders."

"Th-Therra, I wasn't..." stammered Parkel.

"We can't have that kind of attitude now, Therra," Shieda snapped. "Tomorrow we've got to be watching out for each other, working together. If you've got a problem, then get it out now, because I sure as hell don't want to deal with it tomorrow!"

The big warrior woman said nothing right away. Instead, she pulled an eight-inch dagger out of her boot and started digging at the log she was sitting on with it. When she noticed we were all still staring at her, she shifted a little, and said, "If I offended you, you must forgive me. It...it was unintentional on my part. I-I'm not used to...going into battle with...with such a...such an uncertain feeling about the outcome."

"Uncertain? Why?" Shieda asked.

"He...Orlacc...tricked me, tricked us all before," she answered, her gaze distant, her voice quivering minutely. "My instincts, they did nothing to warn me. He...fooled me, completely. I...I fear a man who can do that to me."

For a while, there was silence around the fire. We were all dumbstruck—I mean, Therra, admitting she was afraid? It seemed like a bad omen. On the other hand, it made her seem more human.

Parkel came back and sat down next to her again, but he said nothing, and he did not look at her. He had learned that, with Therra, it was better to proceed with caution. I could tell he was struggling: on the one hand, he wanted to say something, to comfort her, but on the other, he was afraid to face her wrath again, no matter how unintentional it was.

Finally, when I could bear the silence no longer, I said, "Don't feel bad, Therra. I've been fearful practically since I got here. Hell, I was pretty scared of you at first! Remember?"

Now she smiled a little. "Aye, I do. But you must also remember that you are not from a warlike society, little one, whereas I have been trained for battle almost since birth in perhaps the most martial nation on this continent. For me to feel unsure..."

Now Parkel cleared his throat and spoke up. "When Hanez-Ka was teaching me to fight, he told me I would not be able to outfight every opponent. But, he said, if I was willing to study my adversary—especially any who seemed unstoppable—and if I was willing to learn from my mistakes, I could beat any man. You will be able to beat Orlacc."

Therra straightened up a little, and tried to play the proud warrior again. At first I thought she was going to bite Parkel's head off again, for 'daring to address her in such a condescending manner' or something, but then I noticed something different about her look. She was smiling inside, at least, that was the impression I got. She said, "Thank you my friends, for your faith in me, and for...your encouragement."

"I, for one, am not ashamed to admit my fears," Domitrus chimed in. "But I trust we will all do our best tomorrow. Shieda has proved herself a leader. Therra, you and Parkel have devised an ingenious battle plan. And you, Morrelaine, have given me reason to believe in myself again. I really do believe your airship will fly, and that we will win the day, one way or another. It is assured."

"Why, thanks for the vote of confidence, Domitrus," I said. "I only wish I could be as confident."

Shieda sighed, and muttered, "I only wish my father could be here to help."

I don't know why, but her sentiment set me off. "Hey, thanks! We could have ended tonight on an 'up' note! But noooo! Can't you see we're all trying to pull together here? And now you've gotta start belaboring about the help we don't have! How are we supposed to focus with statements like that going around?!"

"I'm sorry. I was just..."

"You were saying before how much you wanted to be a leader. Well a leader has to believe in her own people! But you were none too pleased with Parkel and Therra's plan, and you didn't act too wild about my airship idea either. You don't seem to trust us to do our parts! You...you probably don't even think I'll be able to lead the troops tomorrow either, do you?"

"I...it's..."

"Domitrus here can give me the benefit of the doubt! Why can't you? My own girlfriend has no faith in me! Great!" I noticed everyone was staring at me. I was making an ass of myself, but it was one of those freak-outs where, once it starts to flow, it just doesn't stop 'til the red haze vanishes. And that was starting to happen. Suddenly, I wanted to be someplace else, away from any lights or staring eyes. I let out a rush of air, almost like I was deflating, and said, "Forget it. Just forget I opened my mouth. I'm going to go get some sleep."

Shieda jumped up and followed me as I shuffled away from the fire.

"W-Wait, please!" she said.

"I don't want to argue, okay?" I said. She said nothing else until we'd climbed back up to our tree house. By that time, my anger had subsided, and I was really feeling gloomy. I looked over at Shieda, who was watching me get into bed, and wondered how emotions could get the better of you like that. She was the best thing that had ever happened to me, and yet right now we seemed miles apart. I'd opened a gash in our relationship, and I was worried that nothing I said could repair the damage. Still, I wanted to try. "I'm sorry," I said.

She smiled a little, and came over and climbed into bed with me, as if I had somehow given her permission to walk around in the room. Smiling knowingly, she asked, "So what is it—really—that's bothering you?"

"Well, what do you think? I mean, besides the fact that we're going to get caught up in a major battle tomorrow, and the fact that there's a whole bunch of people around here who are disappointed that I'm not really their great leader, I'm not sure if I'll be in control of my own body tomorrow!"

She began softly stroking my forehead. "You mean you think Morrelaine's mind will take over your...his...body again tomorrow?"

"Well, yeah. It's happened before. Whenever I get into trouble, he takes over and helps me fight my way out of it. Either that, or Argothrex saves my ass. Which isn't much better!"

"Why? If you're able to go on living, what's the problem?"

"I...well, I wish I could take care of myself. That's all. If you can't count on yourself, what can you count on?"

"You know you can count on my love, don't you?"

I sighed. I wasn't ready to give up my anxiety just yet.

"Yes, although I still sometimes worry that that's just a dream, and that, just when I really start to believe in myself, and in you, and this world, I'll wake up and find myself yanked back into my own time again. I'll be alone again, and no one will care. My life will mean nothing."

She leaned over and put her arm around my waist, kissing me in the ear, and said, "It's true. That could happen. And I can't say whether or not it will. But there are two things I want you to remember." When she knew I was listening, she continued, "First, my love for you is as real as anything. I know you feel that, that you know that deep inside, no matter how uncertain you think you feel right now. Second, you have to realize that the world is what you make it. No matter what world you're in, you are in charge of your own life. So what if someone else is trying to strike you down? Strike back! You have that power. And even if someone else is calling the shots, controlling events, they can't control how you react. That's your power, and yours alone. That's how I survived when I got here—and I've been here a lot longer than you have. I decided to learn how to be the best I could be on this world or any other. I don't know. Maybe you were sent here to learn that."

After she'd stopped speaking, we lay there for a while. Finally, I said, "Yeah. Maybe. Though I'm still a little worried...about the future. About whether I'll have any control over it."

"Of course you are. Worry is natural. But it can't help you right now. Leave worry for tomorrow, okay? They'll be plenty of time for it then."

"Alright," I answered. "Let's try to get some sleep."

She was asleep soon after that, but I fought my worries for a time. I finally did fall asleep, but it was not restful. I dreamt of hundreds of thousands of horses' hooves, thundering, endlessly pounding as they tore welts across the land.

And the battered land seemed to hold its breath, for soon it would be bathed in blood.

Chapter Twenty-Seven

The call to arms came sooner than expected.

About an hour before dawn, a pair of scouts tore into the village, bellowing about how Orlacc's troops were on the move and were only about two miles away from the forest's edge.

"This is it," Shieda said, as we yanked ourselves out of bed. "Are you ready?"

"Are you?" I responded, wishing for all the world that I close my eyes and pretend nothing was happening.

She smirked, as she started strapping on her leather armor, and said, "Of course not... let's go."

The whole town was buzzing like a beehive, with people charging this way and that, making last minute preparations, saying good-byes, and gathering into combat units. The archers were rushed out to the front lines first to take up their positions, and, as soon as we hooked up with Therra, Parkel, and Domitrus, we were on our way out there too. But before we went, I checked with Obishku to make sure that the Hunsvang brothers would be given a safe place to continue working. I didn't want anything to happen to our aces-in-the-hole.

When we arrived at the staging area, the sun had risen. One could already tell it was going to be a hot, dry day—perfect for lighting fires. To get to the battle area, we had to cross the trench that had been dug to prevent the second fire from spreading towards the village. The thing must have been at least ten feet wide and five feet deep! Guess the ditch-diggers didn't want to take any chances, which was pretty understandable for a people who were forest dwellers.

Domitrus hurried around, checking several containers filled with his potions. Most contained incendiary mixtures—although all of the wood and leaf piles had already been doused with his flammable chemicals. The others were filled with healing liquids and other concoctions Domitrus apparently thought he might need.

The rest of us headed for the front, where we took up our positions behind the small line of scrub bushes. And there, we waited.

Beyond the Grimnell forest was a stretch of flat, grassy plains. These eventually ran into some foothills, and beyond these were the lower mountains of the Northlands. A difficult pass through these mountains led to Orlacc's kingdom. From what Obishku had said, there was almost no other way that Orlacc could approach the Grimnell forest without adding several days to his journey. This was where he would come through.

Sure enough, we soon spotted great clouds of dust being kicked up by his horses' feet, far in the distance, coming closer.

"Here he comes!" I said. "Get down everybody!"

Shieda nudged me, and hissed, "Louder! Say it louder!"

"Everybody get down!" I hollered at the top of my lungs, and, suddenly, everyone dove for cover.

"Much better, my leader," said Shieda with a smile.

The oncoming army was charging ahead at top speed, and it had taken them just minutes to cross half the distance from the foothills to where we were. Now, we could make out the shapes of men on horseback, of lances and swords, piercing the air, and we could hear their war cries, whooping with the sounds of mad berserkers. In my mind, I started to question what we were doing, keeping as low to the ground as possible where they could trample us in seconds, but then I remembered our plan.

"Hadn't you better get into position?" I asked Shieda, now feeling strangely breathless. "That isn't exactly the safest spot for you, is it?"

"I'll be fine," she answered, and then she turned to one side, closed her eyes, and began to chant. Of course I couldn't hear her over the hoof beats—they were almost on top of us.

Shieda's spell worked. All at once, a wall of flame shot up from the ground only yards away from us. Or, at least, it looked like a wall of flame. I turned back towards Orlacc's troops. This was the part where we were expecting them to stop. The fire would frighten them. They'd halt, and be in disarray, and our archers and army would set upon them, confusing them, coaxing them into the jaws of our trap.

That's what we were expecting.

But as the men reached the fire, Orlacc kept screaming at them to "Go! Go! Go!" They charged right through it, looking a little nervous, but obeying their leader's orders anyway. And our people behind the first fire line were taken by surprise.

"My wizard warned me of your tricks!" screamed Orlacc, as he approached our position, laughing. His men were cutting our army apart—they had no choice but to fight, but Orlacc's forces had the advantage of being atop war-horses. It had become a massacre!

"Retreat!" I yelled, screeching my guts out. "Get behind the second line!" I looked into the trees, and bellowed, "Archers! Fire at will!"

The trees came to life with the sounds of bows twanging. Some of our arrows found their marks, sinking into flesh, and creating enough of a diversion for many of the Grimnells to escape to the second fire area. Some were still fighting, including Therra and Parkel, and many were falling, wounded or dying. I saw that Shieda had made it to safety, so I yelled, "Get back!" one more time, and then I charged for the rear fire line.

Therra and Parkel refused to heed my pleas—they were holding their own anyway—but most of the others who were able to had scrambled behind our barricade. A soldier asked me if we should ignite the second fire—the true fire—and I answered "yes." What other choice did we have? With a whoosh, the new blaze roared to life in a blazing crescent. Some of our people were stranded on the other side with Orlacc's troops, but there was nothing we could do.

But the second fire had the effect on Orlacc that I'd hoped it would: It caught his attention. I couldn't see him through the flames, but I heard him bellow, "It's another trick! Charge the fire, men! Finish them off!"

And the idiots did just that. The first part of our plan may have failed, but now things were back on track. Screams of agony erupted all around us as Orlacc's loyal horsemen scorched themselves in the inferno. I felt my stomach twist at the smell of seared flesh, but my heart was bolstered with the knowledge that we had evened the odds somewhat. Now to get back on the offensive!

"Devils!" Orlacc screeched. "Devils, with your magic! I'll kill you all!"

Shieda, Trolcott, and I led squads of Grimnells around the u-shaped firewall to attack Orlacc's forces from the rear. As we rushed onto the battlefield, I saw a scene of carnage the likes of which I had never witnessed before. Downed Grimnells and a few fallen Terasskossians littered the area—some of them were even getting trampled by the horses. There were a few knights who were on fire, screaming as they rode around, trying vainly to escape their fates. Some of the invaders' cloaks were burning, and other soldiers were helping pat the flames out.

Parkel and Therra had been surrounded by a band of horsemen, and they were now fighting for their lives. Both were bloody and covered in dirt and sweat. As I saw the tired, nearly beaten looks on their faces, I knew we had to move quickly. I yelled, "Attack!" and we threw ourselves into the fray.

I sort of lost track of things for a while; I was so consumed by the rush of battle. I heard the clashing of steel, the thwooshing of arrows, the clopping of horses' hooves, and the echoing screams of men being dealt mortal blows. I smelled blood and tasted dust. When I next came to my senses, my sword and armor were blood-covered, and my muscles were throbbing. I needed a break. I looked around, and noted that, although we had succeeded in taking out some more of their men, they were again gaining the advantage. The Grimnells were being edged back towards the blaze!

"Th-That's it. We've gotta get out," I said out loud to myself. I tried to take in a deep breath, but I coughed.

Then, I sucked in some wind and shouted, "Get away! Get back! Save yourselves!!!"

But Orlacc knew he was winning. When he heard my command, he issued his own: "Redouble your efforts! Bear down on them! Slaughter them all! If you must, then chase them into the fire. But don't let any escape!"

Grimnells were tearing around on the battlefield, trying to get away. I saw a man get trampled under a black horse's hooves. I saw a few of my fellow soldiers take sword and lance points in the back and crumple to the ground. I looked for Shieda. I spotted her being hoisted into the trees with a rope by one of the archers. Others were being rescued the same way, but it wouldn't be nearly enough to save everyone. We had no hope for an offense any more—even our archers were busy saving others. Not only that, but even they weren't safe in their tree-perches: Orlacc's own bowmen had begun to try picking off our guys.

We could only hope to flee, and pray that few of our comrades would be sacrificed. My hate burned hotter than the fire.

His horse reared, and then Orlacc caught sight of me. Smirking, he said, "So, I see the speck has become their leader. That makes you worth killing then."

"I'll take you out first!" I screamed, my hoarse voice ripping out of my throat. "You've brought enough pain and death here today!"

As his horse snorted eagerly, he snickered, and spat, "You can do little from so lowly a position, flea. Why, I doubt that you can even reach me with your sword from down there."

I was about ready to try it anyway, when he decided to make his move. "I grow tired of even looking at your pitiful form! Let's finish this!" he said, and he kneed his horse. He was charging me!

In the distance, in a dream, I heard Shieda crying out, urging me to run. Then, it seemed like my muscles acted of their own volition again. I turned, and bolted, heading straight for the firewall. Take him with me! I thought, and, sure enough, Orlacc was right on my heels. We were both going to burn! Fine, I thought. At least this'll be over with! And I jumped into the fire.

I came out on the other side, unscathed, but momentarily disoriented. Shieda told me later what happened next. Orlacc pulled back at the last minute, but he still got a face full of flame. He clutched his eyes, and fell backwards off his horse. The animal nearly trampled him, as it reared wildly. The cloth parts of his armor caught fire, but his men could not get close to him to help immediately because of his panicking steed. The whole ordeal lasted several minutes, but finally his men were able to pat out the flames. From his voice, I could tell he was terribly shaken. He was also angry.

"I-I h-ho-hope you are still alive beyond th-the f-ffire, Grimnell, s-suffering as I am!" he shouted, presumably to me, though I was barely with it enough to be able to concentrate on what he was saying. "Your insane lust for revenge has cost you dearly, for not only will you perish in flames today, but your homeland will as well!" Then, to his men he yelled, "Dip your arrows into the flames, archers! Before we leave we'll scorch this forest 'til there's naught remaining but blackened earth!"

I was beginning to come out of my daze. Shieda, down from her tree-perch, and Domitrus were at my side, pulling me by my clothes into a sitting position.

"Come on!" Shieda was saying. "We've got to get you out of here. You're too close to the flames still."

"Madame—how did he survive the flames when he jumped through them?" asked Domitrus, as he took hold of my right arm. "Was it some sort of magic?"

"I don't know. Maybe. Though it was nothing that I did. Help me get him to his feet. We can ask him about all this when we're away from here!"

"L-Look," I stammered, and pointed skyward as a flaming arrow sailed over the firewall directly above us and landed somewhere in the woods. I forced myself to sit up and to look behind me. An area of scrub brush burst into flames where the arrow had fallen.

"Put it out! Put it out!" Shieda commanded, and several soldiers standing near the new blaze ran over to try to stamp it out. "Damn it!" Shieda said. "If we're not careful, his archers will spread the fire past the trench!"

"Omigod!" I gasped, as I scrambled to my feet. "If that happens—"

Just then, another burning missile whizzed over the wall and fell among the trees, starting another blaze. Then, another arrow. And another.

"—we could lose the entire forest!"

We hurried out among the other soldiers, barking orders at them to help us extinguish the fires before they grew out of control. But with the flaming arrows falling all around us like acid rain, there was little hope. Despite our best efforts, there were soon several small blazes, eating up sections of the forest, burning their way towards the Grimnell settlement barely two miles away. If we couldn't think of something fast, the Grimnells' town and resources might go up in smoke!

We'd succeeded in turning away Orlacc's attack, only to have our blundering result in the Grimnells possibly paying for our victory with their homes and everything they owned...

The next 36 or so hours were so bone-tiring and so painful, it's next to impossible for me to write anything about them, even well after the fact. Suffice it to say, once the arrows stopped falling and Orlacc's army had presumably left, every man, woman, and child in the town was mobilized to help put out the advancing forest fire. The soldiers doffed their armor, in most cases leaving it where it fell, and rushed about, franticly whooping the stunned populace into rag-tag firefighting posses. Of course there were no hoses, no firemen, and no helicopters with flame-retardant chemicals around to aid us. We had only people to work with.

Some were put to work digging new trenches. Others acted as runners, carrying bucket loads of water from the nearby river. The amount of water they carried was too small to have any effect on the blaze itself: it was used mainly to soak the brush in the fire's path. Men worked to chop down trees and to clear brush, hoping to create a corridor barren of burnable fuel.

Domitrus threw together some fire-stifling concoctions. He was quite a picture, coughing out orders for substances he needed to confused-looking Grimnells, lighting a campfire, boiling and stirring a metal pot. One moment, he'd be muttering formulae to himself, the next he'd hop to his feet, and zigzag around the village, looking for some essential item. He'd stop jarringly in his tracks and clasp a hand over his eyes, trying to think of a substitute for some element he'd realized he could not obtain, and, once he'd come to some decision, he'd hurry off in a new direction.

Shieda, too, was furiously working her art. She explained to me later that she had whipped up a mystical creation she called an "anti-fire"—it was another blaze, one made of magical energy, that could be made to "eat" the original flames. But this anti-fire was under her control, and she could cause it to blink out of existence when it had served its purpose. Unfortunately, she was not a powerful enough sorceress to be able to maintain the incantation for long, so she could only use it for minutes at a time. She had to spend time resting in between spellcastings.

Meanwhile, I was doing a little bit of everything: I chopped trees, dragged away debris, shoveled dirt, and carried water. I sure wasn't giving any orders then. Instead, I shut off my mind, threw my back into the tasks, and went about the work like a tireless zombie. Whenever my brain flickered back on for a moment, it was only to ponder the thought, "If we can't beat this fire ...."

And then, panicking, I would tell my mind to go hang for a while.

We fought the blaze through the night and throughout most of the next day. As the sun set on the second evening, fully one-fifth of the Grimnell forest had been reduced to a charred, smoking blot. But the fire was gone, and we were all alive.

Still, several had died battling Orlacc, and the Grimnells had lost many of their precious resources. Even the bulk of the remaining soldiers were left without armor or weapons, since most such war-tools had been dropped and consumed by the flames.

Shieda and I found each other, and, propping each other up, we limped back to our tree house, avoiding the bitter gazes of some of the Grimnells. At one point, an ash-covered soldier looked like he was about to charge at us and burst into a tirade, but Obishku put a warning hand on his shoulder, stopping him. But even the old man averted his gaze when we noticed him.

"They feel it's our fault," I mumbled, "and they're right. If we hadn't come to them for help, none of this would have happened."

"What were we supposed to do?" Shieda asked, sounding small and lost. "Were we supposed to take on Orlacc alone?"

"I don't know," I answered. We had reached the ladder that led up to our tree. "I'm not sure of anything, except I need sleep."

And that was the end of our conversation.

Chapter Twenty-Eight

For a while, I couldn't get to sleep—every time I'd shut my eyes I'd see exploding fire. Or I'd see that battlefield, littered with Grimnell bodies, crying out, feeling their lives seeping away, wondering why, why, why...?

But finally, after staring at the shadows and listening to the pounding silence for several minutes, I dozed off. As my tired muscles relaxed, I felt myself falling...

I awoke in a charred field, surrounded by billowing clouds of smoke. There was no sound but the crunching of burnt earth beneath my boots as I stumbled around, trying to get my bearings. I coughed, spitting up ashes.

As if it had heard me, the smoke responded. The clouds ahead of me parted, forming a path, and where the path appeared, the grass became green again. With great effort, I forced my legs to move, to begin walking the path, and soon I saw a small, isolated grove ahead. A tall, slender figure stepped out from the trees.

Of course it was Argothrex.

"Pretty fab trick, eh?" he said, a wry smile on his face. "You know? The bit with the parting of the smoke? A tad too 'Moses,' possibly, but the greening grass was my own invention. What did you think?"

"Where have you been?" I asked angrily.

"Grant, Grant, Grant—there are a lot of other lives I've got to...involve myself in, and, honestly, you were doing a fine job of channeling Chaos without my help."

"I'm really not in a laughing mood right now," I hissed.

Argothrex's smile dimmed, and he came and stood next to me, putting his arm around my shoulders. "Alright, look—I know you think you've messed things up in a big way, but really, you're doing fine. You've come a long way towards learning what you have to learn to be the Master of your own Fate. There's one more thing, though..."

"I don't wanna hear it—not any more," I moaned. I shrugged out from under his arm. "I've wanted to talk to you so many times in the past few weeks, and you choose to show up now?!"

He smiled benevolently. "Well, here I am. So, what do you want to talk about?"

"I dunno. How 'bout why you really brought me here."

He sighed, and said, "I told you before—it's my job. Remember: 'Order must encounter Chaos?' The jewel must be turned? Et cetera?"

"I know what you told me, but all this doesn't make any sense. Okay, so my life was monotonous as hell before. But this life is crazy. I'm barely managing to hang on to my sanity here!"

"We are talking about Chaos," he said, crossing his arms and looking like an impatient first-grade teacher. "How much sense do you expect it to make?"

"Well...I just can't see how my helping destroy all these people's lives is doing me or anyone any good! All I ever wanted to do was figure out where I was supposed to be going in life, but I don't seem to know what I'm doing here any more than I did back home. I just keep reacting to things—surviving each messy situation by the skin of my teeth."

He sighed again, and shook his head. "Ah, my little, addled Grant. There's so much I'd like to explain, so many misconceptions I'd like to clear up. But I haven't the time now, and you're not ready yet anyway. Suffice it to say things happen because they do. Sometimes they're supposed to happen, other times they aren't. But it's in how we choose to see things, and in how we react, that we're defined. That's how we figure out who we are. Then, we either seize the reins of Destiny, or we...exist. Understand?"

"Uh, I am asleep right? 'Cause dreams aren't supposed to make any sense."

"Arrgh!" he growled. "You try to teach people the secrets of the universe, and they just zone out! Fine, forget it! But there is one more thing we've gotta discuss before I go."

"Um, okay."

"Well, speaking of your former life...you've got a choice to make." He put his arm around me again, and this time I was too curious to want to escape him. He actually seemed somewhat serious for the moment. "There's going to be no more sharing bodies with this Morrelaine guy. That's gone on long enough. So, you've got to decide whether you want to go back 'home' to Earth, or whether you want to stay here...permanently."

"Waitaminute! What about the real Morrelaine? It's not really fair to just take his body for myself, is it?!"

A knowing grin flashed across Argothrex's face, and he said, "Don't you worry about him—he, um, couldn't be happier with where he is now. Besides, how do you know all this isn't 'meant to be' anyway?"

"Okay, so I get either a boring, lonely life or an overblown, chaotic one, right?"

He rolled his eyes, and said, "You can do whatever you want with whichever you pick! But here's the kicker—pay close attention here: If you decide to remain in Morrelaine's body, it's yours and yours alone. None of the other Morrelaine's instincts or thoughts will show up to help you out during a fight. It's going to be you and you alone from now on on the battlefield. Capiche?"

"I guess. Boy, you don't make this easy!"

"There are reasons for that," he said, and he smiled. Then, he backed away from me a little, and said, "I've gotta go, so let me tell you what you have to do. When you've decided, hold the jewel I gave you in your hand and say either 'I want to go home' or 'I want to be me.' Okay?"

"Be 'me'? How do you figure...?"

"It's simple: up to now, you've been you and him. If you stay, you'll be all you. You'll truly be 'stepping into the role.' Besides, you should be happy—I could have had you do something really silly, like click your heels together, and say 'There's no place like home. There's no place like home.' Right?"

And suddenly, I felt compelled to do as he said; to repeat "There's no place like home" over and over again. He was laughing, and then everything turned black-andwhite, and spun around furiously.

The phrase was still swirling around in my head when I awoke, though there were no Auntie Ems or Uncle Henrys, sitting by my bedside. In fact, Shieda wasn't even there. I had no idea how long I'd slept, but it was blindingly bright outside, so it had to be at least midmorning. Suddenly, I heard shouting coming from nearby. Great, I thought, as I rolled out of bed. Another day, another crisis!

But when I'd climbed down to see what was up, I realized there was no mass panic. In fact, everyone seemed pretty excited. I spotted Shieda in the crowd, and, shielding my eyes with my hand, I scooted over to where she was standing. I noticed that she, like everyone else, seemed to be watching something going on up in the trees. I would've looked myself, but my eyes weren't ready to handle the glare just yet.

"Howdy," I said, gravelly voiced, to my beloved. "Good afternoon, dearest," she answered, with a slight giggle. I noticed some of the other people were clapping, and many had open-mouthed, child-at-the-circus-like expressions of awe and delight on their faces.

"Uh, I don't get it. What, is someone doing a trapeze act up in the treetops or something?"

But she didn't want to take her eyes off the sky. "Just look at it, luv," she murmured. "Just look up."

Suddenly, something huge blotted out the sun, and I couldn't help but gaze up to see what it was. It sounded like a giant bee, its buzzing hum unnaturally low-pitched, and my first instinct was to dive for cover. Fortunately, I wasn't still so asleep as to make that much of a fool of myself.

I quickly realized then what it was that was floating above me: a blimp, an airship, a zeppelin! The Hunsvangs had pulled it off!

"Well, I'll be damned," I intoned. "It actually looks like something out of the twentieth century!"

Shieda grimaced. "If you say so," she said. "It looks like a piece of a fantasy story to me. It's magnificent!"

She was right about that. The airship was beautiful and, what was more, it was inspiring. Even after all the disasters of the previous few days, seeing the German brothers' creation, sailing above the trees, made me think if they can build a blimp out of nothing, maybe we can overcome Orlacc's superior power and numbers!

Shieda and I embraced, and we watched as the brothers brought their ship lower, dropped a rope ladder, climbed down, and tied their creation to a tree. Everybody seemed about ready to bounce with excitement as the two 'flight mechanics' approached.

Helmut put out his hand to me, and, holding back tears, said, "Zank you for believing in us."

I grasped his hand, feeling a little overwhelmed myself, and replied, "Well, thank you for not making me regret it." Pointing to the airship, I added, "I still can't believe you guys actually did it. And so fast!"

Otto stepped up to me, and, facing forward, staring past me like a soldier at attention, he said, "Like any of my creations, I consider zis ship to be an extension of my own zelf—my child, if you vill. But because you haff made it possible for me to...give birth, I am turning her over to you, sir." Then, looking into my eyes, he asked, "Vhat vill you name her?"

I'm not sure why, but the name just popped into my head: "The Guardian," I said. "The Grimnell Guardian, in honor of these people who came to our aid, and who sacrificed so much to help us, when we needed it." Wow! I was making a speech! Sure enough, all eyes were on me. So, I went with it.

"This is it, people! This airship is what's going to allow us to beat Orlacc. We'll all get our revenge on him, but, even better, you won't have to worry about him or anyone trying to subjugate you with the Guardian around. This thing's a real war-ender."

The crowd seemed unconvinced. "But what about his wizards' magicks?" one shouted.

"And his flaming arrows?" yelled another. "What about those?"

"That's the beauty of it," I said, pointing again to the blimp. "This thing flies too high for them to attack it. Right, Otto?"

"Vell," he said, stepping to my side. "I don't know about zis magic, but ve can fly vell out of the range of zose arrows, yes."

"I'm not sure I understand," said one of the soldiers. "How will our flying around above Orlacc's armies allow us to defeat them?"

"That is where I come in." It was Domitrus, clearing a path through the crowd. He was carrying a large sack over his shoulder. He swung the sack to the ground as he reached us, and smiled. "I have made these." He took out a small, cloth bag from the sack. The bag was tied at its opening with a piece of rope. "The mixtures of elements in these bags are very explosive. All one need do is ignite this twine and drop the bag onto one of Orlacc's battlements, and..." he looked around, searching for the right word, before finally letting out a crashing sound and waving his arms. "Ka-rooosh!!!"

The people started crowding around Domitrus. They seemed excited, but still unsure how it would all work. Some wondered how the tiny bags could produce such a potent reaction. Others asked how we were going to fit all the Grimnell soldiers inside of the Guardian.

Realizing that we were running out of time, I gathered Shieda, Therra, Parkel, and Otto to me. "We need to make some plans," I said. "But we can give them a little demonstration first."

"After all," I said, pointing at the hovering zeppelin, "Even I've never been in one of these things."

We spent the next hour and a half, skimming over the plains, dropping Domitrus's bombs, and blowing up chunks of grass and topsoil. Every time a bag exploded, the Grimnells, watching from the edge of the forest, would erupt, bouncing up and down, cheering, clapping, and hugging each other.

It was quite an experience for those of us riding in the Guardian as well! Of course Otto and Helmut were in their element, so they ran about quite naturally, throwing switches and spinning dials. I had been in airplanes before, but this was a different sort of ride—less noisy, and less jolty. Shieda told me she had traveled by train and by ship, but that she'd never ridden on anything that flew through the air, even though planes, balloons, and even primitive airships had begun making appearances on Earth before she'd left it. Parkel, who had cleaved the ocean's waves at furious speeds throughout his youth, seemed fairly comfortable in the blimp, but Domitrus and, especially, Therra, looked far more uncertain. Though she tried to maintain a stoic expression on her face, the huge warrior woman kept her stance wide, as if to steady herself, and she always held on to something—a wall, a machine, or the wooden railing—with at least one hand. Domitrus would sort of cower in one place for a while, and then, when he was called upon to do so, he'd rush over to the bomb chute (basically a hole in the floor of the zeppelin's chassis) and drop a lit sack of explosives.

Well, anyway, some of us were having a lot of fun, but the realization soon dawned on us that we had an attack to plan. We had agreed earlier that it would be best to mount our invasion as soon as possible—before Orlacc's men had had a chance to completely recover from our last confrontation, and before the singed monarch found an opportunity to mastermind another assault on us. I turned to Helmut and asked him to "take this boat back to port."

"Yes, of course," he said. "Otto...?"

Soon, the Guardian was parked, we had eaten, and were sitting around a fire, sharpening our swords and finalizing our game plan.

"So, not that I'm all that great at math, but let me take a stab at summing things up," I said, trying to keep things light. "According to Belgear, we've got 24 captive horses in our pens. If Therra and Parkel each take a horse, and if we put three Grimnell warriors on each of the remaining steeds, which we can do because we're pretty darn small, we can send an army of almost 70 to attack Orlacc on the ground. Correct?"

"Correct," Domitrus and Belgear answered simultaneously, each looking somewhat embarrassed that he might have spoken out of turn.

"And we can take about 30 fighters on board the Guardian?" I continued.

"Yes," Otto replied. "Any more, and ve shall be too heavy."

I rubbed my chin, and concluded, "That's an amazingly small invasion force!

"Pitifully small," Therra said.

"Disturbingly small," agreed Domitrus.

"Depressingly small," Parkel groaned.

"Er, dauntingly small?" Shieda added, meekly. Trolcott, who had lost a hand in the last battle, slammed his bandaged stump on his knee, and cried, "Very well, I'll say it: hopelessly sm-"

"Vait vun moment here!" Otto spouted, leaping to his feet. "None of you seem to realize you are actually quite vell off in zis matter! Vit zee Guardian, our great creation, on your zide, you have an amazing advantage! You have established air zuperiority! Zee enemy has no vay to fight against it! Zey vill run screaming ven zey zee our Guardian bearing down on zem! Trust me! I have zeen it before. Und ve shall triumph, I promise you!"

We were all too ashamed to say anything for a little while. Clearly, we'd offended Otto, though we hadn't meant to. He sincerely believed in his machine, and who were we to say he was wrong? Anyhow, we had little choice—we could forget the few horses we had and launch a larger army on foot, and we could build more zeppelins, but it would cost us precious time. Orlacc might be back to finish us off in less than a week. We had the advantage of surprise now, and we had probably better use it.

"Well," I muttered after a time. "As small as our force is, it'll have to do, and that's that."

Everyone—even Trolcott—grunted in apparent assent.

"Please, allow me to say something," Obishku said solemnly. He took the sword he had been sharpening and used its tip to stir the dying embers of the fire. When he saw that we were all waiting for him to continue, he said: "I am old now, but I remember a story my father told me when I was young, almost seventy years ago. It was the story of how my grandfather's brother died. You see, a Terasskossian knight had led a raid on our village, and my great uncle, Gorremma, spearheaded a retaliation against the Terasskossians. We had not made such a move for decades, because we knew the enemy had superior forces, but Gorremma and others were determined to not let these frequent raids go unchallenged.

"Those were more glorious days, Grimnells, and we had more warriors in our army. Gorremma gathered almost 1600 men for his assault on the Terasskossian stronghold. The battle was a bloody one, and it lasted 11 days. Gorremma's men made many gallant sacrifices, and they killed many Terasskossians, but, in the end, our army could not overcome the enemy's ruthless knights and giant war horses. Also, the Terasskossians had always had more advanced weaponry. Gorremma's assault was repelled.

"As Gorremma, with tears in his eyes, led the remainder of our army—some 350 soldiers—back to Nornlunn, no one realized he had been mortally wounded. He persevered until he reached our village square, and then he collapsed to the ground. As he lay dying, he told my grandfather, 'While we Grimnells strive to master many disciplines, the Terasskossians are giants in war and terror, and in nothing else. Only an otherworldly miracle could ever allow us to best them in combat.' Gorremma died then and there, and that was the last serious attempt we made to challenge the Terasskossians on their home ground.

"For years, many of us 'old ones' held on to the belief that the miracle Gorremma spoke of would come one day."

He turned, and pointed at the silhouetted sky-ship, bobbing prodigiously above the trees. "Mine aged eyes behold that flying machine, and I muse to myself that there are no better words to describe it that 'otherworldly' and 'miracle.' If ancient Obishku, grand-nephew of Gorremma, is willing to put his faith in this object built by off-worlders, how can any of you do any less?"

The assembled soldiers clapped and let out a hearty cheer. Wow! Who wanted to say anything after that speech! Certainly not me. Luckily, Shieda stepped up to bat.

"I think the matter has been decided," she said. "We will put our plans in motion starting tomorrow morning. Now, we should finish our preparations and get some rest."

She was right, of course. Humbly, everyone headed off in their own directions. Of course I can't speak for anyone else, but I had a pretty good idea of the thought that was on everyone's mind: one way or another, tomorrow would be the beginning of the end.

Phase one of our attack—our ground forces—left early the next morning. Our aerial group waited around for a day and a half to give the first wave a chance to get near Orlacc's castle. We spent the time rehearsing maneuvers, making practice runs in the blimp (though we had to be careful to conserve enough of the Hunsvangs' salvaged fuel in the engines to be able to carry out our mission), and grabbing some downtime. But we were itching to go

– Otto, Helmut, Domitrus, Shieda, and I were all dying to get into the air and fighting while we were still fired up enough and convinced that we had a chance of winning.

Finally, it was time to leave. We were going to board the Guardian at dusk, then fly through the night and arrive in time to strike Orlacc's castle just before dawn.

All had been prepared—the swords, bows, spears, and Domitrus's makeshift bombs had been carried aboard the zeppelin. I watched as 30 harried-looking Grimnells—many in battered and fire-scarred armor—gulped down their fears, said goodbye to their loved ones, and scaled the ladder to our sky-ship. None of the uncertainties of previous days showed on their faces—now, they seemed proud and determined to put an end to Orlacc's tyranny against their people.

Then, Domitrus and Helmut were ascending, Shieda was on the ladder, and Otto was waiting for me to start my climb.

"Are you coming, hon?" Shieda asked from ten feet off the ground.

"I will...in a minute."

Otto nodded, then said, "As captain, I should be zee last aboard. Unless...unless you vish othervize."

"You two go on ahead," I said. "I'll be up soon."

Shieda hesitated, but then turned and made her way up the ladder. Otto saluted me, and then he, too, climbed aboard. I was proud of my little army, my band of raiders. I was proud ...

Alone, or at least feeling that way, I finally allowed myself to breathe in the feeling which had been haunting me for roughly the past 72 hours. What was it? Fear? Doubt? Uncertainty? Dread?

There was something about this approaching fight that felt different. I knew deep down that this wasn't to be just another in our long line of battles against Orlacc.

No, this was it. The turning point. Do or die, win or lose, me or...him.

Yes, that was it. I still wasn't sure where I stood—I had my feet in two worlds! And I was sharing a body with another guy. But where was my heart? Here? Or back home?

Argothrex's words replayed themselves in my mind, and the faces of my friends danced in front of me. They believed in me. They knew who I was. Why couldn't I?

Now was the right time. I had to make my decision. And I knew what I wanted at last. I grabbed my jewel in my hands, and looked up at the proud ship Guardian, where my friends were waiting for me, and I said the words.

"I want to be me."

Chapter Twenty-Nine

Finally, we were on our way, skimming about forty feet above the treetops, or so Helmut informed me. Not long after we had begun our voyage, the portly first officer/navigator waddled off and lit two lanterns on the front of the Guardian's hull. The light was barely enough to illuminate the forest-line twenty feet in front of the cruising blimp.

Helmut caught me shaking my head. "Vhat is amiss, sir?" he asked.

"How can you guys tell where we're going?"

"Ah. Zat is a good qvestion. You see, many of ze navigational methods ve use on Earth do not vork vell here for various reasons." He reached into his pocket and pulled out a clunky box-shaped thing with a dial on top. It appeared to be an old compass. "Fortunately, zis vorld zeems to have a magnetic pole, much like ours back home. Zis compass should guide us zafely there!"

By the seats of our pants, I thought. "I guess I should leave the driving to you, eh?"

He was absorbed in his navigation. "Pardon, sir?"

"I, um, I guess I'll go back and check on things in the cabin...see how everyone's doing."

"Very good, sir," he answered, clubbing the compass with his gloved palm. "I vatch things here. Yes, I vatch... "

I left Helmut to his navigating as I passed through the curtains into the cabin, which, by now, was almost pitch dark. As my eyes adjusted, I could make out the shapes of the soldiers, huddled under blankets and cloaks against the zeppelin's walls. I saw Domitrus, too, with his back rigid against the wall—he appeared to be meditating. And I located Shieda, gazing out a window into the night.

"I think I like these blimps of yours," she whispered playfully as I approached. "Perhaps we should own one of our own someday?"

I put my arms around her waist and looked out the window with her. "Probably should let the Hunsvangs keep this one when we're done with it, though. Don't you think?"

"Of course," she said, and she turned and kissed me. It steadied my racing heart. "What's the matter?" she said, apparently sensing some deep worry inside of me, before I even became aware of it.

I searched my mind for an answer. Finally, it came to me: "Well, I was thinking, 'What if this is our last night together?'"

"Oh," she muttered, looking away. Then she held my face in her hands. "It won't be," she said.

"But...how do you know that?" I groaned. "I mean, no one knows their destiny."

She sighed, and thought about it a minute before she spoke. "Some people believe they do know their destinies, and, well...I, for one, don't believe either of us is destined to die in one of these blimp thingies. Do you?"

She seemed strange about it, like she knew something she wasn't telling me. But maybe she was only trying to lift my mood—again! God, I was always such a wet blanket!

"Yeah, you're right," I said, trying to recover my cool. "I can't be thinking like that anyway...especially now."

"Now? What do you mean?"

"Um, I mean now that we're finally heading for our attack," I said.

I had barely caught myself. I really didn't want to tell her about the whole I-want-to-be-me-jewel thing until after the battle. No sense in letting people know that the real Morrelaine's reflexes wouldn't be coming to anyone's rescue tomorrow. Best to just see how things go. It did strike me as strange then that neither Shieda nor the Hunsvangs had apparently been commanded by some superior being to make the same choice I had. Maybe I'd have to ask Argothrex about that when this was all over.

She still seemed a little distant. "How 'bout you?" I asked. "You seem a bit worried yourself."

Her green eyes caught a glint of the scant starlight coming through the windows, and I could tell there was something weighing on her, something that had been weighing on her for some time. Finally, she said, "It's a few things, really. I know I'll have to face that sorcerer of Orlacc's again. The last time we faced him, I could feel his power. I know there's a lot he can do, and there's no way I can prepare for it. If I were half as adept ast my adopted father was...

"And that's the other matter: Once this battle is done, I'll need to get on with my life, finally realizing that my father isn't coming back. I dread having to do that."

"I know," I said, pulling her close again and giving her a squeeze. "This fight has carried us through a lot. Who knows what'll happen to all of us when it's over with?"

Something brought a slight grin to her face. She said, "A moment ago you were worrying that this might be our last night, and now you're worrying about the future. Perhaps you should pick one scenario, and we'll both worry about that?"

"Hey, y'know, it's a good thing we've got this time to air our worries, because we sure won't have time for it tomorrow. I think it's a good time to be...reflecting."

"I know," she said. "I'm just attempting to find some humor in all of this. But, truly, I'm very glad we have this time to cuddle up and bolster each other's confidence." Wryly, she added, "It makes going off to war that much more pleasant!"

We stood there for a while, watching the world slip by outside our airship.

"Well, uh, if this was to be our last night, I do know what I'd like to be doing," I said when I felt the urge to doze creeping over me.

"And what's that?" she asked.

I put my arms around her again and sank to the floor. We sat against the wall, intertwined, and pulled our capes over ourselves. When we were about as hidden away and as close together as we could get, I put my face against hers and said, "This is pretty much it. Maybe there'd be more, y'know, if other people weren't around but..."

"I get the picture," she said. "Here's my only criticism."

And she kissed me long and hard and drove the rapacious fears from my troubled soul. We were one, and we stayed that way, as the night whispered by.

It seemed like it was only a short while later when I awoke to Otto, standing over me.

"Helmut just voke me," he muttered, a pale, sober expression on his face. "It is almost time for ze rendezvous."

Some of the soldiers were up already, and those who weren't were being nudged awake by the others. It was still dark outside, but a thick fog had rolled in overnight. Wisps of bluish cloud moved through the forest below like giant, lurking ghouls through a graveyard. It looked like it was going to be a gloomy—perhaps even a rainy day.

"Is this going to make it tough to navigate?" I asked Otto, as he was about to head into the control room.

"Not really. Ze fog vill make it difficult to see, but ve still have our compass. Und I do not imagine dere is much chance zat ve vill collide vith another airship, do you?" Not waiting for an answer, he poked his head out through a small window and sniffed the air.

"Hmmmm. I do hope, though, zat dere von't be any lightning or heavy rain."

Domitrus, who had just caught up with us, looked out the window and grimaced. "That 'fog,' as you call it, will make it difficult to target our bombs. We won't be able to see what we're striking at."

"It may clear up," Shieda said, stretching and yawning. "Usually, on the plains at least, the sun burns fog away. I don't know if it's like that up here in the mountain region. We'll just have to see, I guess."

With the uncertain mood hanging over us, we braced ourselves and entered the control room. There, a tired looking Helmut was peering out of the front window. He turned and smiled when he saw us. "Good zat you are here," he said, his voice croaking. "I'm afraid my eyes may not be much good now."

"Vhat? No sign of them yet?" Otto sputtered, heading to the window himself. "Ve are still on course, are ve not?"

"You have never qvestioned my navigational skills before, brother," huffed Helmut, his gaze falling. "I am vounded by you!"

"Now, now, Helmut...!" groaned Otto, and he started to say something in German, but then Shieda interrupted.

"Look, the tree canopy is quite thick below, and there's still the fog. We might not be able to see their fire until we're practically on top of them."

As if in response, there came a banging at the control room door. A gasping soldier came clattering into the room.

"A couple of us just saw a light, sir," he said, addressing me. "We passed over it only moments ago!"

I immediately turned to the Hunsvangs. "Well?" "Are ve going to trust ze vord of a foot soldier, Brother?" Helmut asked when Otto sped towards the controls.

"Ve have no choice," Otto growled. "If ve miss our rendezvous, all our plans vill be ruined!"

We all held on as the blimp lurched and came about at Otto's command. Soon, we were all hanging out of the windows, desperately hoping to avoid missing our ground troop's fire signal a second time; after all, daybreak was getting closer.

The wait wasn't long: Through the pillars of mist, Domitrus soon caught sight of a flickering glow. It was our party! As we sailed over their position, we saw them breaking camp and mounting their horses in pairs. They let out a cheer as we floated over them. By the time we had come about again, they were mobilized, riding towards

Orlacc's fortress a mere two miles away. The Grimnells, who were not used to riding into combat, clutched their bows, swords, and spears as the horses leapt into action, following Therra's and Parkel's lead.

"Well, this is it, I guess," I said to our group when the ground crew had disappeared into the still-dark forest. "Now we circle around for a while, right?"

"Correct," Otto answered, too busy really working the controls to talk. The plan was that we would make a wide circle around the area to both get a fix on the castle's location and to allow our first wave to begin their attack. The waiting was almost over.

Locating the castle proved to be an interesting experience—we knew about where it was supposed to be, but we couldn't actually see it. This was because the fog became extremely concentrated around the area where we knew the castle ought to be standing.

Shieda's expression grew grim.

"This could be that wizard, Frouder's, doing," she muttered. "If he can influence the weather..."

"Besides making it harder to target our bombs, how if that fog going to affect our attack?" I asked Otto.

"Vell. . . " he said, not taking his eyes off of the fog bank. "I vould say ve must go in lower zen ve had planned, just zo ve can get zome zort of view of vhere ve are attacking."

"Then let's do it. We'll manage," I said. I turned to Domitrus, and added, "Can you get those explosives ready to drop?"

"Gladly," he answered. "I've been waiting a long time to do this."

Suddenly, our ship jumped jerkily, as it was battered by several sharp gusts of wind, coming in waves.

"What was that?" I yelled. Everyone had become alert as we were jolted.

Otto shrugged. "I am not sure. Ze air has been calm until now."

"The fog down there, and now the wind up here," Shieda mumbled in a trance-like voice. "He must be controlling it."

She was losing it, and I could see that we were all getting the jitters. We had to move, I figured, or we'd never get this operation underway.

"Alright," I said. "Let's go in low, but not too low." Otto and Helmut zipped to their controls, and everyone else besides Shieda took their battle positions. The Guardian descended confidently after a few more gusts, and we headed straight into the thickest of the fog, where, we knew, the house of our enemy lay.

In seconds, we saw a gray spire, poking through the fog, and we knew we had arrived. Unfortunately, the thing was pretty damn close to us! A team of three archers and two spear-throwers were crowded around the tower's narrow walkway. When they spotted us, they yelled, and let loose a volley. We were still a good fifty feet away, but one of the arrows struck the side of our gondola.

"Pull up! Pull up!" I shouted. "We're too low!"

Worried-looking, Otto glared at me. "If ve go any higher, ve shall not be able to see vhere ve are bombing," he said.

"Und ve could hit our own peoples on ze ground, if ve are not careful," added Helmut.

As Otto steered the ship to avoid the tower, I turned desperately to Shieda. "Shieda, honey, you've got to try to do something about the fog. Can't you...?"

"I'll try," she muttered somberly, "but water and wind aren't my strong suits."

But before she could even start conjuring, we were battered by more sledgehammer-force winds. Once we had regained our footing, we saw that our ship was hurtling towards the spire.

"Ve'll be split in two!" screamed Otto, as he furiously worked the controls, but to no effect.

Then, Domitrus came running forward with the explosive bags in his hands. "Take us just a little higher," he said. "We'll take care of that tower." He waved some of the soldiers, who were also carrying bombs, to his side, and they gathered at the windows. The men on the tower were rearming, but they hesitated when they realized the ship would knock them off their platform if it hit. As the collision loomed, Otto and Helmut were struggling to gain altitude.

"Now! Away!" shouted Domitrus, and the men hurled their payloads. Looking out a window, I watched as several of the bombs bounced off the stone spire and fell to the ground below. But two of the bags landed on the tower platform.

"Uh, are we gonna be too...?" I wondered, but then the bombs exploded. We were hit with another gust, but this time it was a shockwave of our own making. When we all opened our eyes again, we quickly moved to the windows. What we saw—or didn't see— lifted our spirits. The tower—the top of it at least—was gone. We all cheered and hugged each other. "Maybe we can do this!" I shouted, as the others reached similar conclusions.

"Let us get more ready," Domitrus instructed the soldiers. Meanwhile, Otto was bringing the Guardian about.

"I think we can go in low for this run," I said to him.

"There's liable to be more towers," Shieda said.

"Then we'll blow 'em away too."

Outside, the fog began thinning as we descended—after all, Orlacc's wizard probably didn't want to make things too confusing for the Terasskossian armies on the ground. We started to be able to make out courtyards, buildings, and the castle walls.

"We've gotta hit the walls with our bombs," I said. "Therra and Parkel's team are gonna need our help."

But before I'd even finished speaking, my friends were whirling into action. Otto and Helmut pointed the ship towards the area where most of the sounds of battle were coming from, and Domitrus led the soldiers in preparing more explosives. I was going to say something to Shieda, but when I turned towards her, I saw that she was concentrating, working her magic. On what, I had no idea.

When I looked out the window again, I got my answer: She was mentally setting fire to the giant front door of the castle, which stood in the way of our army's entry into the court.

"Now we're playing with power," I muttered.

As we zoomed over the wall, Domitrus's team hurled away. Enemy troops on the walls looked up just in time to see our Guardian whoosh over their heads before the fiery bags blew away chunks of stone beneath their feet. And then, we were outside the castle. We could see our troops, charging, yelling, and throwing everything they had at the soldiers atop the ramparts. Our guys had landed a few grappling ropes, but so far no one had been able to scale the 100-foot-high walls.

My heart sank when I saw several Grimnells—either wounded or dead—lying on the ground. Obviously, laying siege to a well-fortified castle with a barely-armed contingent of about 70 warriors was not the safest thing to do, but I guess I had been clinging to my 21st Century-born hope that no one would have to die for us to win. I suppose maybe I'd seen too many superhero movies.

I did catch sight of Parkel and Therra, bruised and bloody, but still mounted, and still commanding the troops. They had noticed that the door was aflame and were calling for the army to mass in front of it.

"We've got to hit that door with our bombs," I said, turning towards the others.

"It vill take me a few minutes to turn zee ship around," Otto said.

"After that we should think about getting some of our guys on the ground," I went on, "so we can help Parkel and Therra, and get this thing over with."

Soon the ship was headed back towards the castle, and Domitrus and crew were standing ready with another barrage. By now, the top quarter of the door was engulfed in flames, and our army was fashioning a battering ram from a fallen tree to help smash it in. We had almost made it!

As we flew back over the wall, I heard Domitrus bellow, "Away!" Almost 20 bombs fell near the door and the front wall, and the resulting explosions sent splinters of stone and wood flying everywhere. When the smoke cleared, we could see that the door was on fire on both its bottom and its top. And Orlacc's men were scattering, running for cover. Vengeance was to be ours!

"Let's take out some of those buildings!" I shouted, but then, something seemed to land on top of our ship. We started losing altitude. It felt like a giant hand was pushing us toward the ground.

"What the hell...?" I said, and I looked at poor Otto.

He was furiously steering, but to no effect. "Zere's nothing I can do!" he yelled.

"Look!" Shieda said, pointing out a window. On top of one of the ramparts a lone figure stood with his arms above his head. "Frouder!" Shieda hissed. "He's doing this!"

"C-can you do anything...?" I asked, squirming, as we started falling faster.

Suddenly, the unseen hand gave us a shove, and the whole craft dropped about thirty feet in seconds.

"H-hold on everyvun," said Otto, his teeth chattering with fear. "I try to land us zafely!"

Everybody was gripping the side of the ship, waiting for another blow. Thing was, we couldn't withstand another, and we all knew it.

"Shieda...?" I groaned.

"T-trying...but I...can't...concentrate."

I mentally put my hope into her, projecting the thought, I believe in you. She was struggling, wrestling her self-doubt and her fear of Frouder, a more experienced wizard. Then, we started to level off. It was working!

"I'll try to bring us in," said Otto.

Our taste of victory was short-lived. The powerful, mystical hand struck again with even greater force, and we started plummeting.

"Mein Gott!" Helmut shouted. It was the last thing I heard.

Chapter Thirty

I have no idea how long I was unconscious. When I came to, I was inside our zeppelin—or what was left of it. It was fairly dark inside the twisted carcass of the airship.

I tried to get my bearings. No one appeared to have died in the crash, but there were others who, like me, had been knocked out and were recovering slowly. I heard groans as some of them tried to shake themselves awake. At least the Guardian did not appear to be on fire—it was no Hindenburg, thank goodness!

As I raised myself up, I saw Domitrus, Helmut, and Otto, sprawled on the floor at the front of the ship. They were waking up too. Poor Domitrus was moaning in anguish—it looked like he had broken his leg or ankle.

Shieda was nowhere in sight!

"Are you all right?" I asked the three, once I'd made my way over to them past the jagged swath of debris.

"As vell as can be expected," Helmut huffed. "But our poor ship is ruined! Ve'll never repair her now!"

Otto put a comforting arm around Helmut's shoulders. "It is all right, dear brother. Ve shall build another one. You must excuse him, sir—he is a zentimentalist."

"That's okay. I'm just glad you're both okay. Did you see where Shieda went?"

They all shook their heads. "Perhaps she left with some of the soldiers?" Otto said. "It seems many of them are gone. Do you vant us to...?"

"I want you to stay here and help Domitrus. You guys aren't really trained for fighting anyway. I'm going to go outside and see what's going on."

The scene outside was pure chaos. Our men must have grabbed the remainder of Domitrus's bombs, because, every so often, I'd hear an explosion and see a stone structure crumble to the ground. The front gate had been burned to a crisp and battered down, and our ground team had long since breached the castle walls. There were skirmishes going on all around me, but I couldn't spot Shieda, Parkel, or

Therra anywhere. I ran off towards the main palace—at least one of my friends would have headed there, I figured.

As I huffed and puffed my way across the open grounds, the sounds of battle and the pounding of my heart assaulted my ears. I was possessed by a feeling of urgency—as if I might have missed something, or that I might be too late. I sped up as much as my armor and my sore muscles would let me.

I rounded a corner and saw the palace steps, which were littered with a dozen or so bodies of the dead and wounded. But still, my friends were nowhere to be seen. There were shouts coming from just inside the castle doors. Perhaps there...?

But no—there were not even any guards. I supposed the regular sentries had long ago joined the fray.

I continued inside, passing through a short hallway and an antechamber, before reaching an archway. Through the archway, I stepped into a large hall. It was one I immediately recognized, for it was in this same chamber that we learned of Orlacc's treachery for the first time. I heard the clang of swords, and, yes, as I turned to look in the direction of the throne, I saw three figures, two of them engaged in combat.

As I tore across the vast room, I assessed the situation. Parkel was on the ground. He appeared to be wounded. Therra was hacking at Orlacc with one hand, but she kept looking over to check on Parkel. Orlacc was trying to hold off Therra, while at the same time looking for an opening when she was distracted.

"Hang on, Therra! I'm coming!" I shouted as I neared them. Therra ignored me, but Orlacc looked startled when he heard my voice.

"Ah, so the toad arrives at last," he hissed defiantly. But he looked worried. When Therra turned back to check on Parkel again, Orlacc spun on his heel and fled the room.

Once Therra saw that he'd left, she flipped out. "Dog!" she shouted, and she started to go after him. But then she hesitated.

When I reached them, I realized that Parkel was in a bad way. Someone—Orlacc, I imagined—had stabbed him right through his shoulder. Blood was seeping through several openings in his armor. Therra dropped to her knees.

"What happened?" I asked.

"The little fool," she answered, as she began to work at removing his armor. "He tried to help me."

Parkel moaned as she moved his arm. "He...he was going to s-stab her in the back," he said hoarsely. "Can't...can't lose Therra..."

Therra's gaze softened a little when he spoke her name. It was clear that, despite her best efforts, she'd grown to care for him.

"Look, maybe I can watch over him if you want to go after Orlacc," I offered.

She raised an eyebrow. "I know enough about you, Morrelaine to know that you know nothing about bandaging wounds. Leave it to me. You follow Orlacc if you want."

"But I...are you...?"

"Hurry!" she shouted. And how could I argue? This was a changed Therra I was seeing, and she was sure enough of herself to know what she wanted and levelheaded enough to keep focused on the big picture, even during the heat of battle. She'd still like nothing better than to see Orlacc punished, but not at the expense of Parkel's life. How could I not want to encourage that?

Besides, I had a six-pack of "whup-ass" I wanted to unleash on Orlacc. And I needed to find Shieda. I shut my mouth and tore out of the room.

Outside of the door there was a stairway leading up. I mounted it, sure that Orlacc was heading for some secret passageway, or at least for higher ground. I could hear boots clopping on the steps.

Up three flights. Then four. Off of the next landing, there was a room. As I reached the top stair, someone slammed a huge wooden door in my face. After catching my breath for a moment, I kicked the door. He'd locked it—it wouldn't budge.

"Why don't you come out so we can end this, Orlacc?" I bellowed, sounding as threatening as I could. "You know one of us will catch up with you sooner or later!"

"Not that I'm afraid to face you, miscreant, but I'll give you a choice," came his muffled reply. "I'll open the door so we can duel to your death, or I will tell you where your precious Shieda is!"

I kicked the door a couple more times for good measure. I had to figure out how to break through! "Well, what's to stop me from busting in there, defeating you, and making you tell me where she is? Huh?" Ouch, my foot was killing me!

"Perhaps the knowledge that she is even now engaged in a death struggle with my court wizard, hmmm? How does that strike you?"

"Where? Where is she? You...!"

"On the top of my tallest tower, pig! Run up these stairs, all the way to the summit. You just might get there in time to hear her death screams! Now, what is your choice, eh?"

I could hear that he'd moved right up close to the door. I

pounded it one more time, hoping to scare him, and then I turned and ran up the steps.

"Ha Ha! Just as I expected!" he yowled from below.

Later, I thought to myself.

It had been difficult enough for me to jog up the few flights to Orlacc's room before, but now I had to make it up many more. I stopped counting after ten. But I had to keep going. I kept hoping Orlacc was wrong about the 'death duel.' I knew my beloved was strong, but in magic, she didn't have much confidence in herself. Why did she have to go off and face Frouder on her own? Was it because of her father?

Suddenly, I felt the air change around me. There was the scent of sweet-smelling smoke, and a crackle in the atmosphere. I was nearly there!

"Shieda!" I yelled, barely able to get the word out with my gasping breaths. Then, I felt a rumble. What the hell was going on?

I finally reached the top of the stairs, and came to another door. This one was slightly ajar, so I kicked it open (well, I sort of fell into it with my foot, actually). I came out on top of a narrow tower, high above the rest of Orlacc's stronghold. And there was my honey, bathed in sweat and on her knees, panting. Frouder was standing nearby. He raised an eyebrow, acknowledging my presence, though he did not turn to look at me. Shieda started coughing, her back heaving.

"What the hell did you...?" No! Shut up and take him out! I thought to myself, and I hurled my body at him.

Now, he looked at me, but his gaze seemed to zoom at me, like he'd launched his thoughts my way. I flew back into a wall as if I'd been slammed with a battering ram in my stomach.

"Leave him out of this!" Shieda croaked, having climbed to her feet again. She still looked wobbly, though. Frouder turned back to her, and let out an annoyed sigh.

"I agree: Let this be between us wizards. We'll leave these brutes to their hacking and slashing, won't we?"

Shieda merely scowled, and lashed out at him with a barrage of fire tendrils. As the molten bolts materialized and snaked towards Frouder, I thought I might be blinded by the glare. But the evil wizard laughed, and moved his hands hyper-quick windmills, plucking the fireballs out of the air and re-directing them in other directions. As fast as they had appeared, they were gone.

"The winds always control the flames, feeding the fire, and, yes, changing its course," Frouder said condescendingly. "Do you yet see it, girl? You could make a fine magician one day, but you are no match for me now."

He was about to continue, when, suddenly, he jumped. I hadn't noticed—and neither had he—that the bottom of his robe had caught fire. He yelped, and looked helplessly around.

"I dare you to throw that away so easily," said Shieda, smiling.

Frouder attempted to congeal moisture around his hemline, but the flames kept licking away at his clothes. Then, he abandoned his conjuring altogether, and tried patting the flames out with his hands, gasping all the while as his hands were singed.

I realized that, instead of sitting there laughing, we ought to press our attack. I was about to say so to my beloved, when I saw her hefting a chunk of the castle wall that had been blasted apart by our bombs. She held the stone in both hands, and lifted it slowly over her head. It started to glow, as she infused it with the heat of her magic fire. After a moment, she tossed it at Frouder. It hit him with a 'thunk.'

He fell to the ground, dazed. Looking at her with his mouth agape, he said, "Are you mad? Do you see what you are doing to me?" He held up his hands, which were now red and blistered. "How can I defend myself...this, this isn't fair!"

Reaching for another rock, Shieda replied, "Of course it isn't fair—I'm no match for you. Remember?"

I pointed my sword at him, and said, "Let's finish him off, eh?" I was so psyched—we had him!

Frouder looked disgusted and worried. "Loyalty can only be strained so far," he muttered. "There will be other chances." And with that, he turned his blackened palms towards his own body. With a rush of air, he vanished.

"Wow!" I said after the air had calmed down. "Do you know how to do that?"

But Shieda dropped the rock, and slumped against the wall. I rushed to her side.

"I-I'll be okay in a minute," she said, her voice small and weak. "He hit me with a lot before you arrived. If you hadn't distracted him..."

"Shh. You can just take it easy now. I don't think he's coming back, at least not right away."

"The fool," she sneered. "Too modest and uptight. I would have flung my clothes off rather than burn my hands!"

"I'm sure you would have," I said, giving her a squeeze. "That's one of the reasons you thrill me so much."

"Well, this should be fun!"

The voice came from behind me. I whirled, and beheld Orlacc, standing in the doorway atop the stairs. He had taken the time to put on his full suit of armor, and he'd gathered a ten-foot lance in addition to his sword.

"Oh great," I muttered.

But of course he had to gloat. "I can either gut you, cut you, or hurl you off the tower. Ah, choices, choices." Shieda was sitting against the wall, and I knew she needed time to recover. This was my test. It was up to me. If I couldn't at least hold him off, we'd both be dead soon.

Make him mad.

"So, you decided to quit hiding in your room, eh Orlacc?"

His face trembled and reddened, but he held his fury in check. "It... will be so... grand to be rid of you!" he said, and then he lunged at me with his lance. I ran, knowing I had to draw him away from Shieda, and he kept right up with me. He was too fast—had longer legs and a wider reach. I headed for another section of wall. As I slowed and turned, his lance shot towards my chest. I clamped it between my arm and chest, and the tip struck the wall, nearly jarring my teeth out. But I'd avoided being skewered.

He tried to yank his lance back, but I held on, feeling it pull at the side of my body. If he managed to rip it away, he could take a chunk of my flesh with it.

"Think you can hang on?" he shouted. "Very well!" He reached back to unsheathe his sword. I grabbed for mine too. Since mine was shorter, I got it out first, and swung at him. But he was out of my reach. Grinning madly, he swung his at my face. I jerked my head back, but his swordpoint caught me on my chin.

"Ouch!" I yelled, losing concentration and my grip on his lance.

"Weakling!" he snorted.

Now, I was down, against a wall, and he had a lance and his sword, ready to attack. He paused for a couple of seconds. He had to decide which to use. I realized it was my one chance.

I jumped up, and landed on his lance, slamming it to the ground with my feet. Before completely losing my balance, I threw myself at him, and I threw my arms around his neck. Surprised, he stumbled backwards, and we both hit the ground hard. I held on to his neck for all I was worth, while he struggled to free himself, finally managing to wrench my arms apart. He held me in the air, away from him, for a moment, before flinging me to one side. We both scrambled to get to our feet and regain our weapons.

We stood at last, facing each other, chests heaving with the effort and swords at the ready.

"Little weasel that you are, you put up a good fight," he said, spitting the words out between breaths. "I should never have underestimated you. No matter—I will still kill you. Have you any last words?"

Dozens of chaotic thoughts were bubbling just below the surface— a spate of glorious, demigod-like platitudes, ready to spill, as I'd seen done in movies, comics, and TV shows. But all that came out was: "Yeah—why don't you eat my shorts?"

I have no idea if he knew what I meant, but he got appropriately mad, and hacked at me with his sword. I parried as best I could, holding my weapon above me with both hands. It did little good. Three or four blows, and I realized I couldn't keep my defense up for long. He was just too much bigger and more powerful than I was. I started faltering under the strain.

I caught a glimpse of Shieda. She was trying to get up to help me, but she kept falling back. Poor thing had spent too much energy already.

"Ha! Ha!" Orlacc was screaming as he bashed my steel, spitting on me, his sweat dripping on me. What should I do? I wondered, and then my sword broke.

I fell back, and crawled as far from him as I could get. The lip of stone at the tower's edge was all that was left between my back and a long, hard fall. Smug and triumphant, the armored giant swaggered towards me.

"Now, small one. Now do you have anything to say?"

"How about 'die, bastard?'"

I had opened my mouth to speak, but these words had come from another source, behind Orlacc. As he turned, a blade fell out of the air and sunk into his left shoulder. He bellowed, and fell back from the force of the blow. It was then that I saw Therra standing behind where he had been standing, ripping her blade from his shoulder. She strode towards Orlacc, her sword at the ready.

"Cursed bitch!" Orlacc yowled, watching the blood seep down his arm. "Why won't you give up and go home to your father?!"

"Why?" she nearly hissed, grimacing as she circled him. "First of all, I have no father. My only family is here. And second..." She nodded towards me. "...I could hardly let him strike your death blow when I want to do it myself!"

Orlacc desperately searched for a way out, but there was nowhere he could go. Resigned, he said, "Bah! I can still wield a sword, cow!"

"Then wield one, lizard. Defend yourself! Though it will do little good. Vengeance is mine!"

I scurried over to check on Shieda, but I kept my blade ready, and I kept my eyes on the fight, in case Therra needed my help. Not that that was very likely. She launched herself at him, and, with a series of quick strikes, she kept him on the ground, on the defensive. Suddenly she took a step backwards.

"Oh do get up, you pathetic worm!" she sneered. "At least make a show of trying to fight back!"

But before she'd finished speaking, he lashed out with his sword, slashing he across both legs. The cuts weren't deep, but they must have stung. Until now, Therra had been uncharacteristically calm and calculating in her actions, but, after Orlacc's sneak attack, I began to see traces of her trademark berserker rage burning to get out.

Growling, she lunged at him with her sword, but he dodged, while she nearly went over the edge. When she turned to face him again, he was ready for her. They went at it, thrusting, parrying, evading, and trying to pummel each other with sweep kicks and hammer punches.

In the back of my head was a voice, telling me I should join the battle, help Therra, try to tip the scales in her—our—favor. But my mind also told me it would be a travesty of sorts to interrupt this meeting of perfect opponents. He, the Hun-like warrior, raised by a conquering king to rule a warlike breed, and to be the master of that breed. He had had the best teachers, been fed the right foods, received the top training, and been indoctrinated from birth with the belief that it was his right—his destiny—to crush others beneath his boots. She, too, had been brought up in a warrior culture, but hers was an uncertain life. Her people didn't make war just to dominate others—theirs was a daily fight just to stay alive in the harsh desert. You had to win by whatever means necessary. Using a variety of styles was acceptable. Whereas Orlacc's style was all about discipline and strategy, she had learned to rely on her intuition. For Therra, losing focus and letting rage take over was not only okay, it was sometimes the only way.

Unfortunately, losing her head to rage could also cost her the fight if she let it take her over too much. The problem? Orlacc knew her well enough to know that.

"You...you fight with the abandon of one suffering a broken heart,

Therra," he grunted while evading her blows. "Could it be...that you truly had fallen in love with me? Could it be, indeed, that part of you loves me still?"

Her eyes flashed, and she hacked at him, swinging her sword in wide, chaotic arcs.

"Ah ha! I see we both know the answer!" he continued, easily blocking her erratic attacks. She was hurling her blade at him—the force was massive enough to push Orlacc back, but her lack of focused aim made her strikes simple to parry.

"Well then, you should know that my men and I shared many a laugh over my plan to seduce you, and I joked about going through with a mock wedding, just to see the look on your face when I had you thrown into the dungeon on our wedding night! You were quite the talk of my throne room!"

She chopped down with her blade, roaring with hate, but her swordpoint lodged itself in a crack in the tower's stone wall. Orlacc laughed, and raised his sword to strike. He was poised to hack her arm off. But Therra moved too quickly. She hiked her leg up, and kicked Orlacc squarely in his armored chest with all her might. Gasping for air, he flew ten feet and crashed to the floor. There he lay, trying to catch his breath, and weighed down by the bulk of his armor.

Therra yanked her sword from the wall, and then approached the fallen knight with an unearthly, murderous gleam in her eyes. She straddled his fallen form, which was perched at the edge of the tower, and held her weapon above her head. She had become the Reaper, poised to execute the deserving.

"Now, Orlacc!" she said. "Now I take back my dignity. The pain of that day when I knelt in your throne room, when you admitted your deceit and lorded it over us, when you slapped me and showered me with insults—I give it back to you! And if anyone else feels release at your dying, all the better. I strike for them as well!"

She drew back, and readied herself. I knew what was coming next. Orlacc groaned and closed his eyes. It was a fitting end to our story.

But I just couldn't let it happen.

No more murder, I heard my heart say. This mayhem is for real.

"Hold on, Therra," I said getting up and approaching her. I was surprised that she stopped.

"What?" she asked. "The moment was perfect."

Could it be? A bit of humor from her?

"I know," I answered. "But hasn't there been enough violence? Violence begets more violence. Doesn't solve a thing. Haven't we seen that?"

"At his hands, yes! If I finish him off…"

"Then someone will want to avenge him, and they'll come after you. Or you'll run into someone else who hurts you, and if they push you far enough, you'll want to kill them too. Nah. I think it's time we tried something different."

Shieda was now up and standing next to me. "What do you have in mind?" she said.

Therra cautiously relaxed her arms and let her blade fall to her side. She also looked to me for an answer.

"Something amusing," I said. "Something that will kick his ass a lot more than a quick death."

Things started to settle down after a few hours. Parkel's and Domitrus's wounds had been attended to. Therra, Shieda, and I had tied up Orlacc with some sturdy rope and had dragged him down the stairs. The Grimnell soldiers had done their best to establish order— despite their small numbers, Orlacc's subjects had given them little resistance. None of them had ever seen anything like the explosives we'd used, and those who had not fled the castle had cowered in their homes until our soldiers came to fetch them.

I had conveyed my idea for dealing with Orlacc to Otto, and he and Helmut went immediately to work. By mid-afternoon, they'd fashioned exactly the device I'd requested. From the wreckage of the Guardian and from some easy-to-find materials, they had created a small balloon and had filled it with the lighter-than-air gas they'd invented. Now, it was being held near the ground by tethers, clutched by several anxious-looking Grimnells. I looked around—it was time for me to address the crowd. I stepped up on a low wall and cleared my throat.

"Grimnells, Terasskossians, and the rest of you—first, I want to say that we can avoid any more bloodshed now if we can accept what's happened here today and can agree on a few more things. First, I wish to treat none of you Terasskossians as prisoners. If you give your word that you will not harm my people or my friends, you will be considered free citizens of Terasskos in our eyes."

Many of them grunted their answers, and none looked particularly enthusiastic, but enough of them nodded their heads for me to feel comfortable continuing.

"Second, let me say that we do not wish to execute King Orlacc."

At this, a rumble of disbelief rose through the crowd. No one confronted me directly, but it was clear from their faces that they were confused and uneasy. This wasn't how things were usually done, after all. Shouldn't the usurper kill the usurped?

"However, we have come to the conclusion that Orlacc cannot remain in power, since he cannot keep himself from invading neighboring nations."

"Insanity!" Orlacc growled, off to my side. His long hair was falling in his face, and he had to keep blowing it aside to talk. "I do what I want."

"Therefore," I continued, ignoring him, "today we inaugurate a new rule of law. Instead of snuffing Orlacc's life, execution style, we'll give him a fighting chance. Perhaps, if he has to 'rough it' for a while, he'll think twice about making life rough for others."

The Terasskossian minions now clapped sporadically. I guess they had realized that my friends and I were planning to take over, and that they'd better try to get in good with their new rulers. Either that, or they were truly happy to see Orlacc go.

I turned to the soldiers who were restraining the balloon and said, "Go ahead and attach it, men."

The two solemnly intertwined their tethers with Orlacc's bindings, and then they stepped back. Orlacc immediately started to rise into the air. The soldiers grabbed and held him by his feet. Now, Orlacc looked worried.

"Wh-what are you doing to me, Grimnell?" he whined, glancing around for someone to save him or some way to get out of his predicament.

"What we're going to do now," I said, addressing the crowd again, "is send Orlacc on a little flight. If he's lucky, he'll drift for a while, and maybe he'll come down in a safe place somewhere. Eventually, he may be able to work free of his bonds. Then, maybe, he can start his life over, always keeping in mind that it is easier to make one's way in the world if one cooperates with others, rather than trying to conquer others. That's if he's lucky. If not . . . "

Now, there was what seemed to be some genuinely enthusiastic applause from the audience. One rag-wearing woman with a weathered face and chapped hands cupped her hands to her mouth and shouted, "Hail the Grimnells! Hail Morrelaine!"

Gradually, others joined in the chant, and, soon, the whole plaza was alive with whoopla.

Orlacc looked like he might throw up. I turned to him and smiled.

"How's it feel now, big boy? Anything you want to say before you go?"

As he bobbed up and down and struggled against his bonds, it finally sunk in that we had done it. And I'd done my part. He was screeching the requisite bit about how he'd come back and get me one day, and that he'd carve my heart out with a spoon, blah blah. But I didn't care. The whooping of the united crowd filled me with renewed spirit. And the sunlight felt too good.

"Shall we end this?" I asked, and the loudest cheer yet arose from the throng. I took hold of a tether, and motioned for the soldiers to let go of Orlacc's boots. "Anything anyone wants to say before we bid him farewell?"

"May you drift a hundred years," said Parkel.

Therra spat to one side, and, wiping her mouth, said, "To the last of you!"

Domitrus looked up at the once threatening knight. Then he bowed his head, and said, "May you learn from your mistakes."

Shieda stood next to me, and we intertwined our free arms.

"Well?" she asked.

"I've said all I can think of. What about you?"

She thought about it for a moment, and then turned, squinting, to face Orlacc.

"Eat my shorts," she said.

At that, Orlacc cried out in anguish, and I figured that was the perfect cue to set him free. Up he rose, straight for the sun, it seemed. Soon no one could see him in the glare. Soon, no one even looked.

* * *

About two weeks have passed since our fight ended, and I am now writing what I expect will be the last entry in this book. Oh, I'll continue to recount my adventures (if I have any more), but I feel this chapter of my life is pretty much done. I imagine anyone who reads this will agree.

Let's see…the wrap up. What became of us all?

Well, some of the Grimnell soldiers returned to their forest homes, tired, I suppose, of being away from their loved ones. Some stayed here with us. "Here" being the former Castle Orlacc. Meanwhile, a bunch of less-rooted Grimnells picked up and moved to the castle to stay and interact with the Terasskossians. To keep an eye on 'em too, I'd say.

Figuring our spectacular overthrow of Orlacc to be his last hoo-hah, Obishku handed over the job of overseeing the tribe to Trolcott. I'm not sure what happened to Belgear, but I'm sure they found something for him to do too.

I'm sorry to say, I don't know what became of Liassa either. I hope she finds somebody nice.

The rest of us are hanging around the castle, for now. Otto and Helmut have already started building another airship. This time, they'll get to take their time, so I'm sure it'll be even more impressive than the Guardian. They're working on a new propulsion system that uses "magnetix" (or something) instead of regular fuel, which is pretty hard to come by in these parts. Domitrus is helping them (mostly watching them, right now, while his leg heals).

Parkel and Therra, who have become the best of friends, are already getting restless. Neither one of them is exactly the settling-down type. They have their own sort of "romance" going, I guess, though it's certainly not a conventional one. Oh well. They seem to be happy, though they've talked about heading out to the ocean in the not-too-distant future.

Shieda's here with me, and, happily, things are going well between us. She's practicing her magic, of course, and slowly coming to terms with her father's death. We even erected a small, tasteful memorial to him on the castle grounds.

The two of us are the acting rulers of Terasskos. Okay, I guess I can actually say it—I'm an acting king. Not bad for a guy who's spent most of his life feeling average. I've got a beautiful queen too!

I don't know where fate will take us next, but, for now, we're working to bring the people together, and taking it one day at a time.

Oh, of course! I almost forgot Argothrex! He showed up soon after our big triumph. He congratulated me, and told me that I'd impressed him with my decision and my determination to see things through.

"I bet you knew what I'd decide when you gave me that choice," I said. "Funny—when I woke up in this body, I was so scared that I'd never get to be myself again. But now, after all I've been through, I feel pretty comfortable being Morrelaine."

My observation seemed to amuse him, and with his permanent, knowing grin, he said, "You still don't see it, eh? What if I told you, Grant, that there never was another Morrelaine?"

The possible ramifications of that thought raced through my mind, but I was unable to draw any conclusions.

Then, before I could get any more out of him, he said he might not see me for a long time. Of course I wailed, "No way!" I told him I had hoped to go with him and check out his underground world again, and I reminded him that he'd said he would explain things more fully. Know what he said?

"You're figuring it out for yourself now, Grant. When you're ready for the next step, I'll return for you."

Then he was gone, and I never saw him again.

Anyhow, the moral of the story is... um, well, I dunno. How 'bout, "Get up. Get out of your room before that chair becomes part of your butt, dork?"

Okay, I said I was creative. Never said I was poetic. Gotta go. Shieda's calling.

Epilogue

Dear Mike,

I knew you'd be reading this before anyone. Anywho.

I lied. I saw Argothrex one more time, about five days after I wrote that last bit in the book. He told me that he felt it was right for me to see Earth one more time—to pay my respects, so to speak. So, here I am.

Or rather, here I was. Guess he picked a time when you'd be out, and no one would be around to see us "flash" into or out of the room.

I was just supposed to take one last look around, and I did that. I took in the room, its drab colors and shabby furniture; I gazed outside at the noisy city, which now seemed more polluted and towering than ever; and I even took a gander at the old pumphouse, and the river flowing by. Jeez, I'd changed since the last time I'd looked out that same window!

Well, not to bore you. I just thought I should leave some record of what happened to me. In other words, I'm giving you my book, though I wasn't supposed to bring anything back to Earth with me. I wasn't supposed to leave any trace of what happened. But, I wanted someone to know. Read my story, if you want, and, please, bring it to my parents when you get a chance. I'm sure things are pretty topsy-turvy around there with them since I vanished!

Finally, let me say to you that I'm sorry I was so down all the time before. Believe it or not, I've found this better place where I fit in better than I did at college. And I've learned there are lots of different ways to live your life. You just have to experiment to find out which one is best for you. But don't limit yourself in your search. Anything can happen.

Anyway, I probably won't be back again. If you ever feel like a real adventure, give this book a read. So long, and have an exciting life.

Your friend,
Morrelaine

About the Author

Nathanial W. Cook began life as a bouncy, blond ball in Phoenix, AZ, but he grew up (though some might question his grown-up-ed-ness) in and around Boston, MA. In his efforts to "find himself" and "find his way," he's moved to Los Angeles, Atlanta, Salem (MA), Seattle, Longmont (CO), and back to Salem again, where "himself" and "his way" seem to want to be found.

Now, he shares his life with beloved fellow writer, EC Hanlon, and twin beloved stepkids. He's led a second life, however, always going on inside, and there is where you'll find the worlds he tries to get out through his writing and other creative pursuits. It can be difficult living several lives at once, but he wouldn't trade it for a more mundane life. He's fallen into many things, but, so far, has mainly shuffled into Fate.

www.ingramcontent.com/pod-product-compliance
Lightning Source LLC
Chambersburg PA
CBHW020402210626
46816CB00006BB/2082